A HUSBAND IS HUSHED UP

A VICTORIAN WHODUNNIT WITH A HINT OF HUMOUR

A DUCHESS OF STORTFORD MYSTERY

HELEN GOLDEN

DREW BRADLEY PRESS

ALSO BY HELEN GOLDEN

The Duchess of Stortford Mysteries

An Heir is Misplaced (Novella)

A Husband is Hushed Up

A Dowager is Done In

A Blighter is Bumped Off

BOOKS BY HELEN GOLDEN

A Right Royal Cozy Investigation Series

A Toast To Trouble (Novella)

Spruced Up For Murder

For Richer, For Deader

Not Mushroom For Death

An Early Death (Prequel)

Deadly New Year (Novelette)

A Dead Herring

I Spy With My Little Die

Tick, Tock, Mystery Clock (Novelette)

A Cocktail To Die For

Dying To Bake

A Death of Fresh Air

I Kill Always Love You

Murder Most Wilde

Nobbled at Christmas (Novella)

ISBN (P) 978-1-918308-13-6

Edited by Marina Grout at Writing Evolution

Published by Drew Bradley Press

Cover design by Helen Drew-Bradley

First edition November 2025

NOTE FROM THE AUTHOR

I am a British author and this book has been written using British English. So if you are from somewhere other than the UK, you may find some words spelt differently to how you would spell them. In most cases this is British English, not a spelling mistake. We also have different punctuation rules in the UK. However if you find any other errors I would be grateful if you would please contact me helen@helengolde nauthor.co.uk and let me know so I can correct them. Thank you.

You will see the phrase 'the *ton*' used occasionally in this book. *Ton* means 'fashionable society,' particularly high class society, and comes from *le bon ton*, a French phrase meaning 'good or elegant form or style.' Members of the *ton* were generally upper class, wealthy, and respected. By the late 19th century the phrase was considered a little old-fashioned so although it was still used by the older and more traditional members of society, younger people referred to 'society' or 'high society' instead.

For your reference I have included a list of characters in the order they appear and you can find this at the back of the book.

1

5:10 AM, SUNDAY 31 MAY 1891

A piercing scream shattered the stillness of the night, jolting Alice, the Duchess of Stortford, from a deep sleep. Her eyes flew open, her heart racing as she tried to pinpoint the source of the sound. For a moment, she lay frozen in her four-poster bed. The familiar floral wallpaper of her childhood room at Francis Court, her parents' estate, swam into focus in the dim light.

What was that? she thought, her mind still clouded with sleep. She strained but could hear nothing.

Was I dreaming?

She wiped her hand across her forehead as she sat up. All was quiet.

I must have been dreaming. Unless, of course… A smile tugged at the corners of her mouth. Unless it was the ghost of Agnes, the seventh Duchess of Arnwall, who, rumour had it, roamed the house—

A high, desperate shriek drifted up from somewhere below.

That's no ghost!

She reached for the tasselled cord beside the bed and gave

it a firm tug, then swung her legs over the side of the mattress, wincing as her bare feet touched the cold floor. She snatched up her silk wrap from the bedpost, and slipping her feet into her velvet slippers, she padded across the room towards the door. As she reached for the handle, the door swung open, revealing a wide-eyed Maud on the other side.

"You rang, Your Grace," her maid said, her chestnut curls in disarray. "Are you unwell?"

"No. But did you hear a scream?" She walked past Maud and out through the door. The upper floor hallway was quiet, but the scream lingered in her memory.

"I heard nothing, ma'am." Maud followed her out of the room, frowning. "Are you sure it wasn't a—"

A muffled wail cut through the stillness.

"Oh!" Maud stopped.

"Indeed!" Alice turned to look at her maid.

"What do you think is amiss, ma'am?" Maud whispered, her dark eyes wide.

"I haven't the faintest idea." Her pulse was still racing. "But there's only one way to find out. We must see at once. Come!"

Ushering Maud ahead of her into the dim corridor, they set off down the passage, past ancestral portraits peering from the panelled walls. The plush Turkish carpet muffled their footsteps as they hurried towards the grand staircase.

Maud slowed down as they approached it and turned around to face Alice. "Er, ma'am. Don't you think we should wait and call—"

Waking her father, the duke, or calling a footman would be sensible. Yet, she'd feel uneasy remaining in her room while someone might be in need of help.

She squared her shoulders and walked past her maid. "No, Maud. Someone might be in trouble." She sped up. "Stay by me and do try not to trip over anything—we cannot have both of us tumbling down the stairs in the dark."

"Yes, ma'am," Maud mumbled from behind her.

They approached the top of the imposing grand staircase as another piercing scream made Alice start. Her heart leapt into her throat. Gripping the thin wooden handrail inlaid with brass above the ornately carved and gold-painted balustrade, she peered down at the black-and-white chequered marble-tiled foyer of the Painted Hall.

There, halfway up the stairs, a maid stood stock-still, her hands clamped over her mouth in horror. The girl's cap was askew, and even from a distance, Alice could see her trembling.

Good heavens, what's wrong?

Her gaze followed the maid's terrified stare upwards—beyond the polished banister, to the broad half-landing above. A figure lay crumpled on the shallow platform where the stairs turned, half in shadow.

Her stomach lurched. *Someone has fallen!* But who…?

She squinted. *Why is it so dark?* The main staircase was always lit at night, especially during house parties.

She glanced over to the wall. The wall sconce closest to the second-floor landing—the one that usually cast a soft pool of light down the upper flight—was dark. Not just dimmed but completely extinguished. *It must have gone out…*

She leaned closer, but without the sconce's steady glow, the landing below was cloaked in gloom. She could just make out the outline of a man—one leg askew, one arm stretched out awkwardly—but his face was hidden, his features swallowed by the dark.

A chill ran down her spine as the awful truth settled over her. The man was…

"Oh, ma'am," Maud whispered next to her, her voice trembling. "I think... I think he's…"

"Dead, Maud. Yes, indeed." Her hands shaking, she bunched her robe more tightly around herself, feeling cold despite the layers of fabric. She blinked hard, trying to make sense of what she was seeing. Something about the man's attire tugged at her memory, but she couldn't quite place it.

I need to get closer. Her heart hammered as she took a tentative step down the stairs, towards the body half in shadow, half-illuminated by the dull orange glow of a remaining gas sconce further down the wall. *Who is it?*

Suddenly, her dainty slipper skidded on the slick edge of a tread, and Maud lunged to grasp her elbow.

"Careful, ma'am!" the maid cried, her voice quavering. "The stairs…"

She nodded, grateful for Maud's steadying hand. She moved to continue, but her maid's grip tightened on her arm. "Your Grace, there's nothing to be done," Maud said firmly. "I'll take you back to your room."

Alice opened her mouth to protest, but Maud had already leaned over the side of the banister. "Betty, go and rouse Mr Stokes at once!" The maid flinched at the sound of her name. "Tell him there's been a terrible accident." Maud's tone brooked no argument. Betty nodded jerkily, her skirts flaring as she stumbled backwards, then turned and lurched forward down the stairs.

Alice barely registered the exchange, her attention fixated on the dead man. She took another step down. The figure came into sharper focus. His legs were twisted, knees bent at unnatural angles, shoes resting against the bottom step as though he'd bounced there on impact.

As she stared at the body, dread oozed through her veins, slow and as cold as ice. The flicker of the gaslight caught on the man's coal-black hair. Her breath caught in her throat. "No…" she whispered and took another step down.

Now she could see the well-cut evening coat, the polished boots… the signet ring on one slack hand. Alice's knees threatened to buckle as realisation slammed into her with the force of a runaway carriage. *How did I not recognise him immediately?* She sagged against the banister, gasping for breath that wouldn't come. *It can't be.* Surely, fate couldn't be so unspeakably cruel.

Oh, no. Please no… She knew that side profile, knew every proud plane and chiselled angle. How many times had she gazed upon them in frustration, in fury, in… Bile seared the back of her throat. *No! Not here. Not now.* The broken body heaped on the stone half-landing between the first and second floors, blood oozing from his head where it had hit the wall, was none other than her husband.

Vance, the Duke of Stortford, was dead.

2

TWO DAYS EARLIER...

E xtract from *The Society Page* broadsheet, dated Friday, 29 May 1891:

Fenshire Beckons: Who is Who at Francis Court

With invitations formally extended and trunks dispatched, society's attention now turns fully eastward to Francis Court, the ancestral seat of His Grace, the Duke of Arnwall, as preparations for his sixtieth-birthday celebrations enter their final, glittering stages.

The guest list—closely guarded, of course—has taken shape, and many of the capital's most intriguing personages will be in attendance.

Foremost among them is the Duke's daughter, Her Grace, the Duchess of Stortford, who is expected to arrive from London in advance of the festivities. Of equal note is the anticipated arrival of her husband, the Duke of Stortford, whose recent absence from both Town and his wife's side has not gone unnoticed by the ton. *That the two shall be reunited beneath the same roof for the first time this year has stirred considerable interest—particularly as Lady Forthington, the Duke's cousin-by-marriage and alleged companion in rural diversions, is also said to be attending.*

Adding to the anticipated tension is speculation around the possible attendance of the newly titled Earl of Rivershore, whose admiration for the Duchess has been politely remarked upon in select circles. Whether his presence proves to be merely a rumour or not remains to be seen, but there is no doubt his appearance, should it happen, would cause no small discomfort to the Duchess' husband.

Also among the gathering will be the Duke of Arnwall's heir, Lord Tilling, and his wife, the Countess—and co-hostess for much of the event—along with her brother, Lord Rushton, long regarded as one of society's more elusive bachelors. The Duke's younger son, Lord James Astley, will also be in attendance, no doubt lending his characteristic energy to the weekend's affairs.

Further distinguished guests include the wealthy and always-watchful Lady Granville, whose eye for opportunity is matched only by her eye for scandal, and Lord and Lady Hawthorne, recently returned from the Continent and certain to bring tales of foreign splendour.

With so many names of note assembled under one roof, we can only wonder: will the weekend prove a triumph for the house of Arnwall—or something rather less harmonious?

3

EARLY THAT AFTERNOON...

The train gave a final shuddering sigh as it pulled into East Felsham, steam billowing in damp clouds along the platform edge. Rain pattered steadily against the window-pane of the first-class compartment, and Alice released a long breath as the carriage juddered to a halt. *The boys would have loved this*, she thought as she stood and collected her things together.

Of course, Harry, her eldest at thirteen and a half (he was adamant that no one forgot that all-important half), would've tried to disguise his excitement with a practised scowl and a muttered, "So we're here then." But his eyes would've given him away, darting eagerly across the platform as porters hurried busily through the swirling white mist. Meanwhile, Freddie—eighteen months younger and incapable of pretending to be unimpressed—would've been pressed to the window from King's Cross onwards, pointing out to her every cow and signal box with breathless delight.

Alice blinked hard. *Goodness, how I miss them.* Her arms ached for the warmth of their unruly hugs and her ears for the thundering of their footsteps as they tore down the corridors.

Although, she was never sure why boys had to run everywhere. She even missed the sound of their squabbling.

She suppressed a sigh. *But perhaps it's just as well they're both away at school in Derbyshire at the moment.* The quiet might give her and her husband, Vance, the chance to talk—really talk—about what came next…

"Well," Fiona, the Countess of Tilling, murmured, lifting the hem of her travelling cloak as she moved towards the door, a teasing smile on her face, "let's hope your father has remembered to send a coach that doesn't smell of damp dogs and cigar smoke."

Her husband, Duncan, grinned as he leaned forward to unlatch the door. "It's very possible, Fee. For all we know, a pony cart could meet us."

Alice smiled wryly. There was an excellent reason she'd sent her own carriage ahead of them—so she could use it during their visit to Francis Court. She'd learned long ago not to rely on her father's standards of comfort. The Duke of Arnwall had no patience for what he called, "London fripperies on wheels". If it didn't carry hounds, hay, or the occasional gouty neighbour, he saw no use for it.

As they descended onto the platform beneath a sea of umbrellas, she spotted George, her first footman, immediately. He stood near the train's luggage van, tall and composed in his waxed coat, issuing calm instructions to two porters hauling down a leather-strapped trunk.

"Your Grace." George bowed as she approached. "Welcome to Fenshire. I trust your journey was tolerable?"

"Tolerable enough," she replied, brushing a curl of moisture from her brow. "You made good time. And my barouche—?"

"Delivered safely to the stables yesterday morning, ma'am. I oversaw the unpacking myself."

"Excellent. And Aunt Cora?"

Her aunt, the Countess of Dunmore, who lived with her when she resided in London, had taken the train the day before, eager to help her sister, Alice's mother, with the preparations for the party.

"She arrived yesterday as planned and is settled comfortably at Francis Court. Her ladyship has already taken charge of the housekeeper." He gave a meaningful pause. "And the footmen."

Of course she has. Aunt Cora can reorganise a household with nothing but her voice and a withering glance. She exchanged a look with Fee, who gave a knowing sigh.

"I suppose we should prepare ourselves," Alice said. "By now she will have made notes about the flower arrangements and taken issue with the wine list."

George's mouth twitched at the corners. "I believe she has, ma'am."

Her parents rarely entertained anyone other than family, so the duchess would have been happy to hand over many of the tasks to her more-than-willing sister.

The carriage stood a short distance beyond the end of the platform, a glossy, dark-green travelling coach emblazoned with the Arnwall family's coat of arms. The coachman sat still beneath his oilskin cape while a liveried footman opened the door at their approach.

"Well, I take it back. It seems the duke has had the sense to send a decent carriage in this weather," Fee said as she took her husband's arm.

Alice caught George's eye. She raised an eyebrow in question. He nodded before offering her his arm to assist her into the covered vehicle. She suppressed a smile. She suspected her father didn't *know* his best coach had been sent to collect his family from the station.

Inside, the air smelled faintly of lavender polish and wool. As she settled into the leather-cushioned seat, the rain intensified, drumming a steady rhythm on the roof above.

Outside, George oversaw the final loading of the trunks into the accompanying baggage cart.

Maud, her maid, approached the door, her boots slightly damp at the edges and her hat pinned neatly in place.

"Everything in order, Maud?" she asked.

"Yes, Your Grace. Though I overheard a porter say some roads through to Francis Court are waterlogged. It might take somewhat longer to reach the house than normal, ma'am."

She dipped her chin. "Thank you, Maud. I'll see you at the house."

Maud curtseyed and hurried away, towards the luggage coach waiting behind them.

Thirty minutes later, the coach rocked gently as it rounded a bend in the road and passed through the impressive gates to Francis Court.

"Come now, Alice," Fee said, adjusting the pearl clasp on her gloves. "Tell the truth—how do you feel about seeing Vance again?"

She didn't answer immediately as she gazed out at the hedgerows; they blurred past the carriage windows, along the long, winding driveway to the stately home.

How *did* she feel? *Somewhat nauseous!* But she was unsure if that was from the dread at seeing her husband or the swaying of the carriage.

She cleared her throat. "Apprehensive, I daresay. Curious. Mildly braced for disaster."

Fee arched a brow. "Indeed."

"I meant what I said when I wrote to him," Alice said softly, recalling how it had taken three attempts to get the wording right. "That we ought to speak plainly about our future. It cannot continue like this—two polite strangers bound by legal ties and little else."

Her hand drifted to her reticule. Inside, carefully folded and tucked into a small pocket, was Vance's reply to her recent letter requesting they meet to talk about their relationship during the birthday celebrations. She'd read it twice already since they'd left London.

My dear Alice,

You are quite correct in observing that the time has come for plain speech between us. There have been failings on my part—many of which I am prepared to face with candour.

If you are willing, I should be glad of an opportunity to confer in private while we are both at Francis Court. I would not presume too far, but I hope we might explore the possibility of arriving at a more companionable understanding.

Yours,

V.

It was not a letter brimming with sentiment, but then, Vance was not a man given to effusions. Still, the line "a more companionable understanding" had lingered with her. For Vance, that bordered on emotional transparency. *He must mean something by it.* And yet, any conversation of substance would be rendered exceedingly difficult with her cousin Lady Forthington fluttering about the house… "It won't be easy to speak freely," she said aloud, "with Lilly in attendance."

Alice's brother gave a brief grunt. "I say, it's dashed ill-mannered of Vance to bring her at all."

"She's your cousin, Duncan," Fee reminded him,

smoothing the skirt of her travelling dress. "And a member of the family. Naturally, she received an invitation."

"Still bad form," Duncan muttered.

Alice gave a humourless smile. "I can hardly speak to my husband about repairing our marriage while his rumoured paramour is sipping sherry in the next room." She paused, her fingers tingling. Saying it aloud made her realise Duncan was right. Until now, she'd resisted thinking of it in such stark terms, but yes, it was poor form. Worse, it was cruel. He should've told Lilly to refuse the invitation. She licked her lips. "It places me at a distinct disadvantage," she said huffily.

"I thought as much," Fee said lightly. "Which is why I arranged something that might assist."

She arched a brow. "What have you done, Fee?"

Her sister-in-law had a long history of what she termed "gentle involvement"—a practice that began during their first Season, when Fee had taken it upon herself to prevent Alice from taking the air with a marquess who she didn't, "like the look of", who later turned out to have both a wife and a fondness for absinthe. That particular intervention had been welcome. Others—such as introducing her to a viscount with breath like boiled cabbage—had been less successful.

Still, Fee's heart was always in the right place, even if her schemes occasionally went sideways. A knot of dread twisted in Alice's stomach as her sister-in-law continued, "Guess who arrives later today and is staying with Duncan and me at Francis Lodge?"

Alice narrowed her eyes. "Fee…" She braced herself for her best friend's reply.

Fee's smile grew positively wicked. "Henry Somerset. Lord Rivershore himself."

Alice blinked as a nervous tremor passed through her. "You invited Henry?"

"I merely suggested it. And the invitation was extended."

Henry, here? The handsome earl's attention in London had been flattering, even exciting. *But now? Under the same roof as Vance?* "That's wildly improper," she murmured.

Fee shrugged. "Perhaps. But scarcely more improper than your husband parading about the drawing room with your cousin on his arm and expecting a private reconciliation over the breakfast kedgeree."

She didn't know whether to scold her or laugh. *Henry. At Francis Court.* She'd enjoyed his company far too much recently, and now he would be here, right under Vance's nose. *Well, at least I'll have a backup!* "Fee," she said, her voice dry, "you may have complicated things rather spectacularly."

"I prefer to think of it," Fee said sweetly, "as balancing the scales."

Duncan groaned and folded up the newspaper on his lap. "I am surrounded by madwomen."

But she couldn't help the smile that tugged at the corners of her mouth. *Complicated? Yes. Improper? Certainly. But interesting? Oh yes!* And Alice liked interesting…

4

LATER THAT AFTERNOON...

Alice sank deeper into the plush velvet armchair, her teacup rattling a touch as she set it on the delicate side table. The sitting room at Francis Court was awash in the golden light of late afternoon; it filtered through heavy brocade curtains and cast long shadows across the Persian rug.

Across from her, Fee reclined on a large green sofa, absently twirling a lock of her golden hair as she sipped her tea. Duncan sat beside her, his dark brows knitted in concentration as he perused the newspaper.

Vance will be arriving any moment now. She glanced at the clock on the mantelpiece. The hands hadn't moved far since she'd last looked.

"I simply cannot wait for tomorrow night's party," Fee gushed, her blue eyes sparkling with anticipation. "I don't think Francis Court has seen this level of activity since our wedding; don't you agree, darling?"

Duncan folded his newspaper with a rustle. "I dare say you're right, my dear."

"And such an illustrious guest list," Fee continued. "It's

quite impressive that so many of the *ton* said yes, considering your father and mother rarely entertain."

"Ah, but that's exactly *why* they're descending here like a plague of locusts. It's a chance to see how Francis Court is holding up under its dust covers," Duncan replied, eyeing his wife with a smirk. "There's nothing Society enjoys more than sniffing around a grand house they've not been invited to in a decade—especially if they suspect the cellars are well-stocked."

Fee gave him a playful tap on the arm. "You're so cynical, darling," she said with a wry smile. "What do you think, Alice?"

She forced a smile, trying to ignore the tension gnawing beneath her ribs. Was it dread or hope that was making her feel a shade ill? "Indeed, Fee. It promises to be quite the affair."

"Talking about affairs," Duncan said, rising, "where's that scoundrel of a husband of yours?"

"Duncan!" Fee hissed, then looked apologetically at her. But Alice was used to her brother, who had never learned the art of tact—at least not where those he loved were concerned. He wielded truth like a fencing foil: straight to the point and entirely unapologetic if it left a little nick in the skin.

"I can't wait any longer, Alice. I need to be at Francis Lodge to ensure all is in order for our guests." He turned to her with a kind smile. "You'll be all right, will you not, dear sister? I know this cannot be easy for you."

She swallowed. She simply wanted all this business with Vance over and done with now so she could enjoy the party. "I—"

"I'm staying. I can't leave her to face Vance and that woman on her own."

She smiled gratefully at her sister-in-law. "Thank you, Fee."

"Excellent. I'll leave you ladies to it then." Duncan gave an exaggerated bow and strode out of the room, leaving her feeling both grateful for Fee's presence and oddly abandoned by her brother.

"I am sorry, Alice. Duncan dislikes confrontation, as you well know." Fee's mouth curved with amusement. "Unless he's seated in the House of Lords, naturally—then he'll argue for hours if someone so much as breathes in disagreement about education reform or clean water in the East End." She gave a soft, affectionate sigh. "He's hopeless with emotion but tireless in his principles." Fee reached over and patted her hand. "It'll be fine, darling. And if that rake says one wrong word to you, I'll box his ears myself."

Despite herself, she chuckled. "I'd pay good money to see that, Fee."

As if on cue, the distant sound of carriage wheels on gravel drifted through the window. A jolt of panic seized her. *That must be Vance...* She rose and smoothed her skirts, acutely aware they were creased and wrinkled from the journey.

Not long after, Stokes appeared in the doorway, looking vaguely harried. "Your Grace, the Duke and Lady Forthington have arrived."

Her stomach churned. *This is it.* Fee's hand tightened on her arm, a silent show of support. Drawing herself up to her full height, she nodded at Stokes. "Please show them in, Stokes."

Vance strode into the room, looking impossibly polished as ever in his impeccably tailored coat and polished boots. *Why must he look so very well?* But it was the woman on his arm that made her blood run cold. Lilly Forthington, all honey-blonde curls and coquettish smiles, clung to Vance as if she were already mistress of Manning Hall, Alice and Vance's home in Derbyshire.

Vance detached Lilly's hand from his arm and moved towards Alice. She braced herself. "Alice, my dear," he said, his voice as smooth as ever. He stepped forward, bowed his head a trifle, and took her hand in his. His lips brushed her fingers with the faintest pressure—just enough to remind her —and everyone in the room that she was still his wife. "I trust you're well?"

This man, who had once set her alight with a glance, now barely stirred more than irritation—and a small, traitorous flicker of something else. *Regret?* She forced a smile, aware of Fee practically vibrating with indignation beside her. "Quite well, thank you, Vance. And you? I trust your journey was pleasant?" Her eyes flicked pointedly to Lilly.

Vance had the grace to look slightly abashed. "As cousin Lilly and I are neighbours, it seemed only sensible to travel together."

She's not even your *cousin!*

Lilly gave a short laugh—a breathy, simpering titter that made Alice's teeth ache. She'd forgotten how much she loathed that sound her cousin made. "Vance has been such a dear, cousin Alice, keeping me company at Forthington Manor. It can get so lonely rattling around in a big house all by myself." She simpered up at Vance, her meaning clear.

Alice clenched her jaw. *How dare she come here, to my parents' home, and humiliate me like this?* She glanced at Vance, searching his face for some sign of shame or regret, but all she saw was a weak-willed fool completely under Lilly's spell. *Well, that makes it easy then!* She would hear Vance out as she'd promised. But she'd been foolish to hope. At least now, she needn't waste time mourning something that no longer existed. If this was the man her husband had become, she wanted no part of him.

Vance, suddenly seeming to sense the tension, cleared his throat. "Er, Lilly, perhaps you would like to retire to your room and refresh yourself before dinner?" He rang the bell for Stokes.

Lilly pouted prettily. "Oh, but I was so hoping to spend more time with cousin Alice, Vance."

Whereas I don't want to be anywhere near you!

"It's been such a long while since we were in each other's company, and…" She trailed off at his insistent look, then sighing, she offered Alice the faintest of curtseys and swept from the room, her curls bouncing with indignation.

Alice resisted the urge to roll her eyes. *Thank goodness she's gone. Now to Vance…*

But before she could open her mouth, Fee rounded on him, her blue eyes flashing with indignation. "What in heaven's name are you thinking, Vance, bringing *that* woman here?"

Fee! Although she felt a rush of gratitude to her best friend, she really wanted to tackle her husband herself.

Vance blinked at Fee, seeming genuinely perplexed by her outrage. "Lilly? But she's a neighbour, Fiona. It was only polite to offer her a ride."

Alice frowned. "You could have—"

"Polite?" Fee scoffed, interrupting her. "Is that what you call flaunting her in front of your wife and the entire *ton*?"

Vance spluttered. "Now hold on—"

A knock sounded at the door, startling them all.

"The Earl of Rivershore, Your Grace," Stokes announced as he stepped to one side, and Henry Rivershore strode into the room, all dashing good looks and effortless charm.

Ignoring Vance and Fee, he came straight to her. "Alice,"

he greeted, his voice warm with familiarity as he bowed over her hand. "You look lovelier than ever."

Heat prickled in her cheeks. She was acutely aware of Vance's gaze boring into her. *Let him look. Let him stew.* She had nothing to hide except the sudden, unhelpful urge to laugh at the absurdity of it all.

Fee, meanwhile, looked like the cat who'd got the cream. "Lord Rivershore! We are *so* pleased you could make it."

Henry smiled at Fee briefly, then his eyes returned to Alice's face. "I stopped at Francis Lodge, where I learned that you ladies were here. I couldn't resist the chance to see you again, Your Grace." She took a shallow breath, then he turned back to Fee. "And of course, Lady Tilling, I am under strict orders from your husband to escort you back to your home."

Fee's delighted laugh rang out, a stark contrast to the tension thrumming through Alice's body. She couldn't help but wonder if Vance had heard the rumours about her and Henry in London. She quickly glanced to her right. *Oh dear!* Judging by Vance's thunderous expression, it seemed he had.

"How... thoughtful of you, Henry," she managed, her mind whirling. *This is all so embarrassing...* She looked at Fee. *Help!*

"Oh, where are my manners?" Fee chirped with exaggerated cheerfulness. "Lord Henry Rivershore, may I present His Grace, the Duke of Stortford?"

"And Alice's *husband...*" Vance added gruffly.

The air in the room seemed to thicken as the two men sized each other up. Alice held her breath, half-expecting pistols at dawn to be declared on the spot.

"Charmed," Henry drawled, his smile not quite reaching his eyes as they exchanged a stiff handshake.

"And how do—" Vance began.

The door opened. Her stomach gave a fresh twist as

Baxter, Lord Rushton, stepped into the room with the unhurried assurance of a man entirely at home at Francis Court.

Naturally! Of course he would arrive *now*—just as Vance and Henry were engaged in the sort of silent masculine standoff that made women roll their eyes and footmen flee. And now Baxter, her childhood friend and Fee's older brother, was here to complete the set.

He'd always treated her like a younger sister in need of sturdy guidance, even long after she'd become a duchess with opinions of her own. Protective to a fault and completely impervious to hints, she could already feel the weight of his disapproving gaze preparing to land squarely on her shoulders.

Out of the corner of her eye, she caught Fee fighting a grin. She recognised the look on her brother's face too—and clearly found it every bit as predictable as Alice did.

This is all I need—one more man trying to manage my life!

5

A SHORT WHILE LATER...

Alice's limbs felt oddly heavy, her breath catching somewhere high in her chest. The sitting room suddenly seemed a little too warm, a little too loud, as though her senses were folding in on themselves. She wished they would all simply vanish—Vance with his polished charm, Henry with his relentless intensity, and now Baxter, looming with a fraternal concern like some avenging angel. It was like watching a stage play from behind a pane of glass—she was present but not quite *in* it.

Fee shifted closer, her hand brushing lightly against Alice's back in a gesture that was both subtle and grounding. "Breathe," she whispered low enough for only her to hear.

Alice inhaled deeply. *You will* not *fall to pieces over this, Alice. Not today.* She exhaled slowly.

Meanwhile Fee blinked at her brother. "Baxter, what are you doing here? I thought we agreed you would meet us at Francis Lodge."

Baxter's brow lifted a touch. "I came to escort you there, of course. Given the weather and the company" —his eyes flicked briefly to Vance, then Henry— "I thought it best."

Fee's eyes darted between them. "Baxter, this is Henry, the Earl of Rivershore. He has also come to escort me back to the lodge. Apparently, I require a full guard this evening."

Baxter turned and offered a polite bow to Henry, who returned the gesture smoothly.

Fee turned to her with an exaggerated smile. "I had no notion one needed this many escorts to walk a few hundred yards. Has a band of highwaymen begun roaming the park here at Francis Court?"

The tension left Alice's shoulders as she looked into the gleaming eyes of her friend. Trust Fee to lighten the atmosphere and deflect the tension away from her. "Not that I know of, my dear," she replied, her voice dry, "but I dare say if one were lurking nearby, he'd find himself sorely outnumbered."

"Well then, Fee," Baxter said, turning to his sister, "I believe it's time we took our leave. Lord Rivershore and I can escort you home now."

"But—" Fee began, glancing at her.

"It's fine. You need to be at your house, Fee. You have guests," she said quickly, giving her sister-in-law's arm a reassuring pat even though she'd rather face a firing squad than another minute of Vance's simmering disapproval alone. "I'm well."

Henry turned and took her hand again. "I look forward to seeing you again later, Your Grace. Perhaps we can take a stroll in the gardens after dinner?"

"That would be—" She hadn't finished her reply when, suddenly, Vance muttered an oath, then turned on his heels and departed from the room, leaving a ringing silence in his wake.

Blast! She shot Henry a look. His blue eyes danced with mischief as he gave her a curt bow.

Fee clapped her hands. "Well! That was bracing. Come on, Henry! Alice, I'll see you at dinner." And with a swish of her skirts, she was gone, an amused Henry trailing in her wake.

She blinked at the now-empty doorway. *Well, at least they've all gone…*

Baxter cleared his throat loudly.

Why is he still here? "Should you not be—"

She got no further as Baxter closed the door, shutting them in. "Damn it, Alice, what are you playing at? Inviting Rivershore here, with the whole *ton* watching?" He raked a hand through his hair, frustration clear in every line of his body.

She bristled at his tone. *Why is this my fault?* She hadn't asked Henry here. Anyway, that wasn't the point… "Oh, you mean like how Vance brought his… his… Lilly here? Funny, I didn't hear you scolding him."

Baxter shifted uncomfortably. "That's different. Lilly is your family. There's no impropriety in her being here. But you and Rivershore…" He trailed off, his meaning clear.

A hot flush rushed to her cheeks. The injustice of it. *How dare Baxter tell me off while Vance—* "She's his mistress, Bax! In what world is that proper?" She advanced on him, her voice rising. She wasn't the sort to shout, but apparently today, was making exceptions of everyone. "And hang propriety! Vance parades his infidelity in front of everyone, but I'm the one who gets a lecture on decorum? And from you, who's not my father *nor* my brother?"

Baxter held up his hands, his expression softening. "Alice, please. I'm not trying to scold you. But I'm worried about you. I don't want you to be made a fool of in front of—"

"The *ton*. I know!" She took a deep breath, her anger

leaving her as she exhaled. "I fear you're too late, Bax. This whole situation is impossible. Fee thought inviting Henry would help, but I think she's made everything even worse."

Baxter snorted. "That's Fee for you. She means well, but…" He gave a small smile.

Despite everything, she felt a smile tug at her lips in return. *He hasn't changed.* The same cheeky grin, same maddening confidence. And still, somehow, her ally. "Do you remember the frog-pond incident?"

Baxter groaned. "I've been trying to block that particular memory for the last two decades, thank you very much. And do you remember," he continued, a grin splitting his face, "when she decided we simply must learn to waltz before the Harrington's ball?"

Laughter bubbled up in her throat. "Oh, good heavens! How could I forget? I'm not sure poor Stokes has ever fully recovered from being used as her practice partner."

They both laughed, the tension between them easing fractionally. For a moment, she could almost believe they were children again, carefree and unburdened, running around the fields and woods that separated their parents' estates.

But all too soon, the moment passed, and Baxter's expression grew serious once more. "Alice, what do you intend to do about this... situation?"

She sank onto the couch, smoothing her skirts absently. "I hardly know, Bax. On one hand, Vance has been…" She trailed off, searching for the right word.

"A nincompoop?" Baxter supplied helpfully.

"Precisely," she agreed, a rueful smile playing on her lips. *Has he been talking to Aunt Cora?* "But he's also the father of my children and my husband in the eyes of God and society. I can't simply cast him aside, no matter how tempting the notion might be at times."

Baxter nodded thoughtfully, pacing before the fireplace. "You know, for all his faults, I couldn't fail to notice how Vance looked at you earlier. And the way he glared at Henry? If I didn't know better, I would say your esteemed husband is rather jealous."

Her eyes widened in surprise. "Surely, you jest?"

"Not at all," Baxter replied, his tone earnest. "Perhaps my dear sister's scheme was not entirely misguided this time. Have you considered that Vance might still harbour powerful feelings for you?"

Is that possible? Could there *really* be anything left beneath all the bitterness and bruised pride? After everything that had transpired between them, was there still hope? "We're to speak privately—to determine how we may proceed," she told him.

Baxter continued, his voice gentle, "My advice is to hear him out, Alice. But make your expectations clear. You deserve nothing less than complete devotion and respect."

Yes. He's right. I do… "Thank you, Bax. Truly."

He gave her a wry smile, then turned and headed to the door.

She called out, "Do play nice with Henry, won't you?"

He paused at the door, a roguish grin spreading across his face. "Now, where's the fun in that? Besides, he's far too young for you, my dear."

Her indignant, "Baxter!" was met only with his retreating laughter echoing down the hall.

6

THAT EVENING...

A lice descended the main staircase of Francis Court, her gloved fingers resting lightly on the polished mahogany banister. The soft *swish* of her skirts echoed faintly in the stillness—a contrast to the unsettled beat of her heart. *After this night, will Vance and I be reconciled?*

After all these months, could an exchange of letters truly bridge the distance between them? Or was she simply setting herself up for heartbreak once again?

Earlier, in her bedchamber, just as she'd been reaching for the bell to call for Maud to help her dress, a quiet knock on her door had disturbed her. Opening it, she'd been surprised —but not unpleasantly so given their childhood connection— to see Tom Gresham, a long-standing footman at Francis Court.

He'd bowed deeply. "Your Grace, I'm sorry to disturb you."

"Not at all, Tom. It's good to see you. How is your father enjoying his retirement?" Tom's father had served the Astley family for over fifty years until he'd retired a month ago.

He'd replied that his father was still helping out occasionally, most likely to keep out of his mother's way. Then he'd explained that he'd been assigned as her husband's valet for the duration of the duke's stay. His hazel eyes had been downcast as he'd extended a folded piece of paper towards her. "His Grace… He asked that I wait for a reply, ma'am."

She'd broken the seal with a frown.

My dear Alice,

I regret the tone of our earlier exchange and wish to offer my sincerest apologies. It was never my intention to cause you further discomfort, particularly at such a significant family gathering.

Might we speak privately later this evening, once the gentlemen have withdrawn from the dining room? I shall await you in the library.

Let us set aside past discord. I believe, perhaps foolishly, that there may yet be a way forward for us. I should like to try if you are amenable.

With the hope of a fresh understanding,
V.

With trembling hands, she'd penned a quick reply, agreeing to meet him. She'd made no further comment and nothing in her tone had conveyed encouragement—her feelings had been too muddled. Tom had taken her note with a respectful bow and discreetly withdrawn.

Now, at the foot of the grand staircase, she stepped into the Painted Hall. The black-and-white marble tiles gleamed beneath the flicker of candlelight, stretching out in orderly perfection beneath the elaborate painted ceiling—a sweeping vista of classical gods, floating cherubs, and fabled figures all rendered in bold, romantic brushstrokes.

The faint echo of laughter and tinkling glasses drifted from the drawing room, mingling with the rustle of her emerald gown.

Her nerves prickled, sharp and persistent. She drew herself up. *I will keep my composure. I will smile at Lilly, and I will behave with the decorum expected of a duchess.*

Turning into the east corridor, she walked with steady steps towards the staterooms, the sound of her heels muffled against the thick carpet. Outside the Green Drawing Room, she paused for a moment and drew in a deep breath. Her corset rose and pinched. *Ouch! And out...* She pressed a gloved hand briefly to her waist, then, summoning her most serene expression, she inched forward.

The Green Drawing Room was already bustling as she entered. The high ceiling was adorned with intricate plaster-work and the faint sheen of gilt. Rich green damask lined the walls, and tall windows were framed with matching drapes. The magnificent marble fireplace—a commanding presence carved with mythological creatures and trailing vines—crackled with warm cheer, casting golden shadows across the floor.

Almost at once, George appeared at her side. "Your Grace," he murmured, bowing, then offered her a crystal flute of champagne.

"Thank you, George," she replied warmly, happy to see the familiar face of her footman. "I didn't expected to see you here tonight. I thought you would still be settling the luggage."

A faint smile tugged at a corner of his mouth. "Mr Stokes asked if I might lend a hand this evening, ma'am. With so many guests, he thought it best to draft in familiar help."

She gave him a knowing look. "And I suppose it is hard to refuse one's own father."

"There is that, ma'am." He stood a little straighter. "But it's also good to be back. I cut my teeth here, so I owe it a great deal."

Her expression softened. "Well, Francis Court is lucky to have you back again." She tilted her head, a wry smile on her face. "But don't get an idea that you want to stay, please. I need you with me at Darby House."

He offered a quiet bow. "Of course, ma'am. I suspect it is too… er, quiet for me here anyway," he said with a faint grin before slipping away.

Disguising her own smile, she sipped her champagne and scanned the room for Duncan and Fee. Her heart sank. Her older brother and his wife didn't appear to be here yet. When her gaze found her other brother James though, she brightened and moved towards him. He was deep in conversation with a tall, confident-looking young man, whom she recognised but whose name eluded her. She stopped in front of them. "Hello, little brother," she said warmly as she reached out to him.

"Alice!" James turned with his usual easy affection, taking her offered hand. "You look amazing, as always."

His companion coughed.

"Oh, Alice," James continued quickly. "Allow me to introduce Mr Sebastian Hawthorne. He's Lord and Lady Hawthorne's son." James' head inclined towards an older couple talking to her parents over by the fireplace.

Of course! That was why she'd recognised him.

Sebastian bowed with a flourish that seemed a touch too practiced. "Your Grace, it's a pleasure." He smiled slyly. "Your brother hardly does you justice with his remark."

Ew! She fought the urge to pull a face. *What is it with the overly smooth ones? Do they all rehearse their lines in the mirror before emerging into Society?* "Mr Hawthorne," she said, inclining her head. "Your generosity does you credit, sir. But it would be unwise to believe everything my family says. They're most unreliable where praise is concerned."

Sebastian blinked, caught off guard for the briefest of moments before offering a laugh that was rather too loud to be entirely natural. *He's handsome, certainly, but there's something slightly off-kilter about him—he's too polished looking, too eager to please.* It surprised her that James, who was usually discerning in his friendships, seemed to be enjoying his company.

As the two men resumed their conversation, she glanced around the room. Her gaze settled on Lilly Forthington, who was talking animatedly with one of their other cousins. She was clad in a daring gown of rose silk, which clung to her rather more than was strictly proper. *Typical!* Her honey-blonde curls were piled high and artfully arranged to appear almost accidental. *Well, at least she's not with Vance,* Alice thought as she looked away, across the room to where Lady Cordelia Granville was deep in conversation with another lady.

With her tall, dramatic silhouette draped in a lavender gown, Cordelia cut an imposing figure. Her raven-black hair was coiled atop her head in an intricate style, and her luminous grey eyes glinted as she chatted with her companion.

Their voices were little more than murmurs beneath the rustle of fabric and the clink of glasses, but that hardly mattered. Alice had long since realised she could follow a conversation by watching the shape of a person's mouth, the twitch of a lip, the curve of a vowel. She hadn't thought much of it over the years— it was just one of those things she'd done ever since the shooting accident that had left her temporarily deaf when she'd been younger. It was proving really rather useful these days — some people really ought to be more mindful of their mouths. She studied the two women's lips more closely…

"…I've heard he's already growing tired of Lilly Forthington," Cordelia said, her mouth curving into a smirk.

Alice stiffened. She knew no good came from eavesdropping, but she found herself unable to look away.

"She clings to him like ivy on stone, and he's complaining about it, apparently," she continued.

A bitter taste rose in Alice's throat, though she didn't quite know whether it was from humiliation or indignation. The idea that Vance was already airing complaints about his mistress was bad enough. That others were discussing it—with that arch, self-satisfied tone of Cordelia's—was quite another.

The other woman gave a conspiratorial smile. "I hope you have no aspirations there yourself, Cordelia. Everyone knows the duke would never consider divorcing his wife."

Never consider divorcing his wife, indeed! Well, perhaps I'll divorce him!

She hoped no one noticed the flush she couldn't quite control, but she kept her posture composed, her gaze cool.

Cordelia looked smug. "Not for Lilly, no. But for the right woman…"

So Cordelia fancies herself as next in line, does she? She suppressed a huff. *And what am I? A public seat to be claimed the moment it's vacated?* She turned her head, her lips tightening. She was unsure whether to feel insulted, intrigued, or simply weary of it all. What was it about Vance that inspired such delusions in otherwise sensible women? Had she grown so used to his charms that she no longer saw what they saw?

At that moment the door opened. *Fee?* Her stomach clenched as Vance entered. Where was her best friend when she needed her?

Her husband was, as always, immaculately dressed, his black hair brushed back to reveal the distinguished silver at his temples. He moved with the confidence of a man thoroughly aware of the impression he made.

No, she thought, *he may not possess Henry Rivershore's striking features, but he has presence—undeniable and effortless.* But presence wasn't character. She recalled a comment he'd made during one of their last arguments in London—how "overfamiliar" it was for her to allow a footman like George to speak so freely in her presence. As if kindness were a failing. As if loyalty from the staff was something to be curbed, not earned. It had stayed with her. The coldness in his tone. The way he'd dismissed her trust as naïveté.

Their eyes met. For a fleeting moment, everything else receded. Then Vance's expression darkened as his gaze shifted to James and Sebastian at her side.

A shiver ran down her back. *What's that all about?*

Before she could ponder it further, Lilly swept across the room with the urgency of one fearing displacement; at that precise moment, Cordelia detached herself from her companion. The two women converged at Vance's side like debutantes vying for the first dance. A smile twitched on her lips. *Oh, ladies!*

At that moment, the door opened again, and in came Duncan, Fee, and Baxter. Her shoulders dropped. *At last!* As the trio made their way over to her, she realised someone was missing from their party. *Henry...*

Beside her, Sebastian Hawthorne excused himself to James. He made his way to join his parents right as her other brother's party stopped in front of them.

"Alice," Fee said brightly, taking her hand. "That dress is sensational." Duncan followed with a warm greeting, and Baxter, ever the stoic, offered a polite bow.

"James." Duncan drew his brother aside. "We must speak."

She leaned towards Fee. "Where's Henry?"

Baxter replied for his sister, "Henry has exercised good sense and chosen not to attend this evening."

Her skin prickled as her eyes narrowed. "And I suppose you had nothing to do with his decision?" she asked, her voice dripping with sarcasm.

Baxter's lips quirked into a smirk. "Now, now, Alice. I merely suggested it might be prudent given the... er, delicate nature of this afternoon's events."

She bit back a retort, knowing—much as it galled her—that Baxter was probably right; yet, the knowledge did little to temper the simmering irritation she felt at being so neatly managed. She lifted her chin and said coolly, "I'm quite capable of managing my own affairs, Lord Rushton."

Baxter folded his arms, his smirk deepening. "Someone has to think about your reputation, and it is plainly not going to be you."

"You're infuriating," she muttered, unable to keep the edge from her voice.

"Only when I'm right," he said smoothly, entirely unrepentant.

Fee gave an exaggerated sigh and stepped between them with the ease of long practice. "Must I separate you two like unruly children again? Honestly, I begin to wonder if we need to place you at opposite ends of the dinner table." She gave them both a pointed look, one brow elegantly arched. "Do try to behave like civilised creatures, at least until after dinner."

Baxter gave Fee a mock bow. "As you wish, dear sister. I

shall be the very picture of decorum—though I cannot speak for Her Grace."

Alice huffed, lifting her chin with mock dignity. "I'm perfectly civil," she said, fighting the corners of her mouth as they twitched.

As infuriating as he might be, the biggest problem with Baxter was he was not often wrong. *And he knows it!* She shot him a sideways glare. "I'm beginning to understand why you've not found anyone else to marry you all these years."

Fee rolled her eyes heavenward. "And they wonder why I drink sherry before dinner."

Baxter opened his mouth to reply but was stopped by the approach of Alice's parents, the Duke and Duchess of Arnwall, and Baxter and Fee's parents, the Earl and Countess of Langdon.

As the neighbouring families exchanged greetings, Alice turned her head and saw Vance. He was laughing at something Cordelia was saying, his hand lightly resting at her waist. Alice's ribs squeezed. *Is he really ever going to change?*

Aware prying eyes were watching her with interest, she turned away but not before, with no small amount of satisfaction, she saw Lilly hovering at the edge of Vance and Cordelia's conversation, looking as though she'd just swallowed a lemon whole.

7

LATER THAT EVENING…

Alice's heels clicked on the polished wood floor as she made her way to the library at Francis Court, her mind swirling with thoughts of Vance and their impending meeting. The murmur of conversation and the clinking of post-dinner coffee cups faded behind her as she moved further away from the drawing room. Each step felt deliberate, like the beat of a drum leading her into battle.

Dinner had passed with merciful decorum, if not ease. Fee had looked ready to faint when she'd seen the place cards—Alice had been seated beside Baxter. But their long friendship had always rebounded quickly from quarrels, and tonight had proven no different as they'd fallen back into their usual rhythm easily enough.

They'd talked of their boys—Albert, Baxter's son, known as Bertie to his family, was at Eton, and Harry and Freddie were at Vance's old school in Derbyshire—who, similar in ages, enjoyed spending time together in the summer when they visited their respective grandparents in Fenshire. As dinner had progressed, she'd found herself studying Baxter afresh. He'd cut a dashing figure in his evening attire, dark hair gleaming in the candlelight. Unbidden, her earlier jibe about his unmarried state had drifted back to her. Why had he never remarried? It couldn't have been grief; his marriage to his late wife, Charlotte, had been brief and dutiful, not a great love story. *He's handsome enough and wealthy, if a little overprotective. But a lot of women* like *that, do they not?*

As she'd contemplated Baxter's bachelor status, her eyes had caught Vance's directly across the table from her. His gaze had been intense and unreadable. It had sent a confusing jolt through her chest, as though he were plucking at an old wound that had healed long ago. *What does he want with me?* she'd wondered.

At least Cordelia and Lilly had been far down the table, too distant to do more than cast the occasional glance Vance's way. Although, Alice had caught Lilly's more than once: sharp, assessing, and perhaps a little desperate?

And, of course, Vance had been next to Aunt Cora. That pairing had not been accidental. She was quite certain of it. Her aunt had made her views plain before she'd left for Francis Court: Vance was a nincompoop, yes—but he was Alice's nincompoop, and she ought to do her best to patch things up, if only for the sake of Harry and Freddie. "A duchess has certain obligations, you know, my dear," had been her final say on the matter. *Obligations indeed! As if I could ever forget.* She'd grimaced. Had Aunt Cora passed along the same speech to Vance between bites of pheasant and potatoes, reminding him that a husband's affections are best kept under one roof and ideally aimed at his wife?

Now, as Alice paused near the heavy oak door of the library, she smoothed her skirts and took a steadying breath. "Come now, Alice," she murmured to herself. "You've faced far worse than a conversation with your own husband." But even so, her stomach twisted as though she were heading into court, not conversation. The weight of their strained marriage, of unspoken words and growing distance, seemed to press down upon her shoulders.

As she stood there, Baxter's words over dessert echoed in her mind. "I know you're uneasy about this meeting with Vance, Alice." His tone had been gentle, devoid of their usual teasing. "But you'll be fine. Hear him out, but don't let him sway you with charm or guilt. Stand firm about what *you* need. You deserve respect. Don't settle for less."

Respect. Yes, she deserved respect...

She drew a breath and straightened her shoulders, one hand smoothing the fabric of her skirts. *Enough stalling.* With a steadying exhale, she turned the knob and pushed open the door.

She paused a little way inside the room, her eyes adjusting to the warm glow of the gas lamps. The scent of leather-bound books and polished wood enveloped her, a familiar comfort in this moment of uncertainty. The fire crackled low in the hearth, casting amber light across the bookshelves and writing desk. Vance stood by the hearth, one hand tucked into his pocket, the other cradling a glass of brandy.

He turned as she entered, his expression warm but guarded.

"Good evening, Vance," she greeted formally while wincing inwardly at the stiffness in her voice.

"Good evening, Alice," he replied, his tone softer than she'd expected. "Thank you for coming."

She inclined her head. "I said I would."

The fire popped softly in the hearth. The ticking of the ornate clock on the mantel seemed to thunder in the uncomfortable silence. Alice steadied herself. *Breathe...*

Vance cleared his throat. "Would you care to sit?" He gestured to a pair of wingback chairs nearby.

"Yes, thank you," she murmured, carefully lowering herself onto the soft leather seat.

"Brandy?" He placed his glass and poured her one from a decanter on the sideboard. He handed it to her, then picked up his own again and sat down opposite her.

Her fingers itched to fidget with the hem of her sleeve, but she forced them to remain still in her lap. "I suppose we have much to discuss," she ventured at last, breaking the tense silence.

Vance nodded gravely. "Indeed, we do, my dear. Indeed, we do." Then he exhaled, his expression sheepish. "Alice, I owe you an apology—for this afternoon. And... for far more besides."

Here we go.... She said nothing, biting back the instinct to scoff. *An apology? Or merely a tidy excuse?*

"About Lilly. In hindsight, I should have asked her not to come," he said, his voice steady, "but she *was* invited by your parents—by your father, I believe, and quite separate from me."

Of course, an excuse. "How convenient," she murmured.

Vance winced. "Perhaps I deserve that. But it's the truth, Alice."

Well, you still should have stopped her coming!

"But I *am* sorry for any embarrassment her being here is causing you," he continued.

At least he was acknowledging the impact it was having on her... She took a breath. "You said in your note that you wanted a fresh start. What does that mean to you, Vance?"

He met her eyes, and for a moment, something unguarded flickered there. "It means I'm tired of pretending we're strangers. I miss the life we were meant to build together. And I miss… us, Alice. I would like us to try again."

She tilted her head, assessing him carefully. "Try again? By which you mean I'm to return to Manning Hall and pretend the past few years didn't happen?"

"No," he blurted. "No pretending. I know I've made mistakes. But I'm willing to do better." He raised an eyebrow. "But it will take both of us, Alice."

She bristled, then remembered that she, too, had to take some responsibility for where they were now. She took a sip of her brandy. It hit the back of her throat with a fierce, smoky warmth, stealing her breath for a moment before settling into a slow, heady burn in her chest. She welcomed the sensation; it gave her something tangible to focus on, something to anchor her against the tangle of emotions tightening inside her. "I suppose we should both acknowledge the path we've chosen these past few years, Vance. It has been... less than ideal."

Vance's hazel eyes met hers, a flicker of something— regret, perhaps?—passing through them. "Yes, I believe we must. Alice, you know I've tried to make Manning Hall a home for us, for our boys. But you never seem to want to be there unless the children are present."

Her chest tightened a little. She hated to admit it, but he was right. "It's true, I've struggled to embrace country life. The endless talk of hounds and horses, the rustic pursuits... It's not who I am, Vance."

He leaned forward in his chair, his voice earnest. "I understand that, Alice, but Manning Hall is not simply our home. It's an estate that needs managing, that provides livelihoods for countless families. I cannot simply abandon my responsibilities there."

Good heavens! She'd never heard Vance talk about

managing his estate in such terms. She'd assumed he spent all his time hunting, fishing, and shooting. *Have I misjudged him?*

Vance's expression softened as he continued, "There's much to do, Alice. And you could make a real difference."

Me? Do country things? She suppressed a shudder. "You want me to play the benevolent lady of the manor, handing out blankets and hymn books?"

"I want you to be involved," he said simply. "In whatever way you wish. Start a school for the local children if you like. Sponsor the village library. Modernise the tenant cottages; goodness knows they could use it. Bring a slice of your London style to the countryside."

She narrowed her eyes. Flattery? It was how he'd used to get his way before. *Does he really think I'll fall for that again?*

She looked away, studying the flicker of the fire. *But...* The idea of being useful tugged at something inside her—she would have a purpose. She tapped her gloved fingers thoughtfully against the arm of her chair. "And I would have my own projects and make my own decisions?"

"Entirely," Vance agreed readily. "I won't interfere."

He seems sincere. Is it possible that he really means it? "And London? You know how I adore the city, the culture, the energy…"

"You'll have it for the Season," he said, leaning back. "I'll open Stortford House properly. We can be there together —my steward is more than capable of overseeing the estate in my absence for a short period."

Her fingers tingled. *Stortford House?* She'd been unhappy that Vance had refused in the past to open the London house for her to use, arguing that it was too expensive to run and staff for just one person. Much to his annoyance, rather than give up her plans to spend her time in town, she'd taken up residence in Darby House, which she would one day inherit from her mother. She loved Darby House, but it was too small for large-scale entertaining. But at Stortford House she could have balls and soirees galore… A flicker of possibility stirred. *Is it foolish to believe him?* Or was this the compromise she'd never thought possible?

But what about… "Vance, I can't… I won't be the subject of gossip and speculation any longer. It's untenable."

Vance's expression suddenly hardened. "Then perhaps you ought not to parade about with Lord Rivershore."

She stiffened as though he'd struck her. The heat drained from her face. *So that's it. Not remorse. Not affection. Just jealousy.*

8

———

A FEW TENSE SECONDS LATER…

She set down her glass with a deliberate *clink* against the table, her fingers trembling only slightly. Her hand curled into a fist in her lap. *So this is my fault, is it?*

"Parade about?" she repeated, her voice low and scathing. "Forgive me, Your Grace, but I'd not realised that exchanging civil conversation at a family gathering constituted parading."

"And you are sure the *ton* understands that, are you?" Vance snapped back.

Ah… so he has heard the rumours….

"There's no parade, and there's no affair," she retorted, her cheeks hot.

A thought struck her. *Is this why he's doing this?* Was this some power play to show she was his and no one else could have her? Her heart hammered in her chest, but she kept her chin high. "Is it merely that you cannot bear to see someone else appreciate what you've so long taken for granted?"

He flinched, a flicker of pain unguarded in his eyes. "I never thought I owned you, Alice," he said, his voice rough. "God knows, I've given you more freedom than most men would ever allow their wives."

Oh, so you want a medal then, do you?

She shifted in her chair. She knew he spoke the truth—Vance might have whinged a bit at first, but he'd never once *forbidden* her the London life she loved.

His words should have reassured her. Instead, they twisted like a knife because wasn't that the problem? He hadn't cared enough to try?

But then the memory of all the careless humiliations, of whispers behind fans and across salons, surged back with brutal force. She rose abruptly, her skirts whispering against the rug. "Then let us speak plainly, Vance. About Lilly. About Cordelia. About all the *many* others."

Vance pushed to his feet, his hands raised in a gesture of surrender. "I won't pretend I've been a saint," he said, his voice tight. "But we've lived apart for years, Alice, and—" He broke off, his jaw tightening, but after a moment, he exhaled, long and low. "You're right. This... all of it... must end."

He rubbed his forehead. "I will finish things with Lilly. There's no one else." He met her eyes. "In return, are you willing to distance yourself from Henry?"

She folded her arms. "So I must give up even the idea of being admired, but you—"

"I'm attempting sincerity, Alice. Please don't punish me for the effort."

She stared at him. There it was. A sliver of truce, held out like a rare coin. Was she foolish enough to take it?

He raised a brow. "I'm asking for fairness, not control."

Her pulse raced as she gazed at Vance, the weight of their conversation pressing upon her. She could hear the distant ticking of the grandfather clock in the hall. *Time...* Was it time to let go and start again? Perhaps. But first she needed to know this wasn't merely Vance having had his nose put out by her rumoured dalliance with Henry. It had to be more than that if it was to work… "Why are you doing this, Vance?"

He hesitated. "Because I don't want to spend the next twenty years pretending we're strangers. Because I still believe we can be… something more than parents and polite dinner companions at family events."

She fidgeted with the lace on her sleeve, her brow furrowed.

He took a step towards her. "Let's stay on after the party, Alice. Once the other guests leave. Let's talk—without Lilly or Rivershore or Aunt Cora playing audience. Just the two of us. To... work things out."

The lines near his eyes, once softened by laughter, seemed etched deeper now. *Did I do that?* Or was it age? For the first time in a long while, she saw not the charming philanderer or the infuriating nincompoop, but the man she'd once thought she could build a life with.

Could they truly bridge the chasm between them?

"All right," she breathed. "A few days. No promises. But," she added, "you must end things with Lilly. Completely."

"I will," he vowed. "And Henry Rivershore?"

Her stomach clenched at the thought of distancing herself from Henry, but she knew it was necessary. "I'll ask him to back off. It's… for the best."

"Thank you," he said with a deep bow.

She picked up her skirt and walked to the door. When she reached it, she turned back to him. "I will hold you to every-thing you've said, Vance."

"And I'll hold you to that school," he replied, a soft smile cracking his face.

What have I got myself into now? Starting a school in the

country? She paused. *But I might like that…* "We shall see." Then she opened the door and walked out of the room.

As she made her way back down the corridor, the low hum of voices from the drawing room grew louder, but her thoughts drowned them out. Her footsteps were steady, her expression composed, but inside, she felt unmoored. Vance had said all the right things—mostly—and yet, she couldn't shake the suspicion that beneath the olive branches and agreeable proposals, the old patterns still lurked, waiting to reassert themselves the moment her back was turned.

And yet… there had been something different in his manner tonight.

Not simply charm but contrition.

Not merely promises but purpose.

Perhaps that was what unsettled her most of all—he could've meant it. And worse, a part of her wanted to believe him…

9

———

THE NEXT EVENING...

Alice perched on the cushioned window seat in her bedchamber, her forehead resting lightly against the cool pane. She stared down at the lush greenery framing the pathways, at the clipped box hedges, and the neat, colourful blaze of the rose garden beyond. Francis Court's gardens had long been a source of quiet pride for her father, laid out in careful, intricate symmetry—every blossom accounted for, every gravel path raked to perfection. Yet, today, even the riot of early summer roses seemed muted to her eye.

A sigh escaped her lips, misting the glass before her. Only this morning, with the weight of her promise to Vance on her shoulders, she'd dispatched a note to Baxter, pleading for his discreet intervention with Henry. A few hours later, Stokes had announced Lord Rivershore's arrival, and she, heavy-hearted, had received him in the Red Salon.

Henry, with an effortless charm she found so intoxicating, had bowed low before her. "If my presence is a burden to you, Your Grace, you need only say the word," he'd said with a gallant, almost boyish smile. "I would not wish to cause you the least distress."

Alice, her gloves twisting in her lap, had met his gaze steadily. "It's not distress you cause, Henry, but complication. Vance and I… we are attempting to find a way forward. Your being here only clouds the waters." She'd hated how her voice had caught at the end.

He'd accepted her answer with good grace, pressing her hand lightly. "Then I shall take my leave of you. I wish you only happiness, Alice."

As the door had closed behind him, she'd felt not relief but a curious hollowness. She'd enjoyed Henry's attention.

Is that mere vanity, or might there have been something more?

A gentle tap on the door announced Maud's arrival, and the slender maid entered, her chestnut curls bobbing with each step as she carried the evening's gown—a ballgown of silk, the colour of dark twilight skies.

"You'll be the finest lady in the room tonight, ma'am," Maud said firmly as she began lacing Alice into her corset.

As Maud worked, she chatted in low tones, sharing the morsels of gossip that only a lady's maid could glean, and Alice lapped it up as always.

"You might find this rather odd, ma'am, but Tom doesn't seem too keen on being His Grace's valet. Quite out of character for him, I must say."

"Indeed?" She arched an eyebrow. "Tom usually relishes a change in his duties. Whatever could be the matter?"

Maud lowered her voice, almost conspiratorially. "Well, I think he is... disapproving of the duke, which is most unlike him." Suddenly, she clamped her hand over her mouth and shook her head. "Begging your pardon, ma'am," she said as she lowered her hand. "It's not my place to remark on such things. He's your husband…"

"Think nothing of it, Maud," she replied, patting her maid

on the arm. "If truth be told, I share a similar sentiment where the duke is concerned."

A brief smile flickered across Maud's features before she turned and carefully picked up the ballgown. "In other news, Lady Cordelia's maid was sent on an urgent errand today—to fetch a particular perfume rumoured to be quite... enchanting. They say it's made with rare essences that could ensnare a man's heart."

I wonder if it works on recalcitrant husbands? Then her shoulders tensed. Was Cordelia serious about her pursuit of Vance? Up until now, she'd only thought of it as harmless flirting on the young widow's part—she was known "to make the most of her widowhood" as *The Society Page* had commented recently.

The silken fabric of the dress whispered against her skin as Maud helped her into it. The maid's nimble fingers began to work the many fastenings. "And Lady Forthington's maid was summoned upstairs this afternoon. It was quite the to-do," she said, finishing the last button and stepping back to survey her work. "Her maid found her in great distress, threatening to leave altogether. They had to send for her parents to calm the situation."

"Goodness," Alice murmured, smoothing down the folds of her gown. She met Maud's eyes in the mirror, a shared understanding passing between them.

Maud made a final adjustment to her hair, then stood back, a satisfied half-smile on her face as she looked her up and down. "You look every inch a duchess, ma'am."

"Thank you, Maud." Her reflection smiled back at her—a duchess encased in steel and silk—poised to face whatever challenges the evening might bring.

Five minutes later, she descended the grand staircase, the murmur of voices drawing her towards the Green Drawing

Room, where pre-dinner drinks were already being served. As she stepped carefully along the grand hallway, she passed the door to the morning room and heard voices—sharp and urgent. She slowed instinctively, the thick carpet runner muffling her steps.

"…you leave him be, or you'll answer to me." Vance's tone had a clear note of warning threading through it.

She couldn't move. It wasn't the threat itself that shook her but rather the realisation that Vance wasn't protecting himself—he was protecting someone else.

"I've done nothing wrong," said the other person; she immediately recognised the slick tones of Sebastian Hawthorne. "We're merely friends."

"You've caused enough trouble with your little games; I will not have him ensnared further in your debts or schemes," Vance said firmly.

"Vance, old chap, I assure you it's all friendly sport," came Sebastian's smoother, though slightly anxious reply.

"Debts are no sport," Vance retorted. "So I'm warning you. I will—"

Vance must have turned away as she could no longer hear what he was saying. *Who are they talking about?* She lingered only a moment longer, her heart pounding, before continuing down the corridor. She knew her husband—he didn't offer warnings lightly.

Inside the Green Drawing Room, the chandeliers bathed the gathered guests in golden light, their laughter and chatter creating a confusing bubble of noise. She took in a deep breath and focussed on the friendly face of her footman George as he advanced towards her with a glass of champagne held high on a tray. "Good evening, Your Grace." He bowed low as he presented the drink to her.

She took it from the tray. "Thank you, George," she

murmured, reassured by the familiarity of his steady presence. "I see Stokes has pressed you into service again."

George allowed himself the barest smile. "I am happy to lend a hand, ma'am."

She beamed warmly at him, then moved further into the room, quickly spotting Baxter standing by the fireplace, his tall frame easy to see. She glided towards him, then stopped in front of him, offering him her hand. "Good evening, Baxter."

"Alice." He took her hand and bowed over it. "You look concerned. Is everything all right?"

"I overheard Vance speaking with Sebastian Hawthorne," she confessed in a hushed tone, leaning closer so as not to be overheard. "He seemed to be warning him away from someone. Do you know anything about this?"

Baxter's expression darkened. "I've heard rumours Sebastian Hawthorne has been keeping some rather unsavoury company in London. Gamblers. Ruthless men. But I'm not aware of any specifics."

Her mind raced. Vance had said "him". So who was Sebastian taking advantage of, and why had Vance intervened? Before she could give it much more thought, Vance himself entered the room, his presence commanding immediate attention. Sebastian followed in his wake, trying—and failing—to match the duke's composure.

Vance crossed directly to her, his attention unmistakably focused. "Alice." He reached out, took her hand, and bowed over it. "I trust you've had a productive day?"

A tingle danced up her arm as the warmth of her husband's fingers permeated her glove. "I have done some… er, chores I had been putting off."

He raised an eyebrow as he gently released her hand. "I, too, have concluded some… er, necessary business."

We understand each other…

Vance turned to Baxter. "Good evening, viscount," he said, extending a hand to Baxter in a gesture of polite civility. His gaze then shifted back to her, and for a brief moment, warmth flickered in his hazel eyes before being shuttered behind a practiced smile.

"Your Grace," Baxter replied, the handshake brief and formal.

"It is good to see you, Baxter," Vance continued, the formalities over with. "I trust Bertie is well? Our boys are looking forward to seeing him this summer."

Baxter's expression softened. "He's keen to see them too, Vance."

As the two men continued to talk about their sons, Alice caught Lilly's glare from across the room; her cheeks were blotchy with barely suppressed fury.

Even if Vance had not just confirmed it, it was obvious from her cousin's demeanour that he'd told Lilly it was over between them.

———

The chandeliers cast a soft glow over the supper table, glimmering off the silverware and crystal as Alice took her seat. To her surprise, Vance was already there, his dark eyes seeking hers with an unreadable expression.

"Your aunt was most accommodating," he murmured as she settled into her chair. "It seems we have her to thank for our proximity this evening."

Suppressing a smile, she recalled Vance's fluid grace during the quadrille earlier, his movements in perfect harmony with her aunt's practiced steps in the moments between dancing with the other couples. They'd cooked this up together, no doubt. She glanced towards Aunt Cora, who offered a knowing nod from across the room.

"Indeed," Alice replied, brushing a loose strand of red hair behind her ear.

"I hope you don't mind, my dear." His lips quirked into a small smile. "I thought it would be charming to sit next to my wife for a change."

"How very… singular of you," she managed, reaching for her water glass to hide her flushed cheeks.

Before they could exchange any further conversation, they were interrupted. "Your Grace, I simply must tell you how marvellous you looked during the quadrille!"

She glanced past her husband to see Lady Cordelia leaning forward, her grey eyes sparkling with admiration. The woman's raven hair was artfully arranged, adorned with jet beads that caught the candlelight. She was striking.

Alice leaned back. *Here we go…*

"You're too kind, Lady Cordelia," Vance replied smoothly, turning to his left. "Although, I confess, I much preferred the waltz."

Alice suppressed a start. Unbidden, a small smile crept over her face. Her mind drifted back to earlier in the night. She'd been standing with Baxter, Fee, and Duncan, observing the swirling dancers when she'd spotted Lady Cordelia approaching Vance along the far wall. Though too far away to hear, she'd clearly read the woman's lips as she'd asked Vance to dance. But to her surprise, he'd politely declined, saying, "I'm afraid I've already promised the waltz to my wife."

Her stomach had fluttered—they'd made no such agreement. But when he'd bowed to Cordelia and made his way towards her, she'd found herself unable to refuse. And, if she were honest with herself, she'd thoroughly enjoyed their turn about the ballroom. She'd not expected to enjoy being in his arms, yet the rhythm and closeness had left her feeling unexpectedly buoyant.

Now, as Lady Cordelia continued to vie for his attention, she observed her husband's responses. While unfailingly polite, there was a distinct coolness to his manner that hadn't been present in his previous interactions with the lively widow.

Perhaps he is *prepared to change?*

As Cordelia and Vance continued to converse, further down the table, James seemed subdued, poking at his food without enthusiasm. She'd noticed during the dancing that he'd been hanging around the walls of the ballroom, scowling, which had been very unlike her normally vibrant and sociable brother.

Her gaze drifted a few seats down from him, where Seb stabbed at his roast as if it had personally insulted him, a thunderous expression on his face. *Have they had a falling out?*

She turned her attention back to her husband in time to hear him say, "I wonder if I might claim your hand for the two-step after dinner, Lady Cordelia?"

Cordelia's face lit up. "Oh, Your Grace! I would be delighted!" She took a sip of wine and turned to the man on her other side, still beaming.

Vance turned to Alice, a smug smile on his face. "It was the only way I could think to shut her up," he whispered.

We've been married long enough to know that's never worked. She forced a smile. "Indeed," she replied, although she could imagine many alternatives—*including not asking her to dance!*

———

The strains of the two-step filled the ballroom as Alice twirled gracefully in Baxter's arms, her deep-blue gown swirling about her ankles. Despite her partner's amusing conversation, a dull throb pulsed at her temples, and the ballroom's gilded chandeliers seemed suddenly too bright.

"Alice, are you quite well?" he asked, his brow furrowed in concern. "You seem rather subdued?"

She forced a smile. "I'm just..." Her voice trailed off as she spotted Lady Cordelia's pale-lilac gown disappearing through a side door with Vance's tall figure following close behind.

A jolt shot through her chest. *Was Vance's attentiveness earlier merely a facade?*

Baxter's gaze followed hers. "Don't concern yourself, Alice. They are surely only taking some fresh air," he said in a reassuring voice.

She swallowed hard. *Fresh air, my foot!* Her head felt like it would explode. *I need a drink...* The dance finished, and she curtsied to Baxter while her eyes searched for an escape from the heat and noise of the ballroom. As she took his arm, she spotted Tom, now attired in his footman's livery, with a tray of drinks. She steered Baxter towards him.

"Your Grace." Tom handed her a crystal flute. "Some champagne?"

"Thank you, Tom," she murmured, accepting the glass. She noticed his hazel eyes studying her face intently, a flicker of concern passing over his features before he offered the tray to Baxter. *I must look a mess!* "Would you care to step outside for some air, Bax? I'm feeling rather warm."

"Of course." He gave her his arm and steered her towards the open doors leading to the terrace. Stepping out into the cooler air, she inhaled deeply. *And breathe...* But the cool night air did little to calm her racing thoughts as her eyes scanned the gardens, searching for any sign of her husband and Lady Cordelia.

"Alice," Baxter said gently, "I can see something is troubling you. I know I'm not Fee, but you can confide in me, and I'll do my best to counsel you…"

She sighed, her shoulders sagging. "Oh, Bax. I'm so confused. One moment, Vance seems genuinely interested in reconciling, and the next…" She gestured helplessly. "Well, you saw them leave together."

He nodded. "I did. But as I said, there's likely an innocent explanation," he said, although his tone suggested he doubted it.

She shook her head. "What other reason could they have for sneaking off like that?" She gazed out at the moonlit gardens, a sudden breeze chilling her shoulders. "I fear I've been a fool to hope."

10

BACK TO SUNDAY, 31 MAY 1891

Alice clutched the banister of the grand staircase at Francis Court, her knuckles pale against the dark wood, her heart pounding in her chest as she stared down at the crumpled form of her husband. Vance lay sprawled unnaturally on the half-landing below. On wobbly legs, she picked her way carefully down the steps. The house lay cloaked in an eerie stillness, broken only by the echo of footsteps on marble and the ragged edge of her own breathing.

The gaslight from the landing sconce cast eerie shadows across his still face, making him appear almost ghostly.

"Ma'am," Maud whispered, her voice trembling, "perhaps we should retire to your chambers. This is no sight for a lady."

She barely registered her maid's words, her mind whirling as she tried to make sense of the scene before her. The pale morning light seeped weakly through the tall windows, blurring the edges of the Painted Hall into a mist of blue and gold. Everything felt suspended—caught between night and day, between dream and waking—including Alice.

Something isn't right.

Her gaze travelled up the grand staircase to the second floor, then back down to where Vance lay. The angle seemed off.

When she'd first seen Vance's body, she'd wanted to believe it had been an accident. But something deep within her rebelled at the idea.

"Maud," she murmured, her brow furrowing, "does it not strike you as peculiar? If he truly fell from up there, how did he end up... like this?"

Her maid shifted uncomfortably beside her. "I'm sure I would not know, ma'am. Such matters are beyond my understanding. We should go now."

Even as Maud clutched Alice's arm in an effort to stop her from going any closer, some part of her—cold and clear —began taking stock. She forced herself to fix the scene in her memory: the way his body was twisted, one arm thrown awkwardly above his head; the gleam of his polished shoes; the sickening stillness of it all. She looked again. *If he'd stumbled from the top, then why is he not at the foot of the stairs? He's too close to the wall and at a rather odd angle for a fall...* Her stomach twisted. *I need a closer look.* "I must go down to him," she said, her voice brittle and too loud in the vast emptiness.

Maud tightened her grip and let out an exasperated, "Ma'am, please. We really should wait for Mr Stokes."

But Alice shook her off with a sharp movement, already descending, her robe whispering against the marble. There was a chance that if she looked closely—properly—this would reveal itself as some dreadful misunderstanding.

She hesitated halfway down, the shifting half-light blurring the world into uneasy shapes. She clutched the banister until her fingers ached, willing herself to turn away, but she couldn't. For one disorienting moment, she almost convinced herself she was still dreaming—that if she simply turned away, the horror awaiting her would dissolve with the coming sun. Perhaps she would wake up and find herself back in her bedchamber, still planning for the future they'd promised each other only yesterday.

She continued downwards, but as she reached the step above the half-landing, she faltered. Vance was still dressed in last night's clothes: black tailcoat, white waistcoat now dreadfully askew, his cravat a mess. His face, so often flushed with life and laughter—or temper—was grey and slack now. How long had he been lying there unseen? It must be gone five in the morning… Surely, someone would've found him sooner if he'd fallen hours ago. Had he been returning to his chamber after a long night of drinking? Or—her chest tightened—had he been elsewhere first?

She swallowed against the bile rising in her throat. The guest suites on the first floor were so close. Lilly and Cordelia were housed there. Had he been returning from one of their rooms when he'd fallen? The thought scraped raw against her heart.

Still moving as if through treacle, she arrived at the half-landing and knelt awkwardly beside him, careful not to disturb the scene. She forced herself to look closely. The side of his head had struck the back wall of the landing; a large dark-red smear marred the pale plaster. The position of his limbs suggested he had fallen almost sideways. Was that even possible?

The distant sound of hurried footsteps echoed on the marble floor below. She looked down to see Stokes, the butler, climbing the stairs before her with grim efficiency, a dressing gown hastily thrown over his nightshirt. His face, usually composed, blanched as he took in the sight of the fallen duke.

She stood, her throat tight, fighting to maintain her composure. "Stokes," she said, her voice remarkably calm despite the hollow ache in her chest, "have a rider dispatched at once to fetch the rural constable. Tell them... tell them there's been a tragic accident."

Stokes gave a stiff nod. "At once, Your Grace. Young Peter can ride; he's quick and sure."

"Good." She hesitated, then added, "And please have my brother Lord Tilling summoned from Francis Lodge. Quietly. I would prefer as little disturbance as possible." She glanced at Vance's still form, feeling a fierce need to protect what little dignity remained to him. "And please find a… covering or something."

Stokes bowed. "Of course, ma'am."

"One more thing," she said as he turned. "My father must be informed. I leave it to your judgement whether to send to His Grace immediately or to wait until the constable arrives."

Stokes inclined his head once more, his voice low and respectful. "I shall attend to everything, ma'am." He hurried away, his footsteps muffled by the thick carpet beyond the marble floor.

Maud moved down the stairs to join her. "Ma'am, you ought to come away now," she hissed. "There's nothing more you can do here."

But Alice's feet were rooted to the spot. She shook her head, unable to tear her gaze away from her husband's still form. *How can I leave you, Vance?* She shook her head. "I cannot leave him, Maud. Not like this. Not alone."

A cool draft drifted down the stairway, causing her to shiver. She wrapped her arms around herself, her fingers catching on the delicate silk of her robe. The chill seemed to seep into her very bones, a stark reminder of the grim reality before her.

"But, ma'am," Maud persisted gently, "you're trembling. At least allow me to fetch you a shawl."

She nodded absently. "Yes, I suppose that would be wise. Thank you, Maud."

As her maid hurried away, she found herself drawn closer to Vance's body. *Only yesterday, that mouth had curved into a crooked smile when I teased him about his waltzing being rusty.* "Oh, Vance," she murmured. "What happened to you?" They hadn't shared a bed in years, hadn't truly shared a life… and yet, here she was, aching in a way she hadn't expected.

She looked up as if expecting an answer from on high. The house remained silent, but to her, it felt as though it was holding its breath.

She waited, keeping silent vigil over the man who had been her husband, sometimes her adversary, sometimes her companion—and who had, at the very end, promised her a fresh start that would never come.

11

A SHORT WHILE LATER...

T he soft rustle of fabric broke the eerie silence as Stokes, now properly attired, draped a crisp white sheet over Vance's motionless form, obscuring her husband's lifeless face from view. Alice blinked rapidly, feeling as though she were emerging from a peculiar trance. The butler's return had shattered the surreal bubble that had enveloped her.

"Your Grace," Stokes said, his voice low and measured. "I have sent word to your brother at Francis Lodge. The stable lad has gone to fetch the constable, and I have informed your father's valet of the situation. We think it best not to disturb His Grace until the authorities arrive."

She nodded absently, her gaze still fixed on the sheet-covered mound on the landing. "Thank you, Stokes," she murmured.

Maud touched her elbow, her brown eyes filled with concern. "Perhaps you should return to your room to rest, ma'am," she suggested gently. "I can prepare a soothing tea…"

Looking down, Alice's eyes widened as she suddenly

became acutely aware of her state of undress. *Good heavens, I am still in my nightclothes!* Soon the household would be stirring, and the police would arrive. She couldn't possibly be seen like this.

"Yes, Maud, you're quite right," she said, her cheeks flushing faintly. "I must get dressed at once." As she turned to leave, a thought struck her. "Stokes," she said, her voice stronger now. "We should close off the stairs until... Until the duke is moved."

"Of course, ma'am. I'll see to it straightaway," he replied with a small bow.

"And could you arrange for tea and coffee to be laid out in the morning room?" she added. The mundane request felt absurd in light of the circumstances, but she was craving the bitter warmth of coffee to chase away the chill that had settled in her bones.

"Of course," Stokes replied with a slight bow.

As she followed Maud towards her chambers, her mind whirled with the events of the morning. *Good Lord,* she thought. *I am going to need the strongest cup of coffee in all of England to face what's coming.*

———

A short while later, Alice emerged from her room, now properly attired in a sombre navy day dress, her hair hastily pinned up. *I'll need to send to Darby House for mourning clothes later*, she thought as she approached the grand staircase.

She halted abruptly.

A thick rope stretched across the top, adorned with a note in Stokes' impeccable handwriting. "Do not enter. Please use the service stairs," it read, with an arrow pointing to an open door a short distance down the hall.

She inched closer to the main stairs, peering down at the half-landing below. She could make out a sheet-covered mound. She swallowed hard, then she turned away and made her way to the propped-open door leading to the service stairs. As she descended the narrow, utilitarian stairwell, her footsteps echoed hollowly off the bare walls and the air smelled faintly of coal dust and carbolic soap. A cobweb brushed her sleeve, and she swatted it away. "Oh, heavens," she muttered to herself, "what will Aunt Cora say about this unseemly detour?" The thought brought a fleeting, wry smile to her lips.

As she rounded the final bend, a maid bobbed into a curtsy so suddenly she nearly dropped the heavy coal scuttle in her arms. "Beg pardon, Your Grace—I didn't expect—"

"Quite all right," Alice murmured, stepping neatly aside to let the girl pass. "Neither did I."

The maid scurried off, her boots clattering on the stairs as Alice paused for a moment—smoothing her gloves and steadying her breath—then continued down the service staircase.

Finally reaching the morning room, she pushed open the heavy oak door. The familiar space greeted her: pale yellow walls adorned with pastoral scenes, and plush armchairs arranged around a low table, and tall windows with their curtains pulled back. Someone—most likely Stokes—had already seen to the tea table. A silver tray gleamed on the sideboard, bearing polished pots of coffee and tea, a small dish of sugar lumps, and a jug of cream.

"Thank goodness," she muttered, removing her gloves as she made a beeline for the steaming pot. She poured herself a cup, inhaling the rich aroma before taking a sip. The bitter liquid scalded her tongue, but she relished the sensation, the physical discomfort a momentary distraction from her emotional turmoil. *Coffee tastes unchanged—even if everything else has shifted.*

The door swung open, and she turned to see George, her first footman, slightly breathless, his dark hair hastily combed and his livery not quite straightened.

"Your Grace—" He stopped short, his eyes wide. "Forgive me. I had hoped to… That is, I meant to be here to receive you…" He trailed off as he tugged down the front of his coat.

She waved off his concern. "No need for apologies, George. It has been… an unusual start to the morning."

"Indeed, ma'am," he replied, his voice lowering. "I… I wanted to offer my condolences. His Grace was… Well, he'll be sorely missed."

The genuine emotion in his words touched her. "Thank you, George," she said quietly.

The footman bowed, a flicker of sadness crossing his handsome features. "Is there anything I can do, ma'am?"

She hesitated, the nagging doubts about Vance's death bouncing around in her mind. But could she voice such thoughts? *Or am I being fanciful, seeing intrigue where there is only tragedy?* "I… No, thank you, George. Not at the moment." She needed time to gather herself, to articulate her unease in a way that didn't sound like the ravings of a grief-stricken widow. *Widow? Oh my… I'm a widow now…* The word fitted her like a borrowed coat—heavy, awkward, and too large for her shoulders. A wave of something powerful rushed through her. Reaching out with her free hand, she grabbed at the back of the sofa to steady herself.

Just then, the sound of hurried footsteps echoed down the hall, growing louder with each passing second. She turned right as the door burst open, and in rushed Duncan and Baxter, both looking dishevelled and out of breath. Duncan's usually impeccable wavy black hair was a little askew, while Baxter's piercing blue eyes were wide with concern.

Of course they would come tearing in like the cavalry!

They made straight for her, Duncan reaching her first. "Alice!" he cried, his commanding voice tinged with disbelief. "Is it true? About Vance…?"

She nodded slowly, her hands tightening around her coffee cup. "I'm afraid so, Duncan."

He drew her into an embrace, his strong arms offering a momentary refuge. "I'm so sorry, sister. So very sorry." She leaned into his chest.

As Duncan released her, Baxter stepped forward, taking her empty hand in his. "My deepest condolences, Alice. This is a terrible shock." His blue eyes were sombre, his handsome face drawn with worry. His warmth steadied her, grounding her much in the way the coffee had…

"Thank you both," she replied, fighting to keep her composure. "It's… it's been a shock."

Duncan ran a hand through his hair, his grey eyes troubled. "Fee will be here shortly. She's just getting dressed."

She pictured her vibrant sister-in-law rushing to join them. The thought of Fee's warmth and energy was oddly comforting amidst the morning's bleakness.

"Have the police been notified?" Duncan asked, turning to practical matters.

"Yes," she confirmed. "They should arrive soon. Father's valet has been told, but it's been agreed not to inform Father yet. We thought it best to wait for the authorities."

Her brother tipped his head approvingly. "A wise decision. No need to distress him until we've more information."

The ticking of the mantel clock filled the silence, each

second louder than it should have been. She sipped her coffee, grateful for its bitter warmth. She glanced over at George, who was standing by the sideboard. *Should I offer them tea?* "Would you like—"

"I'd like to see him," Duncan blurted out, his voice tight with emotion. "Vance, I mean."

She hesitated, then said, "Of course. I'll take you both. Perhaps... perhaps you could offer your thoughts on what you think might have happened?"

As they moved towards the door, her mind raced. Would her brother and Baxter see the same inconsistencies that troubled her? Or was she truly being fanciful in her shock and grief?

With a deep breath, she led them from the morning room, the weight of uncertainty heavy upon her shoulders.

12

MOMENTS LATER...

Alice's pulse thudded in her ears as she approached the bottom of the grand staircase, her silk slippers barely making a sound on the polished marble floor. A tightness squeezed her chest. *Do I really want to see him again?*

Duncan stepped forward, pulling back the rope that cordoned off the staircase with a decisive motion. Behind him, Baxter hesitated, turning to her with a look of concern in his striking blue eyes. "Are you quite certain you wish to do this, Alice?"

She swallowed hard, willing her voice to remain steady as she lifted her chin and determinedly met his gaze. "Of course I want to come," she replied, infusing her words with more confidence than she truly felt. She gathered her skirts and swept past him, the click of her slippers echoing in the stillness. Following her brother, she focussed on his ramrod-straight back, and they soon reached the first-floor landing. She slowed down, and Baxter overtook her as they continued up to the second floor.

As they reached the half-landing, Alice glanced up instinctively—and paused. The gas sconce nearest the top of the stairs, which had been dark earlier, now glowed steadily, casting warm light over the sheet before them.

Duncan and Baxter exchanged a meaningful glance, their expressions unreadable as they surveyed the scene. Her stomach churned as her brother bent to lift the fabric covering Vance.

I mustn't falter now, she thought desperately, forcing herself to look despite every instinct screaming for her to avert her eyes. She couldn't bear for Duncan and Baxter to see her distress, to think her weak or overly emotional.

As Duncan pulled back the sheet, her gaze traced over Vance's body, once again taking in the unnatural angle of his limbs, the way his once immaculate clothing lay rumpled and askew. But it was the mark on the wall of the half-landing that drew her attention as it had before. *So I didn't imagine it...How did he hit the back wall from a mere tumble down the stairs?* If he'd truly tripped, then his legs would've slipped out below him, carrying him straight down and leaving him near the bottom of the stairs. But he'd fallen with enough momentum to hit the back wall....

Frowning, she studied Vance's hands, noting the absence of any bruises. Had he not even tried to break his fall? The thought sent a chill down her spine. The positioning of his body, the point of the impact... He hadn't braced himself at all. And yet he was on his back, which meant he must've tumbled if he'd fallen face-first... And if he'd tumbled, surely, he would've tried to stop himself?

"How very peculiar," she murmured, almost to herself. "It's almost as though he was..." She trailed off, the word "pushed," dying on her lips as she caught Duncan's sharp look of warning. He dropped the sheet back over Vance once more. She swallowed hard, her throat suddenly dry. She glanced at Baxter, wondering if he, too, saw the inconsistencies, the nagging details that hinted at something far more sinister than a tragic accident. But his face remained impassive, betraying no hint of his inner thoughts.

Her brother's authoritative tone filled the space. "I think it's fairly clear. Vance must have slipped on his way up and taken a nasty topple down the stairs."

She opened her mouth to protest, to point out the discrepancies she'd noticed—the point of the impact on the back wall, the lack of evidence that he'd tried to break his fall—but Baxter cut in before she could speak. "I agree with Duncan," he said smoothly, his blue eyes meeting hers. "It's a terrible thing, but accidents do happen." He looked up. "If he tripped near the top, he'd have fallen with some force. Those stairs are unforgiving stone. A single misstep in the dark…"

Her jaw tightened. *You too, Baxter?*

"Best let the police do their part," Duncan said. "They'll confirm it was an accident soon enough."

Biting her lip, she held her tongue. She loved her brother, but even so, she knew him well enough to recognise the set of his jaw; he would dismiss any alternative theories out of hand. *Better to wait for the police. They will surely notice the inconsistencies.*

At that moment, the shrill sound of the doorbell echoed through the house. Her heart leapt into her throat. *The police!*

"That must be the police," Duncan replied curtly. "Let's go down to meet them, shall we?"

The three of them made their way back down the stairs. Her skirts rustled softly with each step. She couldn't help but notice how Baxter's hand hovered near her elbow, as though ready to steady her should she stumble. The gesture, small as it was, was reassuring.

Constable Peters stood in the foyer, next to Stokes, his oilskin cloak damp at the hem from his bicycle ride across the park. Broad-shouldered and sandy-haired, his ruddy face bore the creases of the nervousness of someone more accustomed to dealing with wayward poachers than sudden deaths in ducal households. He removed his cap and offered a low bow. "My condolences, Your Grace. Lord Tilling. I came as swiftly as I could."

Duncan inclined his head. "Thank you, Peters. I'm afraid it's a rather unfortunate accident."

The constable's eyes darted to the roped-off stairway. "Where…?"

"This way," Duncan said, leading him through to the grand staircase. Alice followed, silently, her gaze fixed on the back of the constable's collar as though willing him to look more closely than she feared he would.

When they reached the half-landing, Peters crouched and lifted the edge of the sheet covering Vance's body.

"He must have lost his footing," Duncan said, his voice calm and matter-of-fact. "He'd been drinking last night, enough, I imagine, that he was unsteady."

The constable nodded, seemingly satisfied. "Yes, well. These stairs are steep, and with the stone"—he tapped the edge of a step—"you wouldn't need to fall far to do some right damage."

She couldn't contain herself any longer. "Constable," she jumped in, ignoring Duncan's sharp intake of breath. "The mark on the wall, where his head struck... Does it not seem strange to you that he hit the back wall? And his hands... there are no bruises, no signs he tried to break his fall."

Duncan, who'd come to stand behind her, spoke gently but firmly. "He may have twisted as he toppled down. Bodies do move in unpredictable ways mid-air."

Peters turned, following the line with his gaze. "Yes.

Quite so. Especially if he plunged backwards. Arms flailing, head turning… It wouldn't take much."

She pressed her lips together. *Another man seemingly disinclined to consider further possibilities!* "Yes. Yes. Tragic," the constable continued as he stood up, brushing his hands together absently. "It does look to be just that. A simple fall."

Her hands clenched around her skirts. *A simple fall,* written off like that. *He's going to report it as a drunken accident, and that will be it.* Vance deserved better than that. *I should protest…* About to open her mouth, she caught a flicker of hesitation in Peters' eyes as his gaze lingered on the wall.

"Still," he added, scratching the edge of his jaw, "it would be prudent, given the status of the deceased and the nature of the household, to have someone from Fenshire headquarters take a second look. Just to be sure."

Her breath caught in her throat.

Duncan's smile faltered. "Is that truly necessary, constable? There's nothing to suggest foul play."

Don't let him change your mind, constable…

"No, my lord," Peters agreed. "But I'd rather err on the side of thoroughness. The public eye may be on this matter, and I do not want any loose ends. I'll send a wire to King's Town—Inspector Meacham should be available."

A rush of hope was preceded by a wave of gratitude towards the man. *At last, someone willing to look beyond the surface.*

"Until then," Peters said, replacing his cap, "I'd ask that no one disturb the scene. No cleaning or moving anything further, if you please."

Duncan's jaw tightened, but he inclined his head. "Very well, constable."

"I shall make for the telegraph office directly." Peters gave a respectful nod and turned to descend the stairs.

A proper detective was coming. *Thanks goodness.* They would get to the bottom of this.

Beside her, Duncan exhaled slowly, his expression clouded with unease. "Confound it!" he muttered under his breath. "Now we'll have the police swarming around the place. Father won't be happy…"

Indeed, he won't. But despite that, she couldn't hide a flicker of hope. It may be inconvenient, but an investigation might reveal the truth about what had happened to Vance. Surely, they owed him that…

13

A FEW HOURS LATER...

The morning room hummed with quiet conversation, the clink of delicate china cups punctuating the sombre gathering. Alice stood by the sideboard, her hands clasped tightly around her third coffee of the morning as she surveyed the strained faces of the occupants of the room.

Over the other side, Lilly Forthington perched on the edge of an ornate settee; her parents hovered anxiously by her side. Her usually bright eyes were now rimmed with red from crying.

Sebastian Hawthorne lounged in an armchair across from them, his languid posture at odds with the tightness around his mouth. Next to him, his parents murmured to each other in low tones.

Lady Cordelia Granville, resplendent in black silk, held court near the windows, her voice a gentle lilt as she offered words of comfort to Alice's parents.

Aunt Cora, standing by the fireplace, caught Alice's eye and made her way over. As she reached the sideboard, she sniffed delicately at the silver coffee service laid out on it.

"Coffee, aunt?" Alice offered, reaching to lift the pot.

Her aunt waved a gloved hand as though fending off a foul odour. "Gracious, no. That dreadful brew sets my nerves jangling. If I wished to lie awake all night contemplating the failings of modern society, I would simply read the papers."

She reached for the teapot instead, inspecting the china with a satisfied nod. "Besides, I never trust anything that can be ground up and drunk before breakfast. *And* it isn't even British."

Tea cup in hand, she turned to Alice, her head tilted slightly to one side, a look of compassion running across her features. "How are you bearing up, my dear?"

She managed a wan smile. "As well as can be expected, I suppose." She glanced around the room, her gaze snagging on an empty chair by the window. Would Vance have been sitting there if he'd still been alive? Something prickled at the back of her eyes. "It all feels so unreal."

In a rare show of affection, Aunt Cora patted her arm gently. "It will feel like that for a while, Alice."

She knew her aunt understood how she felt. Aunt Cora's husband, James, Earl of Dunmore, had died suddenly, less than a year ago from a heart attack.

"And then, I'm afraid to say, it will get worse for a period."

Her eyes sprung open wide. *Worse?* Worse than the empty ache in her heart? Worse than her feeling of disconnection from everything? Worse than the hole in the pit of her stomach that seemed to be getting bigger every minute?

She turned to her aunt, but before she could say anything, Aunt Cora continued, "But then it will get better. Slowly but surely." She patted her on the arm again. "I promise." She sighed wistfully, then glided off to join Alice's parents.

Her chest ached as she watched her aunt. She'd spent many happy times with Aunt Cora and Uncle James in Wiltshire when she'd been younger. Her uncle had been affectionate and fun. What none of them had realised at the time was how easily influenced by the wrong people he'd been. It was only after his death that they'd found out he'd lost a substantial amount of his wealth in bad investments. His estate had been inherited by a nephew, who paid Aunt Cora a small annual allowance while he tried to untangle the mess he'd been left with.

At least I know we'll be financially secure.

After her uncle's death, she'd insisted that she and Vance review all aspects of their financial situation, citing her concern for their sons' futures. He had been unusually cooperative, and together they had gone over Manning Hall's income and outgoings, the details of her marriage settlement, and his shares, bonds, and business investments. They had also discussed Harry's inheritance and the health of the trust that had been set up for their younger son, Freddie.

How fortuitous we did that. Thank you, Uncle James…

She took a sip of lukewarm coffee as her gaze drifted to her brothers. James was slouched on a window seat, his boyish features clouded with confusion as he stared into space. Duncan stood ramrod straight by the door, every inch the responsible older sibling, talking quietly to an equally stern-looking Baxter.

They were, no doubt, ready to pounce on the detective from Fenshire HQ as soon as he arrived. A weary breath escaped her. They were taking over, but she didn't have the energy to resist. *I should be grateful I have them looking out for me, I suppose.*

"Alice, darling!" Fee's melodious voice cut through the

subdued atmosphere as she swept into the room and glided towards her, Henry close at her heels.

What's Henry still doing here? Didn't he leave yesterday? What did he do—turn back halfway to London the moment he heard? She patted her hair and straightened the skirt of her dress. *I must look such a mess…*

Fee wrapped her in a gentle embrace, and she found herself leaning into her friend's comforting warmth. "I came as soon as I could. Are you holding up, darling?"

Her shoulders hunched. "As well as can be expected, consid—" She stopped. Was this going to be her stock answer for the next few weeks or even months? The ridiculousness of it hit her—as well as can be expected considering what? *Considering that my husband was going to leave his mistress, and we were going to rebuild our life together, but now we'll not be able to because he's dead? Or considering that I think my husband was murdered, but no one will listen? Or considering that I'll now need to raise my two sons on my own? Or…* She felt another prickle at the back of her eyes. *My sons!* Her stomach rolled. She would need to let them know about their father…

"Well, we're all here for you." Fee gave her a quick squeeze before she released her.

"Thank you," Alice replied in a thick voice. With the support of her friends and family, she would get through this.…

Henry cleared his throat, drawing her attention. "My deepest condolences, Your Grace," he murmured, his voice low and smooth. "I echo Fiona's sentiments." She was aware of footsteps coming from behind her. "Please do not hesitate to call upon me if there is anything I can do to ease your burden during this difficult time."

Baxter appeared beside her, his blue eyes flashing like

steel. "Lord Rivershore, how kind of you to offer your condolences. I'm certain the duchess appreciates your... Er, concern. However, she's fortunate to have many family and *old* friends she can turn to should she need to."

Henry's jaw tightened, but he inclined his head in acquiescence. "Of course. Forgive my intrusion." With a final, lingering glance at her, he melted into the crowd.

"Really, Bax, that was unnecessarily rude," his sister scolded.

"Yes, Baxter, that was hardly needed," Alice added.

"On the contrary," he replied, his blue eyes darting between the two women. "I believe it was entirely necessary." He turned to his sister. "What possessed you to bring him here, Fee?"

"He wanted to—"

She tuned them out, too drained to muster the energy to smooth the tension between the siblings. She swallowed past the lump in her throat, her grip tightening on her now empty cup. *Vance is gone.* Of course, she already knew that, but the reality of it suddenly pressed down on her, stealing the breath from her lungs. *You must hold it together, Alice, for the sake of propriety if nothing else.* But how could she possibly maintain decorum when her world had been turned upside down? And yet, as she gazed around the room at the assembled guests and family, she knew that was precisely what was expected of her.

Oh, how she longed to scream, to rage against the unfairness of it all. *That's not an option!* With a deep breath, she straightened her spine and plastered on a serene smile just as Stokes appeared in the doorway, followed by a stocky man in a rumpled suit. Her heart quickened. *The inspector!*

"Inspector Meacham of the Fenshire Constabulary," the butler announced.

The inspector shifted uncomfortably, his ruddy face betraying his unease. "My deepest apologies for the intrusion, Your Graces. I will endeavour to be as swift and unobtrusive as possible in my inquiries."

Duncan stepped forward. "I'm Lord Tilling, the late duke's brother-in-law. I'll show you to... to where it happened."

As Duncan led the way, Baxter hurried off after them. Alice made to follow. She wanted to hear the inspector's assessment for herself.

A hand gripped her arm.

"Alice, no." Aunt Cora, her voice low but firm. "It's not appropriate for you to view the body. Not now. Leave it to the men."

Alice stiffened. "But I—"

"Everyone is watching," her aunt added in a whisper, her eyes flickering to the other occupants of the room loitering around, their curiosity barely disguised.

She's right. Half a dozen pairs of eyes were on her, some filled with concern, others simply hungry for scandal. Her jaw clenched. It chafed—no, burned—that she, Vance's wife, was being asked to remain behind while the men conferred and investigated. But Aunt Cora's hand was still on her arm, and her expression brooked no argument.

This is so unfair! She looked to the door, but Duncan, Baxter, and the inspector were already well on their way. *It's too late now.* She could hardly run after them, demanding for them to wait. *Dash it all!* "Very well," she said through her teeth.

Aunt Cora released her arm, her tone brisk as she smoothed her skirts. "Come along, dearest. Let's get you another cup of that dreadful coffee you insist on drinking. I can only assume it scours your nerves clean."

Alice allowed herself to be steered towards the sideboard. "It's French roast, Aunt Cora."

"Of course it is," her aunt said with a sniff. "Trust the French to take something bitter and make it fashionable."

———

The hushed conversations ceased abruptly as Duncan and Baxter re-entered the morning room some time later. All eyes turned towards Duncan as he cleared his throat. "The inspector has concluded that Vance's death was a tragic accident," he announced, his voice carrying through the room. "A terrible loss for us all."

Alice's heart shrank as a wave of disappointment washed over her. She bit the inside of her cheek. *Did I get it wrong after all? Could it truly have been an accident?* The inspector was a professional investigator. *Surely, he would know if there were any signs of foul play?* Perhaps there was no sinister plot, no villain lurking in the shadows. She studied her brother. There was no shadow of doubt in his eyes, no hesitation in his voice—just sorrow and conviction. He believed it. Completely. Had she let grief cloud her judgement?

And yet... Why does this still not feel right?

She glanced around the room, searching for something—anything—in the others' expressions that might echo her own unease.

Lady Cordelia Granville's hand rested around her throat as she slowly shook her head. *She looks... surprised? No, more relieved...*

Lilly Forthington had a handkerchief pressed to her mouth, her shoulders shaking with silent sobs. *Is she truly upset, or are they crocodile tears?*

Seb Hawthorne's lips were parted as he appeared to stifle

a smile. *Surely not.* His gaze met her brother's. James turned away abruptly. *Is that guilt?*

If anything, their reactions muddied her thoughts even further. She needed space. Time to think. Away from watchful eyes and well-meaning reassurances.

"The stairs will remain off-limits for the time being," Duncan continued, "but otherwise, we should endeavour to carry on with our day as normal."

She stared at him, incredulity rising in her throat. *Carry on? How can anything be the same after this?* The thought of normality seemed absurd to her. Her mind wandered back to her sons, Harry and Freddie, at their boarding school in Derbyshire, blissfully unaware of their father's death. A low, dull nausea curled in her belly, as if grief were something she'd swallowed and couldn't digest. She needed to write to the headmaster, asking him to gently break the news to the boys and arrange for them to come home.

As the gathering began to disperse, Duncan, Baxter, and Fee joined her.

"Do you need anything, darling?" Fee asked, her face a mask of concern.

She shook her head. "I must write to the headmaster and the boys," she said, her voice barely above a whisper.

Duncan's expression softened. "Do you need my assistance, Alice?"

Still feeling the overwhelming need for solitude, she shook her head again. "No thank you. I... I'd prefer to be alone for a while."

Baxter's blue eyes met hers, filled with worry. "If you change your mind, Alice, please don't hesitate to call upon any of us."

"I'll stay and oversee Vance's... er, removal, shall I?" Duncan asked.

"Thank you." She gave a small, grateful smile, then left, her steps heavy as she made her way up the back stairs to her private chambers.

Closing the door behind her, she crossed the room to the escritoire in her bedchamber. She sat down, took a deep breath and with trembling hands, she penned a telegram to the headmaster.

14

HALF AN HOUR LATER...

I entreat you to break this news to Lord Treeble and Lord Frederick with gentle care.

Arrangements will be made for their return home as soon as is practicable.

Alice signed the telegraph; the faint scent of ink mingled with the lavender sachet tucked in her writing desk drawer. She let out a soft breath of relief as she put the pen down and massaged her temples. Rising, she smoothed her skirts and crossed the bedchamber to the bell pull. After a brief tug, she sank down onto the velvet settee by the window to await the arrival of her first footman.

Her gaze drifted outside. The grounds of Francis Court stretched out before her, a picture of tranquility that belied the turmoil within its walls. She wished, not for the first time today, that she could simply curl up with a good book and a cup of tea and leave the cares of the world far behind her. *Oh, Vance...* It seemed so impossible that he was gone.

A firm knock on the door announced George's arrival.

"Enter." She rose at the same time as attempting to smooth her unruly red tresses. The door opened and the tall, broad-shouldered footman stepped inside, his short dark hair and formal black livery now perfectly in order.

He bowed crisply. "You rang, Your Grace?" His deep voice resonated around the quiet bedchamber.

"Yes, George." She walked over to her desk and picked up the telegram. "I need this delivered to the boys' school in Derbyshire today if possible. It's… Well, it's telling the headmaster about the duke, so it's rather important."

He stepped forward and retrieved the missive with another small bow. "I shall take it immediately, ma'am. The telegraph office in King's Town offers a Sunday service."

"Excellent." She offered a tired smile. "Thank you, George. Please take my carriage. I shan't be needing it today."

"Thank you, ma'am." He tucked the telegram into his coat.

As he turned to leave, Alice called after him, "Oh and George? Do let me know once it's been dispatched, if you would be so kind."

"Of course, ma'am. I shall inform you immediately upon my return." With a final incline of his head, he departed, quietly shutting the bedchamber door behind him.

As his footsteps faded down the corridor, she sank into her chair in front of the desk. She closed her eyes, willing the tension to leave her shoulders. Now she was faced with the more daunting task of writing to her sons. She pulled a fresh piece of paper towards her, then dipped her pen in the inkwell. *How do you tell two young boys that their father is dead?* She swallowed. *Just get on with it, Alice!* Vance was gone, and now she alone must be there for Harry and Freddie.

· · ·

My dearest Harry,

I write with a heavy heart to tell you that your beloved Papa died quite suddenly this morning. I know this will come as a great shock, and I am so very sorry I cannot be there to hold your hand as you hear this news.

Your father was immensely proud of you, and he loved you very dearly. I trust you will always remember that.

Arrangements are being made for you and Freddie to come to Francis Court very soon. Until then, I know you will look after your brother, just as I shall look after you both when you arrive.

Be brave, my darling boy.

Your ever-loving

Mama

She read it through, then set it to one side. *Now Freddie...* She told him his father was very proud of the fine young gentleman he was becoming, ending with:

You and Harry will be coming home soon, and I shall be waiting to wrap you both in the biggest of hugs. Until then, know I am thinking of you every moment.

With all my love,

Mama

She wiped a tear that had run down her cheek, then blotted the paper before putting each letter in a separate envelope and addressing them.

She leaned back in the chair. *Thank goodness that's done...* Her chest felt splintered at the thought of her poor fatherless boys receiving such news. *If only I could gather them into my arms and soothe their pain.* Exhaustion swept over her like a tide. With a heavy sigh, she rose and made her way over to the canopied bed. *I'll rest for a short while...* Sinking down upon the plush mattress, she leaned back against the mound of pillows and allowed her eyes to drift shut. But the moment she did, Vance's lifeless face swam before her, his glassy eyes staring into nothingness.

Her eyes snapped open as she gasped, her heart pounding against her ribcage. How could this have happened? Vance, dead. It seemed incomprehensible. And yet, the reality of it sat like a stone in her stomach. Her mind began to replay the events of the morning, searching for some clue, some hint of what had happened. Despite Duncan's and Baxter's assurances, her instinct told her Vance's death was more than a simple, tragic accident. The very idea that he would be so careless as to plummet drunkenly to his death felt incongruous with the man she knew. There was more to it, she was sure.

A soft knock at the door interrupted her churning thoughts. "Come in," she called, scrambling off the bed.

Maud entered, her chestnut curls poking out from beneath her cap. "Your Grace, I thought you might need—" She paused, concern flickering in her warm brown eyes as she saw both the bed cover and her mistress in disarray. "Is everything all right, ma'am?"

Alice drew in a sharp breath and let it go with effort, falling back against the pillows. "Oh, Maud. I'm afraid I cannot shake this feeling something is amiss with the duke's death."

Maud stepped fully into the room, quietly shutting the door behind her. "I'll be honest, I was right surprised when I found out the police had dismissed it as an accident, ma'am.

Without an investigation at all!" She pressed her hand to her chest. "It don't seem right to me." She moved over to the chair by the bed and picked up Alice's dressing gown. Moving to hang it up, she continued, "I saw the police inspector when he was leaving. Didn't like the look of him. Weak face, you know. The type that listens too readily to the loudest voice in the room." She paused, then gave her a knowing look. "Which is always a man, of course, but loud doesn't mean clever, I always say."

Alice nodded. "In this case, it's my brother." She sighed. "Men certainly have a way of thinking themselves right by virtue of saying things confidently."

"That's the truth of it, ma'am," Maud agreed with a shake of her head.

Alice rose from the bed and moved to the window, her gaze drifting out over the formal gardens below. "But I saw it, Maud. I saw the smear of blood on the wall—it wasn't in the right place to have come from a stumble backwards or a tumble forward. It looked like he'd hit it with force."

Maud hesitated by the closet, the robe still in her hands. Her eyes widened. "Do you think he was pushed, ma'am?"

"I don't know." She shook her head. "I truly don't. And yet, I do know Vance didn't simply topple down the stairs like an old sack of flour." She exhaled slowly. "It troubles me."

"Have you told Lord Tilling or Lord Rushton what you think?"

"I tried, Maud," she said quickly. "But they've already made up their minds. My brother declared it an accident, and Baxter followed suit." She frowned. "I suspect neither of them felt the need to consider the alternative—that someone might have helped Vance along his way."

"So what shall we do?" Maud asked as she opened the

door of the tall walnut wardrobe and retrieved one of the padded, fabric-covered hangers. She hung the dressing gown up and closed the wardrobe door as Alice returned to the window.

Where to start? The beginning… "We need to piece together Vance's final hours to try to make sense of this."

Maud was quiet for a long moment, her brow furrowed in thought. Finally, she said, "Perhaps... perhaps we ought to have a look in His Grace's bedchamber? There may be some clue, some detail that could shed light on what happened."

Alice blinked. *Why didn't I think of that!* Perhaps because everyone had been so eager to declare it an accident, her own instincts had been trampled under the weight of male certainty. "You know, Maud, I think it's a splendid idea. Let's go at once."

15

MINUTES LATER...

The east-wing corridor of the second floor of Francis Court was unusually hushed, and Alice's and Maud's footsteps echoed loudly in the silence as they made their way to Vance's bedchamber.

As they approached the door, they found it slightly ajar. Exchanging a curious glance with Maud, Alice pushed it open fully to reveal Tom, Vance's temporary valet. His shoulders hunched, he stood bent over, one hand resting on the mantlepiece, seemingly in a world of his own. She cleared her throat.

Tom jerked up straight at the noise, his head whipping around to look at them with startled hazel eyes. "Your Grace. I was... I thought I should…" He trailed off, his gaze flitting away as an unsettling stillness seemed to grip him.

"I am sorry to disturb you, Tom. I know this must be a difficult day for you too."

Tom swallowed hard, inclining his head.

Stepping across the room, she laid a hand on his broad shoulder. "Perhaps you might take a short break? I have a few things to do in here, and you look like you could do with a cup of tea."

For a moment, Tom looked as if he might protest. But then his shoulders sagged, and he nodded. "As you wish, ma'am. I'll just... I'll be in the servants' hall. Should you have need of me, simply ring the bell." With a final, anguished look around the room, he slouched out.

"Did you see the way he was staring at the fireplace?" Maud murmured. "Like he expected it to speak. I don't know what's got into him, ma'am," she said as she closed the door behind him. "He didn't want to valet for the duke anyway."

"It's still been a shock for him, I imagine. Like it has for all of us..." she replied as she surveyed the room. It was a grand room, befitting a duke's station, with a large four-poster bed draped in rich brocades, an intricately carved armoire, and a writing desk of polished mahogany. Heavy curtains framed tall windows, casting long shadows across the richly patterned carpet.

"Where should we start?" Maud asked, rubbing her arms briskly.

Alice's gaze fell on the writing desk. "I'll start here, I think," she said, moving towards it. "There may be something in his correspondence. In the meantime, can you have a look on the nightstand?"

Maud made her way over to the bed while Alice moved to the writing desk and began to methodically sort through the few papers scattered across its surface. Most were mundane —correspondence from the estate manager at Manning Hall, a half-finished letter to one of Vance's cousins in London. But as she shuffled through a small pile of envelopes, one in particular caught her eye. The return address was smudged, but she could make out the name 'Lord Ashford', one of Vance's oldest friends from school.

What's the old gossip got to say for himself? She slid the letter from its envelope and began to read.

My dear Vance,

I hope this letter finds you well. It has been far too long since we last exchanged pleasantries. However, I feel I must raise an issue that has been troubling me as of late.

It has come to my attention that your young brother-in-law, James, has been keeping company with a certain Sebastian Hawthorne. I urge you, old friend, to reconsider this association. Hawthorne is known throughout the clubs as a gambler and a rake of the first order. He preys upon young aristocrats, those with more coin than sense, luring them into games of chance and relieving them of their fortunes. More than one promising young man has been ruined by his machinations.

I hesitate to speak ill of James, but I fear Hawthorne has his hooks in him. I've heard whispers of significant debts, of promissory notes signed in haste. James may be in over his head.

Do be wary, Vance. Hawthorne is not a suitable acquaintance for the son of the Duke of Arnwall.

Your concerned friend,

Teddy

Oh, goodness! Her hand flew to her mouth, her eyes widening. Sebastian Hawthorne, preying on James? *My sweet baby brother?* Her vision blurred for a moment as the full weight of what this meant crashed over her. And then, with a sudden, sickening clarity, the conversation she'd overheard the night of Vance's death came rushing back to her: Vance, his voice sharp with anger, warning Hawthorne to keep away from someone; the clipped, indignant tones of Hawthorne's reply. *It must have been James they were talking about!* Had Vance threatened to reveal Hawthorne's true character in his attempt to protect her younger brother? Her breath caught in her throat. *Did it lead to his death?*

"Your Grace?" Maud's sharp voice cut through the swirl of her thoughts. "Are you quite well? You have gone as white as a sheet, ma'am."

She looked up at her maid, blinking rapidly. She opened her mouth to reply, but the words stuck in her throat. Mutely, she held out the letter, watching as Maud's eyes widened with each line.

"Oh, ma'am," Maud breathed when she finished. "Do you think... Could this have something to do with His Grace's death?"

She swallowed hard, her throat dry. She needed to know more about Sebastian Hawthorne. She would send a telegram to Ben Beaumont. The former police officer turned private investigator had helped her with delicate matters before. Perhaps he could discreetly investigate just how bad things were for Sebastian. Such information might prove crucial if they needed to build a case against him. She slipped the letter into the pocket of her dress. "It could be. Let us see what else we can find," she said as she turned to survey the room once more, her green eyes searching for any other clues that might shed light on Vance's final hours.

Maud's soft gasp drew her attention. "Ma'am, look here," the maid cried, bending to retrieve something from the floor near the bed.

She stepped closer. Maud held up a delicate square of lace-trimmed fabric. *A lady's handkerchief!*

"LA," Maud murmured, tracing the embroidered initials with her finger.

Her heart skipped a beat. *Lilly?* She held out her hand, and Maud handed the white square to her. The scent wafting from the handkerchief was unmistakable—the same floral perfume Lilly Forthington always wore, who, before her marriage, had been known as Lilly Astley. A wave of betrayal, hot and bitter, surged through her. Lilly had been here. In Vance's bedchamber.

"It is… It's quite fresh," Maud said hesitantly, her brown eyes wide with concern. "The scent, I mean. She must have been here recently."

She swallowed hard, fighting back a wave of nausea. "Yes," she managed, her voice barely above a whisper. "Yes, I suppose she must have been."

Had this been where Vance had told Lilly it was over between them? *Of course not, Alice!* Vance was a man. He would've been fearful of Lilly's reaction, so he would've chosen to tell her somewhere much less intimate; that way, she could not cause a scene.

Her lips pressed into a thin line as she turned away from the handkerchief. *If, indeed, he told her at all…* She folded it in half and slipped it, along with the letter, into her pocket. As she turned away from Maud's sympathetic gaze, her attention was drawn to the fireplace. Among the ashes, a scrap of paper caught her eye, its edges curled and blackened but the centre still intact.

"Maud, look, what's that?" She pointed to the hearth as the two of them moved towards it. Maud poked at a small pile of ashes in the otherwise empty grate with the toe of her boot. "A letter?" the maid murmured, bending to retrieve it. Straightening, she smoothed out the fragile paper. "'I need to see you'," she read aloud. "'I cannot go on like'—" She looked closer at the badly burned paper. "That's all I can make out, ma'am." She handed it to Alice. The elegant, feminine script swam before her eyes. *Lilly? Cordelia? Someone else?*

She took the letter out from her pocket and tucked the scrap of paper inside to protect it. *Another clue...*

They continued to look around the bedchamber, but found nothing else of any significance.

"I think we're done here, Maud," she said as she patted her pocket and turned towards the door. A letter. A handkerchief. A scrap of paper someone had wanted destroyed. What clues did they hold to Vance's death?

16

THAT AFTERNOON...

A soft afternoon hush lay over Francis Court, the light mellow and uncertain as it slipped across the damask walls of Alice's room. She sat on the window seat, her legs curled beneath the skirt of her dress as she stared out at the formal gardens of Francis Court. Beyond the symmetrical box hedges and gravel paths lay her favourite area—the rose garden, currently displaying an impressive collection of early summer blooms in the thoughtfully arranged beds. She exhaled, her gaze fixed on the grey clouds gathering to the east. She would have loved a walk among the fragrant roses to organise all of these thoughts in her head. But not if it meant getting wet.

Glancing down at the cushion, she attempted to make sense of all the clues she'd laid out beside it. But the weight of her thoughts pulled at her limbs, making her feel sluggish.

She needed a sounding board. But Maud had gone to attend to her afternoon duties, and George had not yet returned from King's Town. It unsettled her how much she had come to depend on Maud and George—not just for practical matters, but as sounding boards and allies too; they were the only ones who didn't dismiss her instincts out of hand.

Come on, Alice. You can do this... Staring at the items again, she tried to think. The letter from Lord Ashford, warning Vance about Sebastian Hawthorne's hold on James. *Well, clearly, I need to speak with James.* She frowned. What was his relationship with Seb? And how deeply was he in debt? Did their father know? Did Duncan know? Her stomach twisted. Was her younger brother entangled in something dangerous?

She reached out to the handkerchief embroidered with LA, her hand hovering over the delicate fabric. *Lilly!* Why had she been in Vance's room? Had he ended things with her? A memory tugged at the corner of her mind. Someone—was it Maud?—had mentioned that Lilly had been terribly upset yesterday afternoon. That couldn't be coincidence, could it? It suggested Vance had ended it that morning, so why was her perfume still lingering in his bedchamber a day later?

And finally, there was the scorched scrap of paper. Penned by a woman, certainly. But which lady? A discarded love? Or something more sinister? Why had they needed to see him so desperately, and why had someone tried to destroy it?

She rubbed at her temples. She needed to talk it through with someone.

But who? Well, certainly not her brother Duncan, that was for sure. He was convinced Vance's death had been an accident. She knew his resolute nature. He would not entertain an alternative theory unless presented with solid, irrefutable evidence. Her sister-in-law? No. Fee was not analytic enough. She preferred losing herself in a good cause than riddles and puzzles. *And, even if I involved Fee, in her exuberance, she would likely tell Duncan, and he would say I was meddling.*

Aunt Cora? Her aunt had been helpful during that unpleasant business of the missing heir, but this… this was murder. Aunt Cora would be horrified, no doubt deploying that pinched expression of hers and proclaiming that duchesses were meant to host garden parties, not question possible murderers.

Footsteps coming down the corridor outside made her start. "Oh, bother," she muttered quickly as she gathered the items and carefully tucked them away in her writing desk.

There was a sharp knock on the door. "Yes?"

The door opened, and Stokes stepped in. "Lord Rushton is here, Your Grace. He's asked if you're receiving visitors."

She hesitated only a moment. *Baxter…* "Tell him I'll be down shortly, please, Stokes." She rose, and walking past her uneaten lunch on the small table by the window, she stopped in front of the mirror by the door to smooth her hair and check the shadows beneath her eyes.

As she tidied her appearance, she weighed the pros and cons of confiding in Baxter. He believed Vance's death had been an accident, but he might be more open to discussion than Duncan. Still, would he truly support her investigation, or would he deem it inappropriate? *Only one way to find out,* she thought, crossing the room to scoop up the letters for her sons. *If he seems receptive, perhaps I can confide in him. If not… well, I can always retreat.*

Letters in hand, she stepped into the corridor. The staircase, roped off earlier, was now open once more. Her breath caught. *Have they taken Vance away already?* She descended slowly, her hand gripping the banister tightly. The half-landing came into view. Part of her wanted to squeeze her eyes shut to block out the memory of Vance's crumpled form that had laid there only this morning, but a combination of the fear of stumbling and the curiosity of what she would find kept them fixated ahead.

But there was nothing to see. Someone had scrubbed the wall clean. They had tried to erase all traces of him—as if the truth of his death might be mopped away with the blood. The barest scuff of pale paint was all that remained to mark the place where his head had struck the wall. She committed the spot to memory, determined to preserve this crucial piece of evidence.

Vance had been here. And now he was gone.

She swallowed hard, composing herself as she continued her descent.

At the bottom of the stairs, Stokes waited. She handed him the letters. "Can these go by express in the morning, Stokes?"

"I shall ensure they are at the post office the moment it opens," he said, tucking them into a leather folio.

"Thank you." She hesitated, then looked back up the stairs. Her throat tightened. "Is… is the duke's body still on the premises?"

The butler gave a short bow. "Yes, ma'am. The police confirmed it would be tomorrow before they could make the arrangements with the undertaker. Lord Tilling felt it best not to delay too long in removing the duke from the stairwell, so we have… made him comfortable."

"Where?"

Stokes hesitated, then said gently, "In the small parlour off the servants' hall, ma'am. It's cool and rarely used. I thought it would be… private. I have kept the door locked. No one but myself and Lord Tilling have been inside."

She met his gaze. "That was… very thoughtful of you."

"Do you wish to see him? I can take you…"

The question caught her off guard, her breath hitching in

her throat. Did she want to see him again? It seemed morbid. *And yet...* There *was* a desire to remember him as something other than a crumpled heap at the bottom of the stairs.

Stokes seemed to sense her dilemma. "Let me know, ma'am, and I shall arrange it," he offered.

"Thank you, Stokes," she managed, her voice barely above a whisper.

"Lord Rushton is waiting for you. Shall I escort you?"

As Alice stepped inside the morning room, the familiar surroundings did little to calm her frayed nerves.

Stokes took his leave, and Baxter crossed the room to greet her, his handsome face etched with concern. "Alice, are you all right?"

No! No, I am not! My husband is dead. My boys are fatherless. A woman was in Vance's room only hours before he died. My brother is being brainwashed by a scoundrel, and I'm unsure if I want to see Vance's dead body again!

A rush of heat coursed through her body, her composure crumbling under the weight of his gentle enquiry. "No, Baxter," she blurted out, her voice trembling, her hand clenched into a fist by her side. "No. I'm not all right. What I am, however, is certain that Vance was murdered."

17

A FEW MINUTES LATER...

Alice's words hung in the air, as heavy as the velvet drapes framing the morning room windows. She stared at Baxter, the silence between them thick with tension until he broke it.

"Alice, you're obviously upset," he said gently, his blue eyes filled with concern. "It's been a very trying time for you…"

Her stomach twisted. *Why did I blurt that out?* She smoothed her skirts, wishing she could take back the words as easily.

"Perhaps you should rest," he continued, reaching out as if to pat her arm.

She recoiled sharply from his attempt at condescending comfort as heat flashed through her body. *Rest?* What was she? Some delicate flower wilting in the heat? She'd hoped Baxter, of all people, would listen. Instead, he was treating her like she was suffering with nerves.

The memory surfaced unbidden—her sitting in that cold doctor's office, being told by a trio of doctors, all male, of course, that she needed electric shock therapy for her "feminine sensitivities" when she'd finally plucked up the courage to tell someone about the painful noises in her ears that made her jump at every turn. Later, much to her horror, she'd discovered from her mother that they'd diagnosed her with hysteria, when, in fact, it had been damage done by a shotgun going off beside her on a shoot.

"I don't need to rest," she snapped, her hackles rising. "What I need is for someone to listen to me. Why are you so certain it's *not* murder?"

Taken aback by her sharp tone, he blinked. "Really, Alice. Nothing indicates that someone murdered Vance. He'd been drinking all evening. So a fall… er, tragic as it is, is the only thing that makes sense. There's simply no reason to think——"

"No reason?" she interrupted, huffing. "What about the mark on the half-landing's wall? How do you explain that?"

"The police inspector said it was consistent with a fall," he replied, a defensive note creeping into his cultured tones.

Her green eyes flashed as she took in a quick breath. "The inspector said what he thought Duncan wanted to hear! You were both blindly following my brother's lead like... like sheep!"

The accusation hung between them. Her pulse rose as her breaths came in short gasps. *Have I gone too far?*

But she was tired of being dismissed, of having her concerns waved away as womanly vapours. She watched Baxter's face, waiting for his reaction. Would he finally listen? Or had she just made a terrible mistake?

Colour rose in his cheeks. "I can assure you, Alice, I am quite capable of coming to my own conclusions," he said stiffly. He walked over to the sideboard and poured himself a drink.

"Then think carefully about where that mark was, Baxter." Her eyes pleaded with him to consider what she was saying. "It was too far up the wall to have been made by someone tumbling down the stairs in his cups. But if Vance had been pushed from the top of the stairs…" She met his gaze, refusing to back down.

His eyes narrowed as he walked back towards her, a flicker of irritation crossing his aristocratic features. "But why on earth would anyone want to kill Vance?"

Without thinking about whether this was a good time to share her recent discoveries with someone who clearly thought she was delusional, she said, "Well, for a start, there's the letter I found about James."

His brow furrowed. "Letter? What letter about James?"

"The one I found in Vance's bedroom. It was from a concerned friend warning him to keep James away from Sebastian Hawthorne," she replied triumphantly. *That will give him something to think about…*

"You were snooping through Vance's things?" he asked, wrinkling his nose.

Really? Is that what he's going to focus on?

"Vance was my husband." She lifted her chin defiantly. "I have every right to go into his room and ensure there was nothing I needed to know." She let out a sharp breath. "But that's not the point, Baxter." She took a step closer, her skirts swishing against the plush carpet. "The point is that I heard Vance threatening Sebastian. You may recall I mentioned it to you before we went into dinner last night. What if Seb didn't like what Vance was saying and wanted to shut him up?"

He paused, seeming to consider her words. The tension in his shoulders eased a touch, and he let out a long breath. "Very well, Alice. Tell me exactly what this letter said."

As she recounted the contents of the mysterious correspondence, he leaned forward, his gaze intent. He seemed to be truly listening to her.

Emboldened by his apparent willingness to listen, she added, "And there's more. We found a woman's handkerchief with the initials LA on it that smells like it was only there a short while and the remains of a note that someone had tried to burn in the fireplace."

"And who is we?"

"Maud was with me."

"Your maid, Maud?"

"Er… yes. It would not be proper for me to be—"

"Sneaking around?" He raised his eyebrow at her.

She gave him a look. "I trust Maud implicitly."

Baxter sank into a nearby chair, the polished wood creaking slightly under his weight. He ran a hand through his hair, mussing up his usually impeccable appearance. "Good God," he murmured, rubbing his forehead. He took a large gulp of brandy.

She perched on the edge of the armchair opposite him, her heart racing. She watched him intently. He'd always been maddeningly correct, but now he looked just the tiniest bit wild-eyed—and she didn't hate it. She waited for his response. *Will he dismiss my concerns as he did earlier?*

At last, he spoke. "I cannot pretend to condone your methods, but on balance, Alice, you might be onto something." He shook his head as if in disbelief at his own words.

Tears welled up behind her eyelids. *He believes me!* She took in a deep breath. *Right. What now?*

"We should talk to Duncan," he continued. "He will—"

She shook her head firmly. "No, he'll not want to hear that we think Vance was murdered. You know how he is about the family's reputation—he'll not want that kind of attention."

Baxter frowned. "But Duncan's a reasonable man. Surely, if I explain—"

"I love my brother dearly, Bax," she interrupted gently, "but unless we have compelling evidence, he'll not want this pursued."

He sighed heavily but nodded in reluctant agreement. "So what do you propose?"

She leaned forward. "We investigate. We find the evidence to prove someone wanted Vance dead. Then Duncan will have no choice but to listen."

His brows shot up, his eyes widening. "We? I don't think so. It's wholly inappropriate for someone of your standing—and a woman to boot—to be involved in such matters, Alice."

Her jaw tightened as she rose rapidly from the edge of the chair. For a man who liked to pretend he was modern and broad-minded, Baxter had an irritating knack for clinging to antiquated views when it suited him. *Inappropriate? Because I'm a woman?* She'd just lost her husband, found the courage to question his death, and presented three legitimate pieces of evidence—and now she was being told to sit down and embroider while the men sorted it all out? *I don't think so…*

"Wholly inappropriate?" she repeated, her voice as cool as ice. "Well, thank you for the reminder of my place in society, Lord Rushton. How fortunate I am to have a man on hand to remind me I ought to stay in the drawing room and let the stronger sex bumble about while I nod politely from the sidelines." His mouth opened, but she didn't give him the chance. "I'm not asking to join the constabulary. I'm trying to ensure my husband's death wasn't the result of foul play. And I fail to see why it's inappropriate for me to investigate when I'm the one who found him, identified the oddities, and—unlike everyone else—haven't decided to simply blame the stairs." She took a deep breath and carried on, "*And* I'll have you know, Baxter, that I discreetly sorted out cousin Lucy's little issue not long ago; as well as, only a few weeks past, I helped recover a valuable stolen artefact *and* prevented a conman from swindling Henry Somerset and his mother out of their money and his title. I'm a very *capable* woman!"

"Yes, I heard about those incidents," he replied, sounding exasperated. "But it's hardly suitable for a duchess to engage in such activities."

She bristled, her hands clenching into fists at her sides. *The audacity of the man!*

She opened her mouth to retort, but he held up a hand, his expression softening. "Regardless, this is far more serious, Alice. This could be murder we're talking about. You never know what unsavoury details you might uncover, things not meant for a lady's ears."

She let out a disbelieving laugh, one brow arching in incredulity. "Honestly, Baxter—what century are you living in? It's 1891, not the Dark Ages. Women ride bicycles now, we read newspapers, campaign for suffrage, and yes, some of us even solve crimes when necessary." She took a step closer to him. "We're *not* delicate flowers wilting at the first whiff of scandal. If there are unsavoury details to be uncovered, I should think the widow of the man in question has more right than most to hear them."

He opened his mouth as if to reply, but she pressed on, jabbing a finger lightly at his chest. "Whatever truth lies at the bottom of this, I intend to find it—and although I would much rather do it with your help than without it, if I have to, I will investigate on my own."

He let out a groan and ran a hand through his hair. "Good Lord, Alice. You really are exhausting when you're like this."

She gave him a triumphant smile. "When I'm right, you mean."

He looked at her for a long moment, as if seeing her properly for the first time—not as a duchess or a widow but as a woman driven by purpose. He muttered something under his breath that sounded suspiciously like, "insufferable woman," then looked back at her and groaned. "Very well. I cannot in good conscience let you do this alone, Alice. But if *we're* to do this—and I cannot believe I'm saying this—we need to exercise caution. And discretion. You must promise me you will not do anything dangerous."

She hesitated, then gave him a sweet smile while behind her back, she crossed her fingers. "I promise."

He narrowed his eyes. "That smile is not reassuring."

She tilted her head to one side. "You're a very suspicious man, Bax."

He huffed but let it go, folding his arms as they both sat down again. "Right. First steps—"

"We should map out Vance's movements the night he died," she jumped in as her fingers tapped on her chin, "so we can work out who he spoke to and where he went. And I want to know exactly where Lilly was that night. I'm fairly certain it is her handkerchief we found. The smell of perfume was still strong, so it hadn't been in there for long, and yet, Vance said he'd broken off their... er, arrangement, the day before..."

He raised an eyebrow. "And you believe she took it badly?"

She gave a dry little laugh. "Lilly Forthington has never taken disappointment well."

He inclined his head. She continued, "I'll talk to George when he's back. He'll know where everyone was last night and who they were with and if—"

"Your footman?" Baxter's eyebrow shot up. "You want to discuss this with—"

She held up her hand. "George is intelligent and obser-vant, as well as being totally discreet and loyal to me."

"And don't tell me, you also trust him implicitly too?"

She lifted her chin. "Of course."

He exhaled slowly and rose. "All right. And while you're questioning the servants, I'll make enquiries about your brother and his charming new friend."

"And do it delicately, Bax," she said, also rising to her feet. "We don't want anyone else to know we suspect anything at the moment."

He looked over at her, fixing her with a pointed look. "I hope you know what you are doing, Alice."

She offered a sugar-sweet smile and headed for the door, calling over her shoulder, "Not in the slightest. Isn't it thrilling?"

18

SHORTLY AFTER...

Alice's footsteps echoed softly against the marble floor of the Painted Hall in Francis Court. She needed to find George or Stokes so she could start piecing together Vance's last evening. She looked around. *Where is everyone?* The scuff of boots against stone drew her attention to the service stairs, where George emerged, his tall figure silhouetted against the dimly lit passage. *Perfect! George will do...*

The first footman spotted her and joined her at the bottom of the stairs. "Your Grace," he said, bowing briefly. "The telegram has been delivered. I waited at the King's Town office until they confirmed it was sent."

"Excellent," she replied, her mind briefly flitting to her boys and the news that would shatter their world shortly. She took a deep breath. *There's nothing you can do there, Alice. You need to concentrate on what you can do here.* "George..." She hesitated, unwilling to have this conversation in the echoing expanse of the Painted Hall. She glanced around. Where could she be guaranteed some privacy? She saw the heavy wooden door behind the stairs. *Yes, that will do…* "Sorry, would you mind stepping into the library for a moment, please?"

"Of course, ma'am," George said, stepping aside and allowing her to lead the way. He matched her pace perfectly, neither too close nor lagging behind, and when they reached the library, he opened the door for her with a soft creak. The familiar scent of leather-bound books and beeswax polish enveloped them.

Once inside, she turned to face him. "George, what I'm about to say may sound rather… well, rather shocking."

His expression remained attentive but neutral. "I understand, ma'am."

She drew in a deep breath, gathering her courage. "I don't think my husband's death was an accident. I'm of the opinion that he may have been murdered."

He blinked once, then nodded, his blue eyes thoughtful. "Do you believe that he was pushed down the stairs, ma'am?"

"Yes!" She felt giddy. *He's not dismissed the idea.* "And there's more." She told him what she and Maud had found during the search of her husband's bedchamber. "Lord Rushton reluctantly agrees with me, though he took some convincing. We've decided to investigate as my brother is unlikely to consider murder without irrefutable evidence."

"A wise approach, ma'am," George replied, his tone measured. "Lord Tilling is known for his… prudence in such matters."

She bit back a smile at his diplomatic choice of words. Duncan was stubborn as a mule, and they both knew it.

He straightened, his expression resolute. "How may I be of assistance, ma'am?"

A prickle teased behind her eye. *Why can't all men be like George?* He didn't think she was being fanciful or having a touch of the vapours. He simply offered to help. Her lips curved with quiet affection. "Thank you. I'd like to piece together the duke's final evening—his movements, who he spoke with, anything unusual that happened."

"A good place to begin, ma'am. Would you like my observations from the evening first?"

"Yes, please," she said, moving to the leather-bound writing desk. She took a seat, pulled out a sheet of crisp paper, and took the fountain pen from the inkwell. She gestured for him to begin.

"His Grace came downstairs around six, ma'am. I was on duty in the Green Drawing Room, and when he arrived, the only other people already there were Lady Cordelia, two of her friends, and your brother Lord Astley."

Alice scribbled quickly, her pen scratching against the paper.

"I made the duke a drink. Lady Cordelia called him over to join her, but he politely excused himself and went to talk to your brother."

"Did you observe anything unusual about his demeanour?"

"Now I think about it, he seemed... tense, ma'am."

She wrote down 'tense' and underlined it. "Did you happen to hear what he and James said?"

"I couldn't make out the words, only the tone. The duke sounded quite stern."

She added this to her notes. Had he been warning James away from Sebastian Hawthorne? "And after that?" she prompted.

"Mr Hawthorne entered the room, but before I could attend to him, the duke intercepted him, and they disappeared from the room."

She stopped writing and told him about the conversation she'd overheard between Vance and Seb in the morning room that evening. "Now, having found the letter in Vance's room, we have to assume they were discussing my brother."

"Indeed, ma'am. That makes sense."

"So not long after I appeared, my husband and Mr Hawthorne returned to the Green Room." She began writing again.

"Yes. It would have been around six-fifty."

"You recall the exact time?" she asked with a raised brow. "George, are you secretly a walking grandfather clock?"

"I strive for accuracy, ma'am," he replied without missing a beat. "Stokes says it's one of my better qualities."

She smiled. "So after that, we all went into dinner," she said as she made further notes. She'd been at the other end of the table to her husband, but was fairly sure he'd remained in the room for the duration. "What time did we finish dinner, do you think?"

"The guests moved into the ballroom after dinner, ma'am, so around eight-thirty, I would say."

"And was the duke then in the ballroom until supper?" She'd seen glimpses of him, and of course, she'd even danced the waltz with him, but she couldn't be certain if he'd left the room at any time.

"I'm afraid I was on duty in the dining room, clearing the table from dinner, and afterwards, I was setting up for supper, ma'am." George's brow furrowed. "I believe Tom was covering the ballroom."

"Very well. We'll come back to that. Then we had supper…"

He acknowledged her statement with a tilt of his head. "Supper was served at ten-thirty, ma'am. Your aunt and the duke came into the room five minutes beforehand, and she… er, rearranged the seating, then they took their places quickly before everyone else arrived."

She wrote down the times. "Yes. I sat next to my husband during supper, then we returned to the ballroom. What time would that have been?"

"Supper was only two courses, ma'am, so quarter to midnight, I would wager."

"And then not long after, Vance left the ballroom with Lady Cordelia." How could she forget having seen them sneak out together, a triumphant smile on the widow's face? She set down her pen with a sigh, staring at the page before her. Her throat tightened. That was the last time she'd seen him alive—and she'd let him walk away with Cordelia, who'd been smiling like a cat with the cream. *Why didn't I stop him?*

A few minutes later, George cleared his throat. "Can I get you anything, ma'am?"

His request dragged her focus back to the task in hand, and she quickly picked up the pen again. "No thank you, George. Did you see the duke again that evening?"

"I laid out port and cigars in here once I finished clearing up from supper, ma'am, which would have been shortly before one. Lord Astley was here on his own, and the duke joined him around five minutes later as I was leaving. About half an hour later, I was sent by my fa—I mean Stokes to deliver kindling, and they'd been joined by Lord Tilling and Lord Rushton. That was the last time I saw the duke, ma'am. I helped clear the ballroom and then, as most of the guests had retired by then, we were stood down. Only Tom and Stokes remained to see to the gentlemen."

She looked down at the page as she returned the pen to the inkwell. It wasn't much, but it was a start. There were gaps, certainly, but no doubt others had seen Vance during the evening. "Well, that's a start, George. Thank you."

"What next, ma'am?" he asked.

What next, indeed? She rose and moved over to the window. The late afternoon sun was poking through the grey clouds, throwing a shaft of light onto the well-manicured lawn beneath. A flicker of resolve kindled in her chest. She knew what had to come next, even if the thought turned her stomach. *But will George be willing to help me?*

19

A FEW SECONDS LATER...

Alice looked up at George, her green eyes clear with purpose. "I want to see the duke's body."

If her footman was surprised by her request, he didn't show it. "Of course, ma'am. Would you like me to accompany you?"

You really are marvellous, George! "Yes. I think it would be helpful. There may be something I've missed—a mark, a clue. I don't know."

"If you wish, I can get my camera. Photographs may capture details we overlook."

She stifled a laugh, aware of how grisly it sounded. *Baxter would faint if he knew we were photographing the body!* A small, rebellious smile tugged at her lips. "Yes, that sounds like a splendid idea, George."

They left the library together, their footsteps soft on the thick carpet. George peeled off when they reached the main staircase, slipping behind the stairs and through the service door. Alice looked around for Stokes. *The house is so quiet...* A quick glance at the grandfather clock standing along the wall told her it was much later than she'd realised. The day was disappearing, and most of the occupants of Francis Court would be resting before dinner. *Right, where's Stokes?* Reasoning that he was probably setting up for pre-dinner drinks, she moved in the direction of the Green Drawing Room.

As she walked down the west wing corridor, a murmur of voices drifted through a partially open door on her right. She paused. The voices were unmistakably male—and familiar.

She took one silent step closer.

"He cornered me last night. He said he knew… something." Her younger brother's voice sounded agitated.

"He always thought he knew something."

"It wasn't like before, Seb. He was different—serious. Like he meant to act on it."

There was a pause. "And did you say anything you'll regret?"

Another pause. "I don't know."

A chill rippled over her skin as she drew back, pressing herself against the wall beside the doorframe, her heart thudding. Were James and Sebastian talking about Vance?

I'll have to tell Baxter. Whatever they were involved in, Vance had stumbled too close—and now he was dead.

She pressed a hand to her temple. Could they have—? *No!* No, she didn't want to believe it. But still…

A floorboard creaked behind her. She jumped, spinning around to find Stokes standing at a discreet distance. He bowed his head slightly. "Your Grace. My apologies—I didn't mean to startle you."

She smoothed her skirts and smiled. "Not at all. I was…" Her voice caught. "I was looking for you, Stokes." She lowered her voice. "I wish to see my husband's body. Would you be so kind as to take me to him?"

The butler's face remained impassive, though his eyes

flickered with something—concern, perhaps? "Certainly, ma'am. If you'll follow me." She followed Stokes down the narrow service stairs, the wooden steps creaking beneath their weight. The basement was cooler, the air thick with the scent of damp stone and composite candles. As they approached a heavy oak door, George reappeared, a wooden case tucked under his arm. Stokes's eyebrows rose a shade at his son's presence.

"I asked George to accompany me," she said, her tone making it clear there would be no debate.

"As you wish, ma'am," he replied, his face the model of discretion. He placed a key in the lock and turned it with a sharp *click*.

"Has anything been removed from the body since this morning?"

"No, ma'am," he replied. "The coroner will attend to all such matters tomorrow." He pushed open the door and walked across the room to light a single oil lamp that stood on a side table. As the flame flickered to life, it cast long shadows across the whitewashed walls. "I shall wait outside, ma'am."

"Thank you, Stokes," she said, gathering the skirt of her dress as she and George stepped into the dim room. The butler closed the door behind them with a soft, final-sounding *clunk*.

The small parlour had been cleared of furniture save for a long oak dining table positioned in the centre, where her husband's body lay beneath a pristine white cloth. The room was cool—almost uncomfortably so—and smelled faintly of beeswax and camphor. Her footsteps seemed unnaturally loud against the flagstone floor as she approached the table, the hem of her skirt whispering with each step. Vance's glossy shoes protruded from beneath the cloth, their gleaming leather incongruously pristine against the stark white fabric.

Her heart rate quickened, a quiver of apprehension rising in her chest as she stood before her husband's shrouded form. *Again! I seem to have spent more time with him since he died than I did during the last six months he was alive…*

"Are you quite well, Your Grace?" George's deep voice echoed in the almost empty room.

She offered a silent acknowledgement, drawing in a steadying breath. "Yes, George. I'm fine." She paused as a memory surfaced—her grandmother's peaceful face, lined with age yet serene in death, her hands folded over her chest. Alice's thirteen-year-old self had peered into the coffin, trembling with a mix of curiosity and fear.

"It's only a body, dearest," her nanny had whispered, a comforting hand on her shoulder. "The person… Her spirit has already left, so there's nothing to be afraid of."

That simple wisdom had comforted her then, and she clung to it now. *Come on, Alice. You're here as an investigator, not a grieving widow.* "Right. We're looking for anything that might give us a clue about what happened," she said, her voice steadier than she felt. "Shall we begin?"

He nodded, setting his box camera on a nearby chair. "With your permission, ma'am?" he asked, gesturing to the cloth.

"Please," she replied, bracing herself as he gently drew back the sheet. Vance lay as if sleeping, his complexion ashen in the dim light. His dark hair was still a little mussed, and a few strands had fallen across his forehead. She forced herself to look at him objectively, to see the clues rather than the man as George began with the outer pockets of the coat, methodically emptying each one and laying the items found on the edge of the table. A monogrammed handkerchief, perfectly laundered; a slim silver case for calling cards; and a few coins. From an inner pocket, he produced a pair of white kid gloves, folded together with the precision of a shop display. Alice picked up one and pressed it between her fingers. It was stiff with recent use, the thumb worn slightly dark.

George lifted a small silver object from the small pocket of the duke's waistcoat. "This is a strange one," he murmured, examining it in the light. "A badge, I think. Perhaps for membership of some kind."

Alice peered over his shoulder. It was shaped like a closed hand, with a tiny key clutched in its fingers. Smooth, weighty, and oddly official-looking. No name or crest she could see. Alice tried to remember Vance's clubs. He was a member of Whites, she was certain of that. And perhaps Boodles? She recalled him mentioning it once. Possibly it was for one of them... "Should we keep it?" she asked.

George shook his head, placing it on the table. "Best left with the rest of his effects, ma'am. The coroner will want it all."

Alice gave a distracted nod as he said, "That's everything, ma'am." He moved over and rearranged the tripod of his camera with practiced precision. He then moved to the window and tugged the curtain aside. Pale daylight filtered in, soft and grey but steady. Since the room was mostly below ground, it remained private. Anyone wanting to peer in would have to crouch down on the pavers along the side of the house.

"That's better," he murmured, checking the light against his palm.

She stepped closer to the table, her eyes flickering over the items. "That's odd," she murmured, leaning closer. "Where's his pocket watch? I'm sure he had it on him at supper."

George frowned and walked back, checking the waistcoat pockets again. "It's definitely not here, ma'am."

She dredged her memory of the previous evening. "I distinctly remember him checking the time before the second course. He always did that."

"Perhaps he left it somewhere. In one of the rooms he was in?" he suggested, returning to his camera.

"Possibly, although it would be most unlike him. The watch was a gift from his father when he came of age. He was always very careful with it." She made a mental note to look for it later.

George, meanwhile, took off his gloves, adjusted the lens and took a slow breath. "I'll photograph what we have, ma'am."

She gave a short nod and moved to the side. He leaned a little forward, his hand steady on the shutter button. *Snick.* The soft mechanical whisper of the shutter closing was barely audible, but she still flinched at the suddenness of it.

"That's his belongings," he said as he rotated the shaft on the top of the camera, readying the film for another photo. He put his gloves back on and moved to the table. "I'll return them as they were."

As he slipped the items back into the relevant pockets, she leaned closer to examine her husband's hands, careful not to touch them. *Not a scratch.* "Look, George," she said softly. "His hands are unmarked. No bruises. I noticed that earlier. If he'd tried to stop himself from falling, wouldn't there be some?"

"Possibly, ma'am," he said as he paused, his eyes narrowed. "But look, there's something here." He pointed to Vance's right ring finger.

Alice peered closer. The heavy gold band, usually pristine, bore a jagged edge where a tiny stone was missing from its setting. "Yes—I see it. The signet ring. It's been damaged. The gold's scuffed here, and—look—one of the little diamonds is gone. It must have been knocked loose." She looked up, frowning. "Do you think he struck something as he fell?"

George blinked. "Diamond?" He looked puzzled, then shook his head. "No, ma'am—I meant this." He pointed again, more precisely this time. Tangled around the Duke's ring was a delicate white thread, almost invisible against his pale skin.

"What's that?" Alice made to lean in further, but the plea, "Your Grace," stopped her. She looked at him.

"I suggest you let me take a photograph first, ma'am, before we disturb it."

Of course! "Yes. Sorry, George," she replied quickly, stepping back.

He shifted the height of the tripod. *Snick.* The sound of the shutter echoed slightly in the stillness. Afterwards, he fished out a pair of tweezers from his pocket and, leaning in, plucked the thread from the clutch of Vance's ring. He held it up to the light.

She narrowed her eyes as she examined it. It was fine but not so fine as to be silk—more the texture of linen or thick cotton. "Could it be from the lining of his gloves?"

"It appears to be a cotton thread," he said, placing it carefully in a small envelope he produced from his jacket pocket. Then he walked over and retrieved the gloves from Vance's pocket. He examined them meticulously, turning them inside out and inspecting every seam. "No, ma'am. The stitching is intact. There are no loose threads or snags." He returned the gloves once again, then handed the packet to her. "Shall I keep this just in case?"

She inclined her head.

He tucked it into the pocket of his waistcoat as he straightened and glanced once more at the duke's hand. "You're right, ma'am—the ring has been scuffed. It may well have happened when he fell."

"It wasn't damaged before, I'm certain of it. Vance was —" She hesitated, the name catching slightly in her throat. "Very particular about his things. He would never have worn a ring in that state. If a stone had come loose, he'd have sent it straight to his jeweller."

George nodded thoughtfully. "Then we can assume the damage must have happened last night." He glanced towards the door. "When I get a chance, I'll have another look on the stairs. If the diamond came loose there, it may still be lying somewhere nearby."

"Indeed," she said quietly. "Thank you, George."

"Now I'll take a picture of the bod—er, His Grace, shall I?"

"Yes, of course." As he moved away, her gaze drifted to Vance's collar. It was slightly askew, the top button open.

George repositioned the camera and cocked the shutter by pulling the string on the top of it, preparing it to fire. *Snick.*

Something about the way Vance's hand rested—it irked her, like a painting hung askew. Her husband had always been meticulous, even vain. He'd have loathed appearing dishev-elled, even in death. An instinctive desire to set things right, to ensure he looked his best for the coroner's arrival, over-came her professional detachment.

She stepped forward, her fingers moving almost of their own accord, reaching to adjust the fold of his cuff. As she did so, her fingertips brushed against the cool skin of his wrist. She froze, her breath catching. There, just above the line where the cuff ended, was a faint discolouration. Thumb-sized, it was barely visible in the wavering light.

"George," she whispered, "look at this."

He leaned in. "A bruise?"

"I think so," she murmured, her pulse quickening. "I didn't notice it before."

"Perhaps the blood has settled since," he suggested quietly.

She studied it, frowning. "It's in an odd place, don't you think? Not where one would expect an injury from falling backwards down the stairs. His hand, yes, but his wrist..." Her gaze lingered on the darkening mark. "More as if someone had—" She stopped herself.

George's eyes met hers, an understanding passing between them.

"Can you photograph this too?" she asked softly.

She retreated to the other side of the room, watching him work, her thoughts swirling. The missing watch, the damaged ring, the unexplained thread, the strange mark on Vance's wrist—none of it aligned with the story of a simple accident. *We must be on the right track, thinking he was murdered....*

"I think that's everything, don't you?" she said as George finished. He bobbed his head and packed his camera away. As he moved across the room and closed the curtain, she shuffled forward and gently drew the sheet back over Vance's face, her hand lingering briefly on the cool fabric.

"Goodbye, Vance," she whispered as George picked up his case and extinguished the lamp, plunging the small parlour into semi-darkness. As they stepped out of the room, she felt the weight of the new knowledge pressing upon her shoulders—knowledge that confirmed her suspicions but offered little comfort.

20

NOT LONG AFTER...

The library's comforting scent of leather and paper made Alice smile as she sank into one of the wing chairs by the fireplace, her mind still processing what they'd discovered. The white thread, the lost diamond from the damaged ring, the unexplained bruise, the missing pocket watch—each piece a fragment of a puzzle she was only beginning to understand.

"Shall I get you a glass of sherry before dinner, ma'am?" Stokes asked from the doorway.

Dinner? She glanced at the clock to the right of the fireplace. *Gracious! Is that the time?* Maud would wonder where she was. *But wait! My husband has died.* Perhaps she could get away with skipping dinner this evening? "Yes, please, Stokes. That would be very welcome."

The heavy oak door closed behind him, muffling the distant sounds of the household, a stark reminder that despite Vance's death, life in the house carried on.

"I'll get to work developing the plates as soon as I can," George said. He stood to the left of the fireplace, resting the camera bag on his hip.

She looked up, momentarily distracted from her thoughts. "Can you do it here?" During cousin Lucy's 'little issue', she'd allocated a small room in the basement of her London home for him to develop his photographs. He referred to it as his darkroom.

A hint of pride crossed his face. "I can manage, thank you, ma'am. I have a blackout cloth for the window in my room and can use my washstand for the chemical baths. I'll do it late tonight. When the house is quiet, no one will notice the smell, and we should have the results by morning."

She gave a small, approving smile. "How very resourceful, George. Thank you."

He inclined his head. "Is there anything else I can do, ma'am?"

She tapped her fingers lightly against the arm of her chair, the rhythmic sound oddly soothing to her heightened senses. "Well, there's the missing diamond of course, but I'm particularly concerned about Vance's pocket watch. I can't remove the feeling that it's important." She sighed. "The question is, where could it be?" She rose and paced towards the window, her skirts swishing softly against the carpet. "If he had it at dinner, and it's not on his person now…"

"Someone could have taken it," he suggested quietly. "Or perhaps the duke removed it himself."

Alice turned, her green eyes brightening with a new thought. "Could he have returned to his room at some point in the evening?" She glanced over at the notes she'd made earlier, which were lying on top of the writing desk. There were plenty of gaps in the timeline she had for Vance's evening.

"It's possible," he conceded. "He might have gone back to retrieve something or perhaps to change."

She shook her head. "No. He didn't change. He's in the

same… Well, he's wearing what he had on at supper when he also had the watch, is what I mean."

"If you wish, I could ask around and see if anyone has seen it? I could also conduct a… a discreet search of the duke's chambers?"

She was amazed yet again at how unflinchingly he'd stepped into this with her. No doubts, no questions. Just quiet competence. "Yes, that would be most helpful. Thank you, George."

A soft knock interrupted them, and the door opened to reveal Stokes carrying a silver tray with a small glass of dark amber liquid on it. "Your Grace," he said with a slight bow and offered her the sherry.

As she took the glass from the tray, she caught the subtle way his gaze shifted between her and George and the almost imperceptible arch of his eyebrow. "Thank you, Stokes," she replied, keeping her tone light. "George was about to attend to a few matters for me."

George took his cue with practiced ease. "Indeed, ma'am. I'll see to them immediately." He bowed to her, dipped his head respectfully to his father, and left the room, his footsteps fading down the corridor. She took a sip of her drink and set it down.

"Is there anything else you require, ma'am?"

I wonder… Stokes had served the Astley family at Francis Court for decades; he knew the rhythms and secrets of the household better than anyone. If anyone could help her piece together Vance's final hours, it would be him. "Actually, Stokes, I wonder if you might stay a moment? There are a few questions I'd like to ask you."

The butler paused, his expression revealing nothing. "Of course, ma'am. I'm at your service." He closed the door quietly and stood at attention, his hands clasped behind his back.

"Stokes," she said, moving around the desk and sitting down in the chair, "I need to understand exactly what happened last night… um, in relation to my husband. Every detail, no matter how insignificant it might seem or, indeed, how inappropriate you may consider it to be sharing with his wife."

His gaze flickered briefly to the floor before meeting hers again—respectful but wary. *Does he disapprove of me asking questions? Should I have left this to Baxter?*

"I shall do my best to assist you, ma'am," he replied, his voice measured. But there was something else there too—a subtle shift in tone that told her he understood, and he would help her.

"Would you be so kind as to recount for me from the time you first saw the duke last night and everything that occurred up until you last saw him? Alive that is."

Stokes gave a solemn nod, then moved a half-step closer to the desk—his hands still folded neatly behind his back, his eyes cast a little downward in thought.

She reached for the notepad she'd tucked into the leather blotter earlier and flipped it open, retrieving her pen from the inkwell with barely a breath.

"Very well, ma'am. I first saw His Grace yesterday evening, shortly before the dinner hour—at approximately ten minutes to seven. He passed through the main hall from the morning room, where he'd been in conversation with Mr Hawthorne. I offered to assist him with his gloves, but he waved me off and proceeded to the Green Drawing Room to join the other guests."

'6:50pm—seen leaving morning room, talking to Seb… refused help with gloves… went to GDR', she noted rapidly.

"During dinner, I remained stationed in the passage outside the dining room, as is customary, and entered several times with the footmen to oversee the wine service. The duke appeared in good spirits—reserved perhaps but not distressed. He requested claret and asked that Lady Cordelia be served first. I remember this because he was very particular about the order and phrased it as a, 'courtesy deserving of clarity', if I may quote him."

She muttered the phrase under her breath as she wrote it. *'Cordelia seated next to V. Specific about wine service. Calm.'*

"After dinner, the guests proceeded to the ballroom. Later, I observed him dancing with you and again conversing with Lady Cordelia, though at a distance."

She underlined *'Cordelia'* twice.

"At approximately twelve-ten, I saw the duke leave the ballroom with Lady Cordelia. They turned in the direction of the east corridor. I didn't follow, but sometime later, I observed Lady Cordelia returning alone, looking somewhat flustered."

'Flustered!' She underlined the word twice. *I bet she did!*

"The duke returned through the main hall shortly thereafter," Stokes continued.

Alice tapped her pen absently against the margin of the page, then scrawled: *'12:30ish—V'*

"Not long after one o'clock, I brought a fresh decanter of brandy to this very room." He glanced over at the arrangement of armchairs and a large leather couch by the fireplace. "The duke was there, along with Mister James."

'1am — James with Vance in library', she wrote. "And how did they seem, Stokes'?"

The butler cleared his throat. "Er... there was tension, ma'am—one could feel it in the air. As I left, Mister Duncan and Lord Rushton arrived. Thirty minutes later, the bell rang, and Mister Duncan asked for coffee. Mr Hawthorne entered while I was leaving, but the duke dismissed him in no uncertain terms."

"Dismissed him?" she asked, the pen paused in mid-air.

"He told Mr Hawthorne to, 'get lost', ma'am. Mr Hawthorne left at once, slightly red-faced."

She concealed a smirk as her pen flew. *'1:30am—Seb enters library. V dismisses him ("get lost") Seb leaves.'*

"I returned with coffee not long after and served the gentlemen. I remained in the room for a short while and left when Mister Duncan and Lord Rushton retired for the night around two."

'2am —D and B leave. V and'... "So there was only James left with him?"

"That's correct, ma'am."

"Were they talking to each other?" Stokes looked down at his highly polished shoes. She hated interrogating him in this way, but what choice did she have? "Stokes, please. Whatever you saw or heard could be important."

"They appeared to be arguing, ma'am. I heard their raised voices as I walked down the corridor. I didn't hear what they said, but I remained close by in case the duke needed anything further, and I saw Mister James leave fifteen minutes later in an... er, agitated state."

She suppressed a groan as she wrote, *'V and J argued, J left upset.'* What had her little brother been up to? "Thank you for your candour, Stokes. Did you see the duke again after that?"

"Tom and I cleared up the coffee things around five minutes later. His Grace was alone at that point, seated by the fire, glass in hand. He seemed... thoughtful. Composed but with that edge he had when something troubled him."

She nodded. She'd seen that edge in the past.

"I asked if he required anything further, but he said no, he was retiring soon, and told us to go to bed." Stokes' voice softened. "That was the last time I saw him alive, ma'am."

She made one final note. *'Approx 2:20am–V alone in library. Last seen alive by Stokes.'* She sat back and lowered her pen. The page before her was now filled with names, underlines, and timestamps. This would give them something to work on. "Thank you, Stokes," she said quietly, her eyes still fixed on the page. "You've been… very helpful. There's just one more thing."

"Of course, ma'am."

"Have you seen the duke's pocket watch? He may have left it lying around somewhere?"

The butler's brow creased. "I believe he had it on his person when I last saw him, ma'am. I remember he took it out of his pocket and looked at it when he told me he would be retiring soon."

She instinctively looked across the room to where Vance would've been sitting. She rose. "Which chair was he sitting in Stokes?"

"The armchair nearest the fire, ma'am."

She inspected the chair and the small coffee table beside it. Nothing.

"The room has been cleaned since then, ma'am, and the maids have not reported finding anything that I know of. I will, of course, check with Mrs Potts to be absolutely sure."

"Please." She made her way back to the desk. If anything had been found, the housekeeper would have informed Stokes immediately. *So where is it?* If Vance had had it here in the Library then it must have disappeared between then and when Stokes and Duncan had secured Vance's body in the basement parlour. *When was that?* "Er, what time did you and Mister Duncan move my husband's body, Stokes?"

"Around twelve o'clock, ma'am."

Had someone taken it from his body? Or had he left it somewhere between leaving here and when he'd died? It felt very much like the pocket watch was an important clue. If only they could—

Stokes cleared his throat. ""There was one other thing, Your Grace. It may be of no consequence, but I thought it rather odd."

Alice nodded. "Go on, Stokes."

"When I was… covering His Grace," he said carefully, "I happened to notice the wall sconce above the landing. The one nearest the second floor."

The one that was unlit. She nodded. "Yes?"

"It wasn't alight," he said. "That struck me as peculiar because I distinctly remember it was burning when I made my final rounds before retiring. I was concerned the gas might be leaking—though I could smell nothing—so I tested the tap. It had been turned off."

Alice's brows drew together. "Turned off?" *Why would it be turned off?*

"Yes, ma'am. I can't imagine why anyone would have done it."

Her fingers tingled. *Is it related to Vance's death at all?*

Stokes continued, "I turned it back on, of course, once I was satisfied it was safe."

She needed to think about the significance of the unlit sconce. She regarded him thoughtfully. "You did right to mention it, Stokes. Thank you."

He inclined his head. "Very good, Your Grace. Will you be attending dinner this evening, or shall I inform your father that you are… er, indisposed and have something sent up to your room?"

She glanced at the clock on the wall. Everyone would be coming down for pre-dinner drinks soon. Her appetite fled entirely at the thought of entering the drawing room and having to make polite conversation. She couldn't face it. "I think I'll eat in my room, Stokes, if you would be so good as to arrange it with Cook."

"Of course, ma'am. Everyone will understand."

A thought suddenly hit her. *Baxter!* She would need to bring him up-to-date with everything. Could it wait until tomorrow? Her heavy limbs and whirling mind told her it would be best. "Stokes, can you ask Lord Rushton to call in the morning, please? Tell him I wish to speak with him."

Stokes bowed. "Certainly, ma'am. Now, may I suggest I escort you upstairs before your family and the guests descend?"

She looked down at her notes. They were a tangle of arrows and half-finished thoughts, but somehow they made perfect sense to her. She gathered them up and rose promptly. The threat of being seen and having to explain why she wasn't in her room distraught with grief was enough to motivate her to move. Quickly.

21

THE NEXT MORNING...

Alice was already waiting when Baxter arrived at Francis Court. Dressed in a walking outfit of deep navy, trimmed with black ribbon—a compromise between full mourning attire and practical clothing for the outdoors, she stepped forward to greet him. "Thank you for coming so promptly. I hope I haven't disrupted your day too terribly," she said with a small smile, the sun glinting off the brim of her straw-trimmed hat.

"Not at all." His blue eyes studied her face with concern. "How are you holding up?"

"As well as can be expected," she replied, the practiced phrase slipping out automatically. Then, lowering her voice, she added, "The house feels rather like a prison at the moment. Would you mind terribly if we walked outside? The air is fresh, and I find myself in desperate need of movement."

"Ah, so you're dressed for escape," he replied, offering a bow with enough flair to make her smile widen.

She nodded. "Besides, I wanted to speak to you privately." She looked around and lowered her voice. "There are too many open ears indoors."

He extended his arm. "Then let's make a run for it."

They stepped out into the late May morning. The sky was pale blue, streaked with high cloud, and the scent of lilac and warming earth hung in the air. Birds chattered in the hedges as they walked away from the house, circling around the east wing and down a gravel path that led towards the formal gardens.

"I wanted to tell you about some new information I've uncovered," she began.

He raised an eyebrow, intrigued. "Very well. As it happens, I have some things to report as well, but ladies first. What have you discovered?"

They passed the shadowed windows of the basement where Vance's body lay awaiting the coroner's examination. She shivered involuntarily, her mind replaying the stark image of her husband's lifeless form. How would Baxter respond when she told him that she and George had been in that room only yesterday, searching Vance? *Only one way to find out...* "George and I examined Vance's body yesterday."

He stopped mid-stride, turning to face her with astonishment. "You did what?"

Oh dear... She lifted her chin. "We needed to look for evidence."

"Good Lord, Alice." He ran a hand through his hair. "You can't simply... That's to say, examining a body without proper authority is probably illegal!"

"Well, someone had to do it, Bax! The police weren't interested..." She unclenched her jaw and waved a dismissive hand. "Look, can we please focus on what we found rather than the propriety of our methods?"

He exhaled sharply, clearly struggling between exasperation and curiosity. He sighed heavily. "Very well," he said as they resumed walking. "Did you find anything?"

She swallowed. "Indeed. We found some rather significant things. For a start, there's a bruise on his wrist—it's small but distinct."

He was quiet for a few moments, then said. "A bruise on his wrist does sound suspicious. What shape was it?"

"About the shape of a thumb," she replied, touching her own wrist to demonstrate. "Here, just above where his shirt cuff was. It's not at all consistent with a fall backwards down the stairs."

"As if someone might have grabbed him," he murmured, his initial irritation giving way to thoughtful analysis.

"During a tussle before pushing him?"

"Indeed. I must admit, that does support your theory that Vance was helped along his way rather than simply fell."

"Exactly!" She felt a surge of vindication. "Then there's his signet ring; it's damaged and has lost one of its small diamonds."

Baxter shrugged. "That would make sense, wouldn't it? A fall down a staircase—he might easily have caught his hand against the bannister or a wall."

"But there are no marks on his hands that show he hit anything on the way down."

"Well, perhaps he did it some other time? I don't see that it's necessarily related to his fall."

She hesitated. *But Vance wouldn't wear a damaged ring, would he?* Not the Vance she'd known. But then, it had been a while…"Yes… I suppose so." Her excitement dimmed slightly, but she pressed on. "George also found a white cotton thread caught in his ring."

"A thread?" Baxter asked, guiding her around a puddle on the path, where the water had spilled over.

"George thinks it's cotton rather than silk. It was caught in his signet ring."

He wrinkled his nose. "That could have come from anywhere, Alice. A napkin, a handkerchief, even the sheet they wrapped him in. I'm not sure it's relevant."

Is he going to dismiss everything we've found? She suppressed a sigh, then she remembered the watch. *Now that is a clue...* "His pocket watch is missing, which is very odd as Vance was meticulous about his timepiece."

"I don't know," Baxter murmured as they turned the corner. "He might simply have left it somewhere. Perhaps in the library or the billiard room?"

"None of the staff has reported finding it." *Well, not yet...* "George is searching for it," she added. "But if it doesn't turn up, we must consider that it was taken—perhaps by whoever pushed him."

"It's possible," he said nonchalantly as they passed The Cascade, the grand tiered fountain that dominated the front lawn of Francis Court. Water gushed down its stone basins, which were ringed with moss and creeping thyme.

"There's something else that doesn't add up," she said. "One of the sconces on the wall above the half-landing wasn't alight when I found the body, but Stokes said he'd checked it earlier before he'd retired for the night and knew it had been burning. He thinks someone must have turned it off."

Baxter's brows lifted. "Turned off? That *is* strange." He paused, thinking. "But why would anyone do that? Unless they thought there was a leak, or the flame had gone out."

"Stokes said there was no smell of gas," she replied. "But I've been thinking about this. Could it have been turned off to disguise something on the stairs that was there to trip Vance up and then later removed? Or perhaps it was off to hide someone on the second floor, waiting to pounce and push him down the stairs?"

Baxter gave a short, incredulous laugh. "Alice, you've been reading too many sensational novels." He shook his head, though not unkindly. "No one lurks in darkened corridors, waiting to shove dukes down staircases. If someone wished to harm him, there are simpler ways than extinguishing a gaslight first."

He leaned forward slightly, his tone gentler now. "I don't deny it's strange, but there's almost certainly a mundane explanation—a draught, a loose valve, perhaps even one of the footman or maids turned it off and forgot to mention it to Stokes. Everyone is very careful about gas fittings, as they can be temperamental and therefore dangerous things." He smiled faintly. "You're determined to find meaning in everything, Alice."

"And you're determined not to," she replied with feeling. She lifted her chin. "In spite of your scepticism, I'm documenting everything in case we need it in the future. George is developing photographs of the bruise, the ring, the thread, the items he had in his pockets, and his body."

"Photographs?" he barked, stopping abruptly.

Oh dear, perhaps I should've kept that to myself.

22

SECONDS LATER...

B axter looked heavenward, as if seeking divine patience. "You've recruited the footman as your personal detective photographer. Marvellous!"

She removed her arm from his and gave him a fixed stare. "It's George's hobby. It's come in very useful in the past..."

He shook his head slowly, then, putting his hands behind his back, moved forward. The crunch of gravel underfoot was the only sound for a moment.

He'll get used to this soon, won't he?

She caught him up as they entered the formal gardens. The meticulously pruned boxwood hedges created a maze of green paths where tulips and alliums were in bloom, with early roses beginning to unfurl their petals.

"How was dinner last night?" she asked, hoping to steer the conversation to something less controversial.

"It was understandably subdued," he told her. "Lilly kept dabbing at her eyes with a handkerchief—rather dramatically, I might add. Cordelia was unusually quiet, though she did manage to eat a hearty portion of everything served."

She gave a wry smile.

"James," he continued, "was in a real sulk all evening; he barely touched his food. And he seemed to be deliberately ignoring Sebastian, who kept trying to catch his eye."

Have the two fallen out?

"So when the ladies retired to the drawing room, and James announced he was going for a walk, I saw an opportunity to speak with him alone, as we'd discussed. So I followed him out."

She shot him a look of mild surprise. *So he's taking our investigation seriously…*

"I caught up with him near the stables. He was smoking a cigarette. I mentioned he seemed out of sorts and asked if he was quite well."

"What did he say?"

"He said he was shocked by Vance's death, naturally, but also that he'd been let down by a friend. I asked if that friend was Sebastian."

Bold. "And?" she pressed, intensely curious.

"He nearly exploded with anger. 'What did Vance tell you?' he demanded. I assured him Vance had said nothing to me directly, but then…" He hesitated, looking uncomfortable. "I'm not proud of this, but I lied."

Well done, Bax!

"I told him I'd heard rumours Sebastian preyed on wealthy young titled men, getting them into debt, and we were all concerned on his behalf. James was furious. He told me I was as bad as Vance and asked if we all thought he was that naïve. According to James, we've all misjudged Sebastian."

But have we? As much as she instinctively wanted to trust her younger brother, she hadn't taken to Sebastian at all. She didn't trust him…

They rounded a corner in the path, and the rose garden

came into view. Some of the tension in her shoulders dissipated as she entered her favourite retreat at Francis Court. *There's something so peaceful about this space.* The air was perfumed with young blossoms that interspersed the stone benches, nestling them within secluded alcoves. The gravel paths formed a perfect circle around a small fountain. A gentle trickle of water emitted from it, tinkling as it landed in the basin at its foot. She led Baxter to a sheltered bench where the sun was warming the stone. "Did James mention if Vance had confronted him about it?"

"Yes. He said Vance had spoken to Sebastian and told him to leave James alone. He was livid about it. Then he told me he didn't need anyone fighting his battles for him and that we should all stop interfering. Then he stormed off."

Stormed off? It didn't sound like her usually mild-mannered brother. "I can scarcely believe James would speak to you like that." *Although it aligns with what Stokes mentioned about tension in the library last night...*

"I think it explains one thing," he continued. "Duncan and I went to the library last night for a nightcap before returning to Francis Lodge. When we got there, Vance and James were already there. There was a tension I couldn't quite place at the time—like we'd interrupted something. Vance seemed relaxed though. He told us he was looking forward to staying on after the other guests left."

So nothing had happened to change his plans...

"James was very quiet. Then Sebastian came in about thirty minutes later, and Vance stood up immediately and told him to, 'Get lost.' He left without a word, and James looked decidedly unhappy, though I didn't make the connection at the time. Duncan and I left about twenty minutes after that."

She bowed her head slowly, piecing this new information together with what she already knew. *That matches what*

Stokes said. "And that reminds me, I overheard an argument between James and Sebastian earlier that day." She told him the details. "Do you think James might be in financial trouble despite his denials?"

His eyes narrowed. "It's possible."

Her heart rate increased. *Was that it?* "And Vance knew. He threatened Sebastian." Her mind was now racing ahead. "He told him to leave James alone." She swallowed twice before she could speak. "Baxter, do you think Sebastian could've been angry enough with Vance to push him? If Vance had threatened to expose Sebastian's gambling debts, it could have ruined him socially."

He held up a hand. "We have no evidence Sebastian was anywhere near the stairs at the time Vance fell. You're building theories on sand without facts to support them," he said carefully.

But he has a motive... "But if Vance was threatening to reveal something about Sebastian that would dry up his income source, that's a powerful motive to want him silenced."

He cocked his head to one side. "If you want to look at motives, then he's not the only one. What about Henry Rivershore?"

She blinked. *Henry?* "What on earth motive does he have?"

"It's no secret he admires you," he said, not quite meeting her gaze. "With Vance gone, he—"

"That's preposterous," she interrupted, heat rising to her cheeks. "Henry wasn't even at the party."

"Not that we know of," he admitted. "But he is and was staying at Francis Lodge. It wouldn't have been difficult for him to slip over here."

She stared at him, unable to form a coherent response.

Henry sneaking into Francis Court to murder Vance? It was so outlandish she could scarcely process it. She shook her head.

"Lilly then," he continued. "Perhaps when he ended things, she took it… badly."

Her brows lifted. "Now that makes more sense. Lilly does have a temper. And she was distressed at dinner, you said?"

"Quite theatrical about it," he confirmed. "Though that could be genuine grief, of course."

"Or guilt," she suggested, warming to the idea. "And she would've had the opportunity. No one would question her wandering the house, given her connection to the family."

"Then there's Cordelia," he added. "If Vance rejected her advances…"

Good heavens, is there anyone who doesn't have a motive?

He hesitated, then added delicately, "And, of course, if we're looking at motives, we cannot ignore James."

James? Her body went rigid. "That's absurd! He would never—" Her voice rose sharply, but Baxter interrupted.

"You yourself said he was angry with Vance for interfering," he pointed out. "And if he's in financial trouble as you suspect, he might have been desperate to prevent Vance from taking any drastic measures."

This is madness! She shook her head vehemently. "No. I won't entertain that notion for a moment. James is not a murderer. He's my brother, Baxter."

"I'm not accusing him," he said gently.

She huffed. *Well, it sounds like you are to me!*

"I'm merely pointing out, Alice, that if we're discussing purely motive, then we must consider all possibilities, however unpalatable."

Her eyes narrowed. "So who else is on your list, Baxter?"

He blew out a breath through his nose. "I don't have a list!"

But she wasn't listening. "Me? Do you think *I* murdered my husband? After all, Vance betrayed our marriage vows. Was I so angry about him making a fool of me that I cast him down the stairs, do you think?"

Baxter rolled his eyes. "Don't be—"

"Why is that any sillier than accusing James? You've known us both since we were born. How can you think one of us has the capability to murder anyone?"

"Alice!" He rested his hand on her arm. "Listen! Please."

She took a deep breath in, then let it out before snapping, "What?"

"Of course I don't think you or James murdered Vance." His eyes met hers, and she saw sincerity in them. Her heartbeat slowed down. "I was simply trying to demonstrate that motive alone is not enough. We need evidence."

She sniffed. He had a point. She'd accused Sebastian of killing Vance, but there was nothing concrete to suggest he, or indeed anyone else, had been on the stairs with Vance. *He's right. There are plenty of others with a motive.* But she wasn't about to let him off the hook so easily. "I know that!" She paused, stifling a smile. "But you could have simply said so without accusing me and my brother of murder."

His eyes sprang open wide. "I did no such thing," he pleaded, a hot spot of red appearing in his cheeks.

She grinned.

He shook his head. "Alice, you…"

She reached into her pocket and handed him a neatly folded page. "Let's start here. I've made a timeline of Vance's last hours."

He unfolded it and scanned the page. "This is excellent work. It's an excellent start."

"But as you can see, there are still quite a few gaps."

"Well then, next, we need to fill those in," he said, refolding the paper with care. "We should speak with everyone who was in the house that evening, find out where they were and what they might have seen or heard."

She looked at her watch. "Indeed. Luncheon would be an ideal time to begin. Everyone will be gathered, and we can observe their reactions to our casual enquiries."

He rose and offered his arm. "Though we must be discreet. If someone pushed Vance, the last thing we want is to alert them to our suspicions."

"Agreed," she said as she straightened up and wrapped her arm through his.

"And... what about your brother? I still think we need to get to the bottom of what his pal Sebastian is up to and find out what James' argument with Vance was about."

"I think that's best handled by someone... sympathetic."

He looked at her, amused. "You mean you."

She smiled sweetly. "I didn't say that."

He harrumphed as they began walking back towards the house, the gravel crunching beneath their boots.

23

AN HOUR LATER...

Alice stepped into the breakfast room at Francis Court. Laid upon the table were silver serving dishes containing cold beef, pressed tongue, rabbit pie, and carved ham, surrounded by bowls of cucumber salad, pickled beetroot, and an artfully arranged display of early strawberries. A stack of plates stood at one end, alongside silver cutlery and folded napkins and footmen stationed discreetly to assist.

The soft murmur of conversation hung in the air, punctuated by the occasional *clink* of cutlery against china. Through the open French doors, the terrace had been set for luncheon. Small round tables, each covered in crisp white linen anchored by glass vases filled with pale-pink roses, were scattered beneath wide parasols that fluttered gently in the breeze.

She scanned the room. Sebastian Hawthorne sat with his parents at a table near the windows, his shoulders hunched, and his brow furrowed. He pushed food around his plate with apparent disinterest. The worry etched into his features sent a flicker of suspicion through her chest. *Is that guilt perhaps?*

At another table, Lilly Forthington picked at her food, her

usual vivacity dimmed to a quiet melancholy. Her parents flanked her like guards, exchanging concerned glances over her bowed head.

Across the room, Lady Cordelia held court over her table, all sweeping glances and affected grief.

Duncan sat with their parents and Baxter at the family table, their heads bent together in quiet conversation. Baxter glanced up as if sensing her presence. His blue eyes meeting hers, as he gave her a quick nod.

No sign of James. She exhaled slowly, her shoulders drooping. She'd hoped to catch him alone, away from Sebastian's influence. As she was about to turn and search elsewhere, the door opened behind her and James stepped in.

She intercepted him before he'd made it more than a few feet. "There you are," she said, keeping her voice light.

Her brother looked down at her with a tired smile. "Alice. How are you holding up?"

"Still in shock, I think," she admitted, the half-truth coming easily to her lips. "It all feels rather surreal."

He nodded, his eyes sympathetic. "I imagine so. Are you going to join us?" He gestured in the direction of their parent's table. "I can make up a plate for you and bring it over."

She shook her head, seizing the opportunity. "I'm not feeling particularly sociable today. Would you mind terribly if we sat on the terrace, just the two of us? I could use the fresh air."

"Of course," he replied. "You find us a spot. I'll bring our luncheon out."

"Thank you," she said, squeezing his arm as she turned towards the French doors. She caught Baxter's eye as she crossed the room, giving him a subtle smile.

The terrace was warm in the sunlight but softened by a

breeze. She settled into one of the wrought-iron chairs with a quiet sigh. From here, she could see The Cascade through the trimmed hedges and hear the gentle splashing of water over stone.

A moment later, James appeared with a footman carrying a tray containing two neatly plated lunches, chilled lemonade, and a basket of rolls. Her brother muttered a quiet thanks as the man set everything down, then disappeared back inside. He sat down opposite her. "Alice, I... I want you to know how sorry I am about Vance. We may not have always seen eye-to-eye, but he was like another big brother to me. I shall miss him."

She blinked. She'd expected polite condolences, but this seemed genuinely heartfelt. *It's good to hear genuine affection for him.* Her fingers tightened around the lemonade glass. If she was going to move the conversation in the direction she needed to, it had to be now. "I know exactly what you mean," she said, her voice softening. "Sometimes I feel as though I have three brothers—you, Duncan, *and* Baxter. And at least two of them seem convinced they know what's best for me at all times."

His face relaxed into a rueful smile as he picked up a fork and stabbed a slice of chicken with it. "Don't they just? It's maddening how Vance and Baxter both think they have the right to interfere in my life as well."

"It must be difficult," she said, pleased that they seemed to be heading in the right direction.

"I know it comes from a good place," he added as he tore off a piece of bread and placed the chicken on it. "They want what's best for me. But they jump to conclusions without knowing everything."

She took a sip of her lemonade. *Give him time…*

"And why do they all think it's their sacred mission to

steer me through life? Like I'm not capable of thinking for myself," he continued through a mouthful of food.

She hesitated, then added casually, "I couldn't help but notice you're avoiding Sebastian. Is everything all right between you two?"

His expression tightened. "Sebastian is… It's not straightforward."

"In what way?"

He paused, then set his fork down with slightly more force than necessary. "He likes to gamble—nothing wrong with that; lots of men do. But then there are some silly young titled fools who hang about him and follow his example, so now he's got this reputation for leading them astray." He shook his head.

She busied herself with her napkin, keeping her gaze steady as James' fork hovered over his plate. "It's not Seb's fault if these young men lose money," he continued, though something in his expression suggested he wasn't entirely convinced of his own argument. "They make their own choices."

"I imagine it's easy to get caught up in the excitement," she ventured carefully. "Sometimes people lose perspective and bet more than they can afford." *Is James one of those people?*

"Not if you know when to stop."

"And do you?" she asked, the question lighter than the weight it carried. "Know when to stop, I mean?"

"Absolutely," he said with conviction. "I've never lost more than a few pounds in a night, and normally, I'm up a bit." He popped a tomato into his mouth. "I would never risk more than I could afford to lose."

She studied her brother's face, searching for any sign of

deception but found none. Relief washed through her. *James isn't in debt after all.*

"And Sebastian?" she asked. "Is he equally sensible?"

James frowned, chewing thoughtfully before answering. "Seb isn't… as disciplined as I am," he admitted. "I've been trying to help him moderate his behaviour before he loses everything, but I fear he's in deeper than he wants to admit."

Her mind raced. Could this be what Vance had known? Had he threatened to inform Lord Hawthorne of Sebastian's debts? It would certainly provide Sebastian with a powerful motive. But if James was trying to help Seb, then why had they fallen out? "So why the rift between you two?"

He sighed, pushing his plate away. "I've discovered that Seb has done... something I find unacceptable. I'm not sure I want to help him anymore."

Her heart skipped a beat. Could it be that he suspected Sebastian of murder? *No. That's silly. No one else suspects Vance's death was anything other than an accident, do they?* "You implied Vance meddled in your affairs? Was it to do with Seb?"

"Some do-gooding friend of Vance's wrote to him," he said with a scowl. "He told him Seb was a bad influence and not a 'suitable' friend for the son of a duke." He rolled his eyes. "Vance tried to warn me to stay away from Seb. He said…" He trailed off for a second, then shook his head. "Anyway, I told him it was none of his business, but then" — he shook his head in disgust— "I found out he'd spoken directly to Seb. I was mortified, Alice. I know he was your husband, but he really should've kept his nose out."

"And Seb was angry with you because of it?" she asked, her pulse quickening.

"He was at first," he admitted. "But then I found out something and... well. Things are different now." He picked up his fork again, leaving the thought dangling tantalising in the air between them as he ate.

She stifled a sigh. She was desperate to know what he'd discovered about Seb and if it was anything to do with Vance's death.

"Did this all happen the night of the party?" she asked, keeping her tone casual.

He leaned back in his chair, his gaze drifting to The Cascade as if searching for something in the dancing waters. "Yes," he said, his voice measured. "Seb and I had the argument I mentioned after supper—about Vance interfering—and then parted ways."

"I didn't see you dancing. Did you call it a night after that?" she asked. Of course she knew he hadn't, but she wanted to know what he'd done that evening.

"I wish! No, I got collared by the Wyndhams and their daughter. You know how Mrs Wyndham can be—once she discusses the London season, one can scarcely get a word in edgewise." He smiled faintly. "After that, I needed some peace and quiet, so I retreated to the garden room for a while. It's always so pleasantly cool in there, even on summer evenings."

"The garden room is lovely," she agreed. "I often find myself there when I need to escape—"

"Speaking of escape," he interrupted, his tone shifting abruptly. "I suppose you'll be free to be with Henry Rivershore now that Vance is gone. After a suitable time, of course."

The words hit her like a slap. She stared at her brother, heat rising to her cheeks as she struggled to process his suggestion. "I beg your pardon?"

He looked uncomfortable, clearly regretting his bluntness.

"I'm sorry; that was terribly gauche of me. It's just... Well, there have been rumours."

Excellent. Vance isn't even cold and already future romantic affairs are being discussed.

"And what with Vance and Lilly, well, I thought perhaps…"

Really? Did her brother think she would... "James, how could you think that? I…" She took a steadying breath as a little voice in her head reminded her that she had actually contemplated it before she and Vance had agreed to try again. "Whatever you've heard is nonsense. Vance and I were actually planning to give our marriage another try."

"I had no idea. I'm sorry, Alice. But I heard whispers when I was in town last week. People talking about you and Henry, suggesting there was some... understanding between you. And when I saw him in the gardens that evening, I assumed he was there to meet you."

The world seemed to tilt beneath her. She blinked rapidly, certain she'd misheard. "You saw Henry here that night?"

"Yes, the night of the party," he replied, oblivious to the bombshell he'd dropped. "I was in the garden room, and he was making his way through the garden."

Baxter's words from their earlier conversation echoed in her ears. She'd dismissed the notion that Henry had a motive to kill Vance as preposterous, insisting he hadn't even been at the party that night. Yet, here was James, casually confirming he had indeed been on the grounds. *Oh my goodness…*

"What time was that?" she asked, fighting to keep her voice steady.

He furrowed his brow. "It must have been around ten to one," he said after a moment. "I left not long after that, looking for a nightcap. I remember because I was in the library when the clock struck one."

Hours before someone murdered Vance. Had Henry been lurking in the gardens all that time, waiting to get Vance on his own, then pushed him to his death? Her heartbeat slowed down somewhat. It seemed very unlikely.

"Alice, are you quite well?" her brother asked.

"I'm fine," she managed, though her voice sounded strange even to her own ears. "I'm merely… surprised. I had no idea Henry was here that night."

"I hope I haven't upset you," he said, reaching across the table to touch her hand.

"Of course not." She gave him what she hoped was a reassuring smile as she patted his hand. Her thoughts were elsewhere, racing through the implications of this new information. She would have to tell Baxter, of course. The very thought made her cringe with embarrassment. After her adamant dismissal of his theory about Henry, she would now have to admit he might have been right all along…

24

A SHORT WHILE LATER...

The Blue Parlour was a small square room tucked away in the east wing of Francis Court, a quiet corner of the house mostly used by the family for needlework or reading when the weather turned poor. But today, the sun lit up the space through tall, narrow windows, throwing slanted beams across the faded Axminster rug and bringing a little warmth to the pale-blue silk wallpaper. Alice sat in one of the high-backed chairs near the fireplace, where she could see the edge of the rose garden and where, according to James, Henry had been lurking on that fateful night. Her mind struggled to make sense of it. *What possible reason could Henry have had for being at Francis Court at such an hour?* Had he come to find her? And if so, why hadn't he sent word or, at the very least, enquired with one of the staff?

She closed her eyes, trying to piece together the events of that night. James had been in the garden room—next door to where she was now—and had seen Henry outside around ten to one. But that was an hour and thirty minutes before Vance was last seen. If Henry was the murderer, and she was still very reluctant to even consider the possibility, would he have waited all that time? Where would he have been, and why had no one else seen him? Unless someone *had* seen him but no one had said anything yet? She sighed. *No. Henry isn't a murderer.* Sebastian had the strongest motive. *It must be him…*

The soft click of the doorknob broke her reverie. She stood, expecting to see Baxter, but the door remained closed. *What's happening?* Frowning, she moved towards it as it swung open to reveal Baxter himself, looking a trifle embarrassed.

"I do apologise," he said, closing the door behind him. "The handle slipped from my fingers the first time."

"Not at all," she replied, feeling oddly relieved at his presence. "Thank you for coming so promptly."

He glanced around the room. "I don't think I've ever been in this room before."

"It's only really used by the women in the family. I wanted somewhere private," she said, gesturing at a chair. "I have news."

He lowered himself into the armchair opposite her and crossed his legs.

"I've had a most illuminating conversation with James," she said. She would lead with Seb's debt and leave the revelation about Henry for later. *Better to establish Seb's guilt first…*

"Indeed?" He leaned forward, his interest piqued. "Do tell."

She smoothed her skirts, gathering her thoughts. "It seems we were mistaken about James being in financial difficulty. He assures me he's never lost more than a few pounds in a night and is usually up. I believe him."

"That's a relief," he said, his shoulders relaxing visibly.

"Indeed," she agreed. "But what's interesting is what he

revealed about Sebastian. According to James, Sebastian has significant gambling debts—enough, I imagine, that his father would cut him off entirely if he knew the extent of them."

Baxter's eyebrows rose. "And you believe this might be what Vance knew? What he was threatening to expose?"

"It seems likely," she said. "I wonder if the letter Vance received from Teddy Ashford prompted him to dig deeper, but James mentioned that Vance confronted Sebastian directly, telling him to leave James alone. Imagine if Vance also threatened to inform Lord Hawthorne about Sebastian's debts…"

"It would certainly provide a compelling motive," he mused, stroking his chin thoughtfully. "Sebastian would be ruined."

She lifted her chin a fraction. "My thoughts exactly." She'd known it. "James said he had been trying to help him. But recently they've fallen out. James found out Seb did something that he finds… unforgivable."

"Did he say what?"

"Unfortunately not. But it's making him question his whole friendship with Seb." She hesitated, then added, "Do you think he suspects Seb of... of harming Vance?"

He uncrossed his legs and rubbed his hands together. "It seems possible, I suppose."

"He's clearly shaken, whatever it is."

He cast a troubled look at her. "While I'm relieved James isn't the one in trouble. I agree that Seb's still our strongest suspect. However, we lack any evidence placing him at the scene."

Now she needed to tell Baxter about Henry. She swallowed. "There's something else," she said, her fingers fidgeting with a loose thread on her sleeve. She took a deep breath, steeling herself for Baxter's reaction. "It seems I was wrong about Henry Rivershore not being at Francis Court that evening."

He stilled, his gaze sharpening. "Oh?"

"James saw him," she continued, the words tumbling out in a rush. "In the gardens, around ten to one in the morning."

He sat back, his expression a mixture of surprise and—was that satisfaction? "I see."

"I don't understand it," she said, rising to pace the room. "What was Henry doing here when, as far as everyone knew, he was back at Francis Lodge? And at such an hour?"

"Looking for you, presumably?"

She flushed. "Well, if he was, he didn't find me. I'd gone up to bed by then." She shook her head. "No one has mentioned Henry calling. Besides, what gentleman calls at nearly one in the morning? It's most irregular."

"Indeed, it is," he agreed. "Which makes his presence all the more suspicious."

Well, of course you'd think that! "But before you get carried away and mark Henry as a murderer, this was an hour and a half before Vance was last seen. So where was he all that time?"

He frowned. "That's a valid point."

"You'll need to speak to him, Bax."

He gave a slow smile. "Gladly." Then his smile disappeared. "I also have news, and it's not good, I'm afraid."

Her stomach knotted. *What now?*

"I spoke with your parents over lunch. Most of the guests still at Francis Court will be leaving tomorrow morning after breakfast."

Her hand stilled on the armrest. *Tomorrow? That's no time at all. Blast! We should be out there now asking questions. But what questions?* They didn't know who or what to ask yet. *And now we're running out of time…*

25

A HEARTBEAT LATER...

"They're leaving so soon?" Alice sat forward in her chair. "But that barely gives us time to question them properly before they all scatter to the winds."

"My thoughts exactly," Baxter said grimly. "The trail will grow cold quickly once they've gone."

A sharp knock at the door of the Blue Parlour interrupted their conversation. The door opened to reveal George, a leather portfolio tucked under his arm. His eyes widened slightly at the sight of Baxter. "Your Grace," he said, bowing stiffly. "I do beg your pardon. I can return later if you prefer."

"No, no," she replied quickly. "Come in, George. Lord Rushton is fully apprised of our investigation. You may speak freely."

He nodded, closing the door behind him. "I've developed the photographs, ma'am," he said, opening the portfolio on the coffee table between them.

Baxter leaned forward, his expression one of astonishment as he examined the crisp, clear images spread before him. "These are remarkable," he murmured, looking up at

George with newfound respect. "You developed these yourself?"

"Yes, my lord," George replied, a hint of pride in his voice. "I constructed a makeshift darkroom in my quarters."

Alice caught Baxter's eye, giving him a smug look that clearly said, "I told you so." He acknowledged it with a slight incline of his head.

"As you can see," George continued, pointing to one of the images. "His Grace's hands show no marks whatsoever. No defensive wounds, no bruising."

"Suggesting he never hit his hands on the railings or stone steps as he fell," she said, looking at Baxter. "So how do you explain the damaged signet ring and the missing diamond?" She turned back to George. "Do you have a photograph of the ring?"

He slid another photograph across the table to Baxter. "You'll see the damage here—and the missing diamond, my lord."

Baxter leaned closer, studying the image.

"I've found the diamond, ma'am," George told Alice, allowing himself a small smile. "It was on the stairs, just below the sconce. I took a look at the fixture too—there's a scrape on the metal arm that turns it on and off. I'd wager that's where the ring struck, knocking the stone loose—"

"And turning off the light!" Alice completed, a look of triumph on her face.

Baxter let out a low laugh. "Well, well—so it wasn't turned off by a lurking assailant with nefarious intent after all."

"And neither was it absolutely nothing to do with anything, as you insisted," she shot back.

"Which, you must admit, was half right," he said, smirking. "It wasn't sinister—it was just clumsy."

She folded her arms. "Except it still doesn't make sense. If he fell backwards, he couldn't have hit it with his ring unless—"

"Unless he spun," George offered.

"Or was pushed backwards," Alice finished, her tone pointed.

Baxter groaned. "Here we go again. One loose diamond and you've built an entire murder plot."

"But if he fell forward and tried to grab the sconce, he wouldn't have hit it with his ring. He would've grabbed it with his fingers," she said sweetly. "You can't deny this supports my theory."

He chuckled. "You're impossible."

"And you're infuriating."

"Splendid," he said, folding his arms. "At least we're in perfect agreement about something."

George coughed. "Begging your pardon, ma'am, Your Lordship, there's more." He showed them another photograph. "Here is the white cotton thread we found caught in the duke's signet ring." Revealing the final image, he added, "And most importantly, the bruise on His Grace's wrist."

Baxter bent closer, his brow furrowed in concentration. "It's quite distinct in the photograph," he observed. "More so than I would've expected."

"Yes, my lord," George said. "The camera often captures details that escape the human eye."

"All right, I must allow that these photographs support your theory that someone pushed Vance," Baxter said, straightening as he looked at Alice. "Perhaps it's time we brought this evidence to Duncan's attention."

What? She stared at him incredulously. "And tell him what? That George and I examined the body and took photographs of it? I can imagine his reaction, can't you?"

He winced. "Point taken. I suppose we must continue to build our case in secret for now."

"There's something else, ma'am," George said, reaching into his jacket to produce a small object wrapped in a hand-kerchief. "I found the duke's pocket watch."

Alice and Baxter exchanged startled glances. "Where?" they asked in unison.

"In His Grace's bedchamber," George replied, unwrapping the gold timepiece carefully and placing it on the table. "It was in the drawer of his bedside table, tucked under a book."

"How odd." She knitted her brows. "Stokes mentioned seeing him use it not long before he said he was retiring to bed."

"Could Vance have returned to his room after leaving the library, left the watch there, and then gone out again?" Baxter asked.

George cleared his throat. "Er… I inspected it closely, my lord, and the watch has been cleaned. There are no smudges, no dirt—nothing. His Grace would have left marks from handling it, especially as he wasn't wearing gloves."

Baxter looked at her, his brow furrowing. "Would he have cleaned it before putting it away?"

"Surely, that would be his valet's job?" She looked to George for confirmation.

"I initially assumed it might have been Tom," he said. "He was acting as His Grace's valet that evening. But when I asked him about the watch before searching His Grace's room, he told me the last time he'd seen it was when he'd handed it to His Grace as he was dressing for dinner."

"How odd," Baxter mused.

They stared at the watch.

"Someone returned it," she said slowly, "cleaned it, and placed it back in his room."

Baxter raised an eyebrow. "I don't think we can—"

"There's more, my lord," George said gravely. "The watch has been damaged. The glass has a hairline crack, and the mechanism has stopped. Look at the hands."

They leaned closer. The watch had stopped at two-fifty.

Alice's breath caught. "That could be the time of death." A heavy silence fell over the room as the implications sank in.

It was a very specific time. *At last something solid to work to...*"Ten to three," she repeated softly. "If the watch stopped when Vance fell..."

"Then someone must have picked it up and returned it, ma'am," George finished.

"But why?" she asked, bewildered. "If someone wanted to conceal the time of death, why not simply take the watch away entirely?"

"Perhaps they didn't notice it was damaged," Baxter suggested with a shrug. "But the question remains, did Vance die on his way from the library? Or did he return to his room, then leave again for some reason?"

George cleared his throat again. "There's one more thing, ma'am. When speaking with one of the maids, I asked if the fireplace in His Grace's room had been used that evening. She informed me it'd been empty and ready to be laid the next day, as there had been no need for a fire."

So when the letter was burned, it must have been after the room had been cleaned. "Perhaps Vance burned the letter..."

"Or someone who came in after him," Baxter added. "Did Tom mention seeing the letter, George?"

"I didn't ask directly, my lord," George said. "I didn't want to mention it specifically as it's one of our clues. But I did ask if the duke had any visitors or received any notes before dinner. Tom said not that he was aware of."

Alice sank back into her seat, her mind whirling with possibilities. "It's quite the conundrum," she murmured. "We need to determine who wrote the letter." She stood and began pacing. "I think Lilly is our strongest possibility, so I'll see if I can catch her alone. George, can you talk to the servants? See if anyone remembers seeing Vance that evening and who he was with."

"And, George, could you find out if any of them saw Lord Rivershore too? We have reason to believe he was in the grounds at around twelve forty-five the night of the party," Baxter added.

"I'll make enquiries, my lord."

The footman bowed and gathered his photographs, tucking them back into the portfolio. With a final nod to them both, he left the room, closing the door softly behind him.

"And what of me?" Baxter asked once they were alone. "How shall I contribute to our investigation this afternoon?"

She considered for a moment. "I think you should speak with Cordelia," she said at last. "She left the ballroom with Vance that night. See if you can find out what happened."

He grimaced. "Lady Cordelia? Are you certain?"

"Don't tell me she makes you nervous," she teased, noting his discomfort with amusement. "Are you worried she'll weave her widow's web around you?"

"It's not funny."

"It's a *little* funny."

He huffed as he turned towards the door. "I'll attempt to come back in one piece, but if I go missing, promise to search under her chaise longue," he threw over his shoulder as he left the room.

Her smile faded as she looked down at Vance's precious

pocket watch on the table. *Somewhere within the walls of Francis Court, a murderer is walking free.* And they had precious little time to unmask them before the guests departed, taking their secrets with them.

26

HALF AN HOUR LATER...

Alice gazed out the tall windows of her bedchamber, watching as afternoon shadows lengthened across the manicured lawns of Francis Court. Speaking with Lilly Forthington would not be pleasant, but it was necessary if she wanted to uncover the truth about Vance's death.

"You'll want something lighter, ma'am," Maud said, stepping out from the wardrobe with a half-mourning day dress in a soft shade of lavender-grey. "It's warm in the sun, but if you're planning on staying indoors, this'll breathe well enough."

She smiled gratefully at her maid's thoughtfulness. *It's the prefect dress for interrogating my husband's mistress.* "Thank you, Maud. That will do nicely." She moved to the centre of the room and turned, allowing Maud to unfasten the long row of tiny buttons that ran down her spine. "I'm going to try to talk to Lady Forthington this afternoon and find out if it was her handkerchief we found in the duke's bedchamber and—"

"Oh, I can help you there, ma'am," Maud interrupted as her nimble fingers worked quickly, each button slipping free with practiced ease. "I spoke with Lady Forthington's maid."

Her heart quickened. "Oh?"

"Yes, ma'am." Maud eased the walking dress from her shoulders, careful not to disturb her hair. "It seems Lady Forthington asked her to go to the late Duke's bedchamber and search for a handkerchief she believes she left there."

She stiffened. *So it is Lilly's.* And she'd been in Vance's room. Her chest burned. Had Vance arranged to meet her there after everything he'd said to Alice about ending it with Lilly?

"Eliza was properly put out," Maud continued, helping her step out of the heavy skirts. "She said it wasn't her place to be rummaging through a gentleman's private quarters, especially not…" She hesitated, colour rising in her cheeks.

"Spit it out, Maud," she prompted, standing now in her chemise and petticoats, her arms crossed against the slight chill in the room.

"With him being dead and all," Maud finished in a rush, her eyes downcast as she gathered up the discarded walking dress.

Alice moved to the dressing table and sat, watching Maud's reflection in the mirror as the maid carefully hung her dress in the wardrobe. "Did she say anything else? Anything about why Lady Forthington might have been in Vance's room?"

Maud's hands paused briefly in their work. "Not at first, ma'am. But I made it my business to find out."

She raised an eyebrow, meeting her maid's gaze in the mirror. "Did you now?"

A small, satisfied smile curved Maud's lips. "Of course, ma'am. Turns out, Lady Forthington had gone to leave a note, and that's when she must have dropped the handkerchief."

"And when was this?" she asked, a peculiar mixture of relief and curiosity washing over her. If Lilly had merely left a note, then perhaps there hadn't been an intimate encounter in Vance's bedchamber after all. Perhaps he'd kept his promise to end things with her.

"Before she retired for the night, ma'am." Maud began to twist Alice's hair into a more elaborate arrangement for the afternoon. "Eliza said her ladyship came up at about half past twelve, paced around a bit, wrote a note, then left, telling Eliza she would be back shortly. She wasn't gone more than fifteen minutes before she returned, and Eliza got her ready for bed. Do you think," Maud continued, securing a curl with a hairpin, "the letter we found burned in His Grace's fireplace might have been from Lady Forthington?"

She considered this, her mind turning over the possibilities. "It would make sense. If she left him a note, and we found the remains of a note in his fireplace…"

"And the words we could still read—'I need to see you' and 'I can't go on like this'—they sound like something a spurned lover might write, don't they?" Maud suggested, reaching for the lavender dress.

"They do indeed," she agreed, rising from the dressing table to allow Maud to slip the dress over her head. "But why would Vance burn it? And when? According to the maid, the fireplace was empty when he left to go down to dinner."

Maud's brow furrowed as she began fastening the dress. "Perhaps His Grace returned to his room at some point, read the note, and burned it to ensure no one else would find it?"

"I suppose that makes sense," she said slowly, smoothing the dress over her hips. She turned to face her maid. "But I've no idea when. That's why I need to speak with Lady Forthington directly."

Maud finished with the buttons and stepped back to appraise her work. "The colour suits you, ma'am. Shall I deliver a note to her ladyship, asking her to join you for afternoon tea?"

She moved to her writing desk and pulled out a sheet of cream-coloured paper. "That's the perfect excuse, Maud." As she penned the brief invitation, her mind raced ahead to the coming conversation. She would need to be direct but tactful, firm but not accusatory. Above all, she would need to keep her emotions in check. This wasn't about confronting her husband's former mistress—it was about uncovering the truth behind his death.

She folded the note and handed it to Maud. "Thank you, Maud, you've been very helpful." The maid accepted the note with a small curtsy and left the room.

As Maud departed, she reached into her desk drawer and withdrew the handkerchief and the charred fragment of paper they'd found in Vance's room. She tucked them carefully into her pocket. *Will Lilly lie? Or worse, will she confirm the affair had continued?* Alice sucked in a lung full of air. *Whatever happens, I will remain in control. I will not let Lilly see me crumble.*

27

TWENTY MINUTES LATER...

The garden room at Francis Court was one of Alice's favourite spaces—usually. It faced south, catching the warmth of the afternoon sun, and was furnished with light damask-covered chairs and pale-blue walls that had faded tastefully over time. She had chosen this room deliberately—it was isolated enough to ensure privacy, afternoon tea normally being served in one of the more formal drawing rooms in the west wing.

Through the tall sash window, Alice caught sight of movement on the gravel path beyond the terrace. She leaned a little to the side and smirked. There, making their way towards the formal gardens, were Baxter and Cordelia Granville. Cordelia clung to his arm with theatrical delicacy, her head tilted at just the right angle to feign fascination with whatever he was saying—or more likely, to give the impression of intimate interest. Baxter, for his part, looked like a man cornered. His shoulders were rigid, his spine too straight, and even at this distance, Alice could detect the faint air of panic in his gait.

Poor Baxter. She stifled a laugh. It would be interesting to see how much useful information he could gather while trying not to be devoured…

A soft knock at the door announced George's arrival. He entered, bearing a silver tea tray, his movements precise and silent as he arranged the service on the low table between the tall armchairs.

"Darjeeling, Your Grace, as you requested. And some of those small cakes from the kitchen that you favour."

"Thank you, George." She watched as he arranged the cups and saucers with exacting precision.

He straightened and gave a small bow. "Would you like me to stay, ma'am?"

She hesitated for a moment. The idea of having George as a buffer between her and Lilly was tempting. But no—if she was going to get to the truth, she needed Lilly to speak frankly, woman to woman. That wouldn't happen with anyone else in the room.

"No," she said. "But will you wait outside the door, please, and see that we're not disturbed?"

"Of course, ma'am." His blue eyes met hers briefly, a question in their depths. "I shall remain within calling distance."

She gave a slight smile as she caught his meaning. "Yes, please do. I don't anticipate any... difficulties, but one never knows." She watched him go, the soft *click* of the door sealing her in with her thoughts. She needed to know what had happened that night—and if Lilly had been a part of it. The handkerchief and the scrap of burned paper sat heavy in her pocket. She would use them as evidence when the time was right, but first, she would give Lilly a chance to be honest of her own accord.

A firm knock at the door pulled her from her thoughts.

"Enter," she called, straightening her spine and smoothing her expression into one of polite interest.

George opened the door to admit Lilly, then withdrew, closing it softly behind him.

Lilly Forthington's usual vibrant presence had dimmed considerably since her brazen arrival several days ago. Her blonde hair, typically arranged in elaborate curls, was pulled back in a simple chignon, and her complexion had a waxy pallor that even rouge couldn't disguise. But it was her eyes that struck Alice the most—once bright with mischief, they now seemed hollow, ringed with the telltale shadows of sleepless nights.

A surprising pang of sympathy tugged at her heart. Whatever else Lilly might be, she'd clearly cared for Vance. In some strange way, they were united in their grief, both mourning the same man, albeit in different capacities.

"Lilly," she said, her voice gentler than she'd intended. "Thank you for coming. Please sit." She motioned to the armchair across from hers. "Would you like some tea?"

"Yes… thank you." Lilly sank into the chair opposite. "I was surprised to receive your note, Alice."

"I thought it best we clear the air," Alice began carefully, pouring tea into two china cups. "I know you and Vance were… er, close. You must be grieving him too."

Lilly's eyes welled instantly. "I don't know what to do," she said, taking the cup she offered. "I lost Francis… and now Vance. Do you have any idea how lonely it is, stuck out in the middle of Derbyshire with nothing but sheep and gossiping neighbours for company?"

The self-pitying tone grated on Alice's nerves, eroding some of her initial sympathy. She bit back the urge to remind Lilly that she now faced raising two fatherless boys alone.

Instead, she nodded with what she hoped appeared to be understanding.

"I don't even know how I'll get home," Lilly continued, dabbing at her eyes with a handkerchief that was similar to the one Alice had found in Vance's room. "I came with Vance, you see, and now—"

"You may take Vance's carriage," Alice interjected, wanting to move her on from her complaints. "It needs to return to Manning Hall in any case."

Lilly brightened. "That's very kind. Are you returning as well?"

"Not yet," she replied. "I'm arranging for the boys to come here to Francis Court for a while, to be with their family."

Lilly's face tightened, and she huffed, muttering something under her breath that sounded suspiciously like, "Family! That's all anyone ever cares about."

Alice chose to ignore the comment, instead taking a sip of her tea and waiting.

The silence stretched between them until finally, Lilly looked up, a new determination in her gaze. "May we be frank with each other, Alice?"

Alice forced a smile. "I'd prefer it."

Lilly took a sip of tea. "I wasn't happy when Vance ended our relationship. Being with him… it was the only thing that made Derbyshire tolerable after my husband died. And it wasn't like you were rushing to Manning Hall. You were settled in London. Everyone knew about your… er, friendship with Lord Rivershore."

Alice straightened. "They are merely rumours. There's nothing between Lord Rivershore and me."

Lilly arched an elegant brow. "Perhaps. But Vance

believed them. And he wasn't happy about it. Men are strange creatures—they always want what they don't have."

Alice wasn't sure if that was insight or spite on Lilly's part. *Is she suggesting Vance's desire to repair our marriage stemmed only from jealousy?*

"Suddenly," Lilly continued, "Vance wanted to make his marriage work. After years of happy neglect, he developed a conscience."

Yes, that's exactly what she's saying. How dare she…

"Oh, come, Alice, it was hardly a coincidence, was it?" Lilly said with a bitter smile.

She stifled a sigh. *Of course Lilly wants to save face.* And anyway, did it matter what had sparked Vance's change of heart? He'd been sincere in wanting to make their marriage work—she was sure of it. She changed tack. "When did you last see Vance?"

Lilly looked away, her fingers fidgeting with the handle of her teacup. "Oh, sometime during the post-supper dancing, I believe."

The lie was so obvious that Alice almost rolled her eyes. Instead, she reached into her pocket and withdrew the lace-edged handkerchief.

"Come now, Lilly," she said evenly. "There's no point in denying it. I know you were in Vance's room later that evening."

Lilly's eyes widened as she recognised the handkerchief, her cheeks flushing pink. For a moment, she seemed ready to deny it, but then her shoulders slumped in defeat. "Very well. I went to leave a note for him," she said, putting down her teacup. "I wanted to see him, to try to reason with him one last time. The note asked him to come to my room—I gave him the details of where I was staying on the first floor." She gestured at the handkerchief. "I must have dropped it when I was there."

"What time was this?" Alice asked, her heart quickening. So Vance hadn't been there! *There was no rendezvous…*

Lilly shrugged. "Around one in the morning, I suppose. I'd returned to my room at half-past twelve. I wrote the letter, then went to his room."

"Was the grate clean when you left?"

Lilly hesitated, her well-defined brows rising. "Er, yes, it was."

Alice hesitated, then asked the question she dreaded the answer to. She clutched her teacup. "And did Vance come to your room?"

Lilly's gaze dropped. "Yes. At twenty to three. The knocking woke me up, and I glanced at the clock."

Twenty to three—only ten minutes before Vance had died. He'd gone to Lilly's room on the first floor. Alice braced herself for what would come next, afraid that Vance had changed his mind after all and that he'd succumbed to Lilly's persuasions.

"What happened?" she asked, her voice barely audible over the beating of her heart.

Lilly hesitated, seeming to weigh her words carefully. Then she sighed and met Alice's gaze directly. "He told me again it was over. He said he'd made up his mind—he wanted to make things work with you." Her voice caught slightly. "He handed me back the letter, said he was sorry, and left." She looked away, her breath catching faintly. "I suppose I should be grateful he was honest with me."

Relief washed over Alice like a cool wave. *So Vance had honoured his promise after all.* But, of course, it was too late now… "Thank you," she said softly, "for telling me the truth, Lilly. I know that must have been difficult to hear." A new thought struck her. Had Lilly followed Vance in a fit of anger? Had she pushed him down the stairs out of jealousy or rejection? "What did you do after he left?" Alice asked, watching Lilly's face carefully.

"I was upset." Lilly looked away again. "I called my maid —she was sleeping in the room next door—and she came in and gave me a sleeping draught."

Alice made a mental note to have Maud verify this with Lilly's maid. If it was true, Lilly couldn't have murdered Vance—she would have been in her room when he'd fallen.

So had someone encountered him as he'd made his way up from the first floor to the second?

"One last question," Alice said, remembering the pocket watch now safely in her room. "Did Vance have his pocket watch with him when he came to your room?"

"Yes," Lilly replied without hesitation. "He took it out of his pocket and made a comment about it being late as he wished me a good night."

Alice's mind was a whirl. *So Vance had his watch when he left Lilly's room, minutes before his death.* Yet, the watch had been found in his bedchamber, cleaned and polished, with its crystal cracked and the hands stopped at ten minutes to three.

Did someone follow him? Or wait in the corridor? There was no getting away from it. Someone had taken the watch from Vance's body and returned it to his room. *But who? And why?*

28

SHORTLY AFTER...

The door closed behind Lilly with a soft *click*, leaving Alice alone with her thoughts as she stood by the mantelpiece in the garden room, her fingers curled loosely around the cool porcelain of her teacup. Sunlight filtered through the glass ceiling, casting dappled shadows across the Persian carpet as she contemplated what she'd learned. Lilly had been forthright, surprisingly so. Whatever else the woman might be, Alice now believed she wasn't Vance's murderer. The timing simply didn't allow for it.

George entered the room and began clearing the tea things.

"Well, that went better than I expected, George," she said, watching as he gathered the delicate teacups onto the silver tray. "She was quite forthcoming in the end."

"Indeed, ma'am?" His voice was measured, but she could detect a hint of curiosity beneath his professional demeanour.

"Yes. It seems Lady Forthington visited the duke's room around one in the morning to leave him a note, asking him to come to her room. She confirmed Vance visited her at around twenty to three."

He paused, teapot in hand. "That's very close to when His Grace must have died if his watch is anything to go by."

"Precisely. He was only there for about five minutes. He returned her note to her and left. And, this is interesting, George, he had his pocket watch in his hand."

He raised an eyebrow.

Alice paced in front of the fireplace. "She claims her maid then gave her a sleeping draught immediately after Vance left. We should verify it, of course, but I believe her."

George arranged the last of the tea things on the tray, his movements precise but unhurried. "So if Lady Forthington's account is accurate, ma'am, that would seem to eliminate her as a suspect."

"It would appear so."

His brow furrowed in thought. "Ma'am, if I may point something out?"

"Please do."

"If the duke returned Lady Forthington's note to her when he visited her room, then it couldn't have been her letter you found burned in his fireplace."

She stopped pacing, her breath catching. *Of course. Of course.* If Lilly had the letter… then whose words had gone up in smoke? "You're absolutely right. I hadn't made that connection."

"Perhaps it was from someone else entirely," he suggested. "Someone whose correspondence His Grace wished to keep private."

She dipped her chin slowly, her mind racing with possibilities. Before she could pursue this new line of thought, a sharp, urgent knock sounded at the door. Then it burst open. Baxter stumbled in, looking distinctly flustered. His usually impeccable hair was somewhat mussed, as if he'd been running his hands through it, and his cravat sat askew.

Without a word of greeting, he hurried across the room to the window, peering cautiously outside.

"Baxter, what on earth—" she began, but he cut her off with a frantic gesture.

"Shhh!" he hissed, pressing himself flat against the wall beside the window as a familiar figure in dark-grey silk hurried past outside. Lady Cordelia Granville's dramatic silhouette was unmistakable even through the glass and greenery. She paused briefly, scanning the garden as if searching for something—or someone—before continuing on her way with determined strides.

Alice pressed her lips together, fighting the urge to laugh as he remained flattened against the wall, barely breathing until Cordelia disappeared from view. Only then did he exhale, his shoulders slumping in relief. "Baxter, are you hiding from Lady Cordelia?"

"Of course I am!" he said, striding agitatedly across the room to her. "The woman's a man-eater, Alice! I've spent the last thirty minutes trying to escape her clutches, and now she's hunting me like... like a fox after a particularly hand-some rabbit!"

She couldn't contain her laughter. It bubbled up, bright and unexpected, easing some of the tension that had gripped her since Vance's death. Across the room, she caught George's eye, where a twitch at a corner of his mouth betrayed his own amusement.

"Oh, laugh all you like," Baxter grumbled, straightening his cravat with as much dignity as he could muster. "You weren't there when she told me, in excruciating detail, how lonely her bed has been since Sir Reginald passed." He collapsed into an armchair, running a hand over his face. "She'll be back, you know. She's determined. What am I to do if she comes looking for me here?"

George cleared his throat. "My lord? Perhaps I may be of help."

"What do you propose?" Baxter asked, looking up hopefully.

"I believe Lady Granville is heading to the stable yard. I shall intercept her and inform her I saw you leaving to return to Francis Lodge to rest before dinner."

Baxter looked at George with newfound respect. "That's… that's remarkably devious of you, George."

"Thank you, my lord." George inclined his head and exited, the tea tray balanced perfectly in his hands.

The moment the door closed behind him, Baxter rose and strode to the drinks tray in the corner, where he poured himself a generous measure of brandy. He downed it in one swift movement, wincing at the burn, then poured another before dropping back into his chair with a heavy sigh.

I need to tell him what I've learned. "The letter we found burned in Vance's fireplace wasn't from Lilly—"

"—was from Cordelia," Baxter said simultaneously.

They both stopped, surprised, then laughed.

"Well," he said, "it seems we've both made progress. You go first."

She gave him a summary of what Lilly had told her, ending in, "So if she's telling the truth, then she's not our murderer." He gave a quick bob of his head. "You next."

He took a sip of his brandy, seeming to have now relaxed a fraction. "I managed to extract some useful information before fleeing for my virtue," he said wryly. "Cordelia was remarkably forthcoming, perhaps hoping her candour would endear her to me." He shuddered at the thought.

"And?" she prompted, stifling a smile.

"She confirmed that she and Vance went outside for some fresh air during the dancing. They left the ballroom at approximately ten minutes past midnight returning around twenty minutes later." He set his glass down, his expression slightly bemused. "She made no attempt to hide the fact that she was pursuing Vance romantically." He shook his head.

Alice suppressed a sigh. *Of course Cordelia was chasing him too!* It seemed everyone had wanted a piece of Vance. *Even so...* "Even knowing he was married?"

"Especially knowing he was married," he replied grimly. "Her exact words when I asked her why she would pursue a married man were that, 'Married men are easier and discreet and don't expect you to marry them and hand over your fortune.'"

Alice smirked. *Well, she does have a point!*

"Then she told me she wasn't averse to an unmarried man, provided he had his own money. At which point she gave me what I can only describe as a carnivorous smile."

She bit her lip to suppress another laugh. "So what happened after they returned from their walk?"

"She said Vance seemed distracted the entire time and was eager to get back inside. She decided to abandon her pursuit for the evening and retired to her room on the first floor at around a quarter to one." He took another sip of brandy. "And here's where it gets interesting. After her maid helped her prepare for bed, she decided to make one final attempt. She wrote Vance a note asking if they could meet the following morning to discuss some 'business issues' she was having. She openly admitted to me it was a fabrication, merely an excuse to speak with him privately."

She is bold...

"Then she instructed her maid to give it to Vance's valet for delivery to his room."

That must be the letter we found burned in the fireplace. She nodded slowly, piecing together the timeline. "So Vance must have returned to his room around half-past two, finding both Lilly's note asking to speak with him and Cordelia's note about meeting the next morning."

"He was certainly popular," Baxter remarked dryly.

"Indeed." She folded her hands, frowning. "So. Vance returns to his room not long after two-thirty. He finds the note from Cordelia and burns it, although I'm struggling to think why. He also finds Lilly's note, which he takes with him. He goes to her room at twenty to three, leaves about five minutes later with his pocket watch still in his hand. And then…"

"That's when he encountered his murderer on the staircase."

She rose, moving to the window to gaze out at the gardens where Henry had allegedly been seen. "Do you think it's possible Cordelia saw Vance leaving Lilly's room and was so angry, she followed and confronted him?"

He shook his head. "I doubt it very much. Her pursuit of Vance seemed rather half-hearted, more a matter of convenience than passion. And she showed no signs of guilt, regret, or even particular sadness about his death." He swirled the remaining brandy in his glass. "I don't believe she had any reason to want to kill him."

"I agree," she said, turning back to face him. "So that's Cordelia and Lilly both eliminated as suspects."

"Which leaves us with Sebastian and Henry." His voice hardened a touch on the second name.

She sighed, returning to her seat. "I still think Sebastian is our most likely culprit. He had the motive—Vance was likely threatening to expose his gambling debts to his father."

"And yet, we have direct evidence placing Henry at Francis Court that night, against all expectations." He set his empty glass aside.

No, not Henry… "I'm sure there's a simple explanation,"

she insisted. "In fact, we should go to Francis Lodge now and confront him directly."

He pushed to his feet, grim-faced. "No, I'll deal with Henry. Alone."

Why? "But—"

"Alice." His tone was firm. "If Henry's involved in Vance's death, confronting him could be dangerous. I won't put you at risk."

But it's Henry... She opened her mouth to protest but thought better of it. Baxter could be as stubborn as Duncan when his mind was made up. "Very well," she said reluctantly. "But we'll speak again before dinner? You'll tell me everything you learn?"

"I promise."

As he moved towards the door, she called after him. "And Baxter—watch the corridors. The fox might double back."

He groaned. "I'll take the servants' stairs."

"Off you hop then," she said, laughing as the door closed behind him.

29

THAT EVENING...

Alice sat at her dressing table in her bedchamber, watching Maud's practiced movements in the mirror as the maid arranged her hair for dinner. The brush glided through her red locks with a gentle rhythm that should have been soothing, but her mind was far too occupied with the day's revelations to find comfort in the familiar ritual. Beyond the windows, dusk settled over Francis Court like a heavy cloak, bringing with it the promise of another evening of strained conversations and sidelong glances.

"I've added some jet beading at the collar of your dress for tonight, ma'am. It's appropriate but still becoming."

"Thank you, Maud," she replied, her gaze drifting to the gown laid out on the bed. The deep forest-green would suit her colouring, while the black beadwork would acknowledge her mourning state without the severity of full black.

"Almost done." Maud secured the last of her hair with a tortoiseshell pin. She leaned back and caught Alice's eye in the mirror. She winked. "You'll do, ma'am."

Alice sent her a wry look in response as Maud moved to the bed and carefully picked up the green silk dress. "There's quite a stir downstairs, ma'am, I must say. Everyone's packing and making arrangements to leave tomorrow. The house is fair buzzing with activity."

"I'm worried we're running out of time, Maud," she murmured, rising from the dressing table.

"Indeed, ma'am." Maud held up the dress, allowing her to step into it. "Though I've not been idle. I've been chatting with Lady Forthington's maid again, trying to learn more about the night His Grace died."

She stilled, her arms halfway into the sleeves. "And?"

A smile of satisfaction played at the corners of Maud's mouth as she eased the dress up and over her shoulders. "I've already told you Eliza told me Lady Forthington came up to her room around half-past twelve. Well, she didn't call for her —Eliza sleeps on a cot in the dressing room attached to the main bedchamber, you see."

"Go on," she encouraged, turning to allow Maud access to the row of small buttons that ran down her back.

"About twenty minutes later, Eliza heard the door open and close—Lady Forthington had left the room. She was gone only about fifteen minutes before returning and ringing for Eliza to help her prepare for bed." Maud's fingers worked nimbly at the buttons, her voice dropping to a conspiratorial whisper. "Eliza said her ladyship seemed jittery and nervous but wouldn't say why."

"We have to assume it's because she'd already delivered the note to Vance and was waiting for him to respond."

Maud offered a curt nod as she secured another button. "Eliza said Lady Forthington said she was going to read for a bit, so Eliza went to bed in the dressing room. But a knock at the main bedroom door later awakened her."

Alice's heart skipped a beat. "Vance," she whispered.

"Yes, ma'am. Eliza says she heard the duke's voice

speaking to Lady Forthington." Maud hesitated, her fingers stilling on the buttons. "She claims she couldn't hear what was said, but between you and me, I don't believe that for a moment. Servants always hear more than they let on."

She suppressed a smile at Maud's frankness. "What happened then?"

"Eliza says the duke didn't stay long—possibly five or ten minutes at most. After he left, Lady Forthington rang for her. She was clearly upset, clutching a letter in her hand. That's when she asked Eliza for a sleeping draught. It was shortly after quarter to three, she says. She stayed with Lady Forthington until she fell asleep."

She nodded slowly, satisfaction warming her chest. "That confirms what Lady Forthington told me earlier."

"So the letter we found burned in the duke's fireplace can't have been from Lady Forthington," Maud said, securing the final button with a triumphant little pat.

"No, it wasn't," Alice confirmed, turning to face her maid. "It was from Lady Granville. She admitted as much to Lord Rushton this afternoon—apparently, she was pursuing the duke rather aggressively."

Maud's eyes widened. "I was going to tell you that very thing, ma'am! I spoke with Mary—that's Lady Granville's maid—and she told me she was asked to deliver a note to the duke after getting her mistress ready for bed that night. It was about half-one, and Mary was tired and none too pleased about it. She couldn't find Tom, so she gave the note to the hall boy and asked him to pass it along." Maud reached for a black velvet ribbon, carefully tying it around Alice's neck.

"And did Tom receive it?"

"I spoke to him about it, but he was distracted at the time," Maud replied, rearranging the ribbon to sit perfectly against Alice's collarbone. "He was darning one of his gloves and clearly having problems with it, but he said he didn't recall receiving a note."

A thought struck her. "Tom was on duty that night along with Stokes, wasn't he? He might have seen something—or someone—moving about the house at that hour."

Maud stepped back to appraise her work. She leaned in and made a small adjustment to the set of the dress at Alice's shoulders. "I can try again later, when he's less preoccupied, if you'd like, ma'am?"

"That would be very helpful, Maud." She smiled at her maid. "Thank you for being so thorough. We've now confirmed what Lady Forthington told me, which means we can rule her out as a suspect." It ought not to have mattered to her, but it did. Whatever else had passed between them, she didn't want Vance's final moments to have been with Lilly— or ended by her hand.

"And Lady Granville as well, ma'am," Maud added, reaching for a pair of long black evening gloves. "If she'd left her room later, Mary would have heard her…"

"Good point." She slipped her hands into the soft kid leather, smoothing the gloves up to her elbows. "So now we've ruled out two suspects. I think we can call that progress, don't you?"

"Indeed, ma'am," Maud agreed, stepping back to take in the completed ensemble. "There. You look very elegant."

Alice surveyed her reflection in the mirror. The green silk complemented her fair complexion and red hair, while the jet beading added a sombre note appropriate to her mourning. She looked every inch the duchess—composed, dignified, and betraying none of the turmoil that churned beneath the surface.

"Will there be anything else, ma'am?"

"No, that will be all for now. Though if you hear anything else from the servants that might be relevant…"

"I'll come to you at once," Maud promised.

With a last glance in the mirror, Alice squared her shoulders and departed her bedchamber.

The corridor outside was quiet, most guests still in their rooms preparing for dinner. Her footsteps echoed softly on the polished floor as she made her way towards the main staircase. As she approached the top of the stairs, a chill crept up her spine. This was where it had happened—where Vance had fallen to his death only days ago. Had he been pushed by Sebastian, desperate to keep his gambling debts secret? Or by Henry, driven by some misguided passion? Or was there another explanation entirely, one they hadn't yet considered? It seemed that everyone had wanted something from Vance that night. She'd wanted closure. Lilly had wanted love. Cordelia had wanted excitement. But someone had wanted silence. Permanently.

She paused at the top step, her gloved hand resting lightly on the banister. Below, the marble floor of the entrance hall gleamed in the light of the crystal chandelier. She took a deep breath, steeling herself for the evening ahead as she descended the stairs slowly, one hand trailing along the banister. She would not give up. Even if the guests departed without revealing their secrets, she would pursue the truth relentlessly. She owed Vance that much.

30

A SHORT WHILE LATER...

As Alice reached the bottom of the stairs, the Painted Hall opened before her in all its aged glory. The vast space stretched away in three directions, its black-and-white chequered marble floor gleaming like a frozen lake in the golden lamplight. Above, the curved ceiling soared, adorned with frescoes depicting scenes from classical mythology—gods and goddesses frozen in eternal revelry and strife. Time had softened their colours, lending the once-vibrant paint a dreamlike quality that seemed particularly fitting tonight. Four generations of Astleys gazed down from gilt-framed portraits along the walls, their painted eyes following her progress across the floor.

"Your Grace."

She started, turning to find Stokes materialising from the shadow of a marble column.

"Lord Rushton is here," he said, his voice pitched low despite the empty hall. "He wishes to speak with you in the library before dinner if that would be convenient."

Her pulse quickened. This was why she'd come down early. Baxter had returned from the Lodge, which meant he'd spoken with Henry. What had he learned? Had Henry confirmed his presence at Francis Court that night? And if so, why had he been here?

"Thank you, Stokes. I'll see him now."

They crossed the Painted Hall in silence, their footsteps echoing against the marble. Soon, they reached the library door, its polished oak gleaming warmly in the lamplight. Stokes opened the door for her, and she stepped inside.

The library embraced her with its familiar scent of leather and beeswax, with its tall shelves of books rising to the ceiling, containing centuries of knowledge. Baxter stood by the hearth, his hands clasped behind his back. He turned as she entered, his face unreadable.

"May I bring you something?" Stokes enquired from behind her. "A glass of sherry, perhaps, before dinner?"

All she wanted right now was to find out if Henry was still a suspect. "No thank you, Stokes. That will be all for now."

The butler bowed and withdrew, closing the door silently behind him. For a moment, neither of them spoke; the only sound was the ticking of the long-case clock in the corner. *Come on, Baxter. Tell me!* She crossed to the armchair where he was standing. "Have you spoken to Henry?"

"I have." He sat down, his face still unreadable.

She settled into the chair opposite, arranging her skirts carefully. *Is he drawing this out deliberately to unsettle me?* "And?" She braced herself.

"He denied it at first," Baxter said, resting his forearms on his knees, "but I told him he'd been seen. He admitted it then."

Her stomach twisted as she leaned forward slightly, her hands clasped tightly in her lap. "Why was he here?"

"He claims he was feeling rather put out at being left

behind at the Lodge while everyone else attended the party. He dined alone, had a few too many glasses of claret, and got it into his head you were making a terrible mistake in reconciling with Vance."

Heat rose to her cheeks. "I see." *So he came looking for me...*

"He decided in his somewhat inebriated state, he should come to Francis Court and speak with you directly. He wanted to tell you not to go back to Vance."

A tangle of emotions unfurled in her chest—gratitude, guilt, a flush of awkwardness. *Oh, Henry!*

"He said he was walking through the gardens when he saw Vance and Cordelia arm in arm, heading back into the house," Baxter continued. "He claims the sight only reinforced his conviction you deserved better than a husband who flaunted his indiscretions so openly."

His gaze was steady, but was that a slight quivering of his lips she could see? "He continued on, determined to find you and—I quote—'help you see reason'."

She looked away, unable to meet his eyes. Had she encouraged Henry's attentions too much? He'd clearly developed feelings strong enough to drive him to such a reckless act.

"So where did he go next?" she asked at last.

A small, wry smile touched Baxter's lips. "He didn't get very far. It seems our impulsive friend's mission was thwarted before it could properly begin. According to Henry, he managed to reach the terrace doors leading to the ballroom when he was intercepted by a footman."

"A footman?" Alice repeated. "Which one?"

"He didn't know." Baxter shook his head, a smile still on his lips. *He's enjoying this...* "In any case, this unnamed footman apparently asked him his business, and when Henry explained he wished to speak with you, the footman informed him rather firmly that you were with your husband and unavailable to visitors."

She frowned, thinking back to that evening. She'd retired early, leaving Vance in the ballroom. Who would've told anyone she was with her husband? And which footman had been on duty at the terrace doors?

"Well, it can't have been George," she said slowly. "He would've told me if he'd seen Henry that night." She cast her mind back, trying to recall the staff arrangements that evening. "Besides, George mentioned he was clearing away from supper at that time, not attending to the ballroom."

"Whoever it was, he did you a service," Baxter said. "Henry admitted the encounter sobered him somewhat. He realised how inappropriate his behaviour was and decided to return to Francis Lodge immediately."

"And did he?" she pressed. "Return there, I mean."

He nodded. "Of course, James saw him on his way back at twelve-fifty, but I've also confirmed it with the butler there. Henry arrived back at precisely one o'clock and didn't leave again that night. The butler is quite certain—as he was waiting up for the rest of us also staying at the lodge to return."

She slumped back in her chair and exhaled deeply. "So Henry couldn't have been involved in Vance's death."

"No," he agreed, giving her a wry smile. "We can eliminate him as a suspect. Which only leaves us with—"

"Sebastian Hawthorne!" she finished. The relief of clearing Henry was immediately replaced by the weight of what this meant. If not Henry, then their only remaining suspect was Sebastian. And yet, they still had no concrete evidence placing him at the scene.

"Indeed," he said grimly. "Though we're no closer to proving his involvement."

"And time is running short. Most of the guests leave tomorrow, including Sebastian and his family." She rose restlessly, moving to the window; night had fallen completely, turning the glass into a dark mirror reflecting the room behind her. "If we can't find evidence against Sebastian before he leaves—" Her words were interrupted by a knock at the door. Before either of them could respond, the door opened to reveal George.

"Your Grace, my lord," he said, bowing. "I do apologise for the interruption, but a telegram has arrived for you, ma'am." He held out a silver tray, on which rested a folded piece of paper. "It's from Mr Beaumont, and I knew you were waiting for it."

She crossed the room quickly, her heart racing as she took the telegram from the tray. Ben Beaumont could be their last hope.

"Thank you, George," she said, her voice steadier than she felt. She turned the telegram over in her hands, keen to know its contents, her fingers trembling. *Please let this help us find Vance's murderer…*

31

A FEW SECONDS LATER...

"George, who was on duty in the ballroom on the night of the party?"

Alice paused, her fingers hovering over the stiff paper. She looked at Baxter. *Can't this wait until after I open the telegram?*

"Tom and Edward, my lord. They covered the late evening until the dancing stopped."

Oblivious to her glaring at him, Baxter continued his questioning. "Did either of them mention speaking to Lord Rivershore around ten to one? He said a footman stopped him from entering the ballroom."

"No, my lord," George replied after a moment's consideration. "Neither mentioned any such encounter to me. Would you like me to enquire?"

"Yes, please do," he said. "Discreetly, of course."

"Of course, my lord." George bowed and left the room.

Baxter turned to her. "And who exactly is Ben Beaumont?"

Her lips twitched. "Mr Beaumont is a former police officer who now works as a private investigator. I've employed his services on occasion when... discretion was required."

His eyebrows shot up, his expression a mixture of alarm and fascination. "You regularly employ a private investigator? Whatever for?"

"Not regularly," she corrected, smoothing her skirts with one hand. "Only when circumstances demand it."

"And these circumstances arise often enough for you to have a preferred investigator on hand?" He pressed his hand to his chin, looking increasingly concerned. "Alice, surely, you see how irregular this is?"

She lifted her chin. "Not at all. Many people in our position require help with delicate matters from time to time."

"And, of course, you trust this man implicitly?" His tone held a note of sarcasm.

"Yes, I do." She met his gaze steadily. "Ben Beaumont has proven himself both capable and discreet on multiple occasions."

He threw up his hands in a gesture of exasperation. "First examining bodies and taking photographs, now private investigators—I fear to ask what other unconventional pastimes you've developed, Alice."

Oh, for heaven's sake! "Perhaps you'd like to hear what Mr Beaumont has discovered before dismissing his usefulness?"

They locked eyes, then he huffed, waving his hand at the telegram. "Go ahead."

She flipped the paper open and began to read aloud:

"'*Inquiries confirm SH owes considerable sums to notorious gambling figure Mr Halstead, who runs Thornfield Club, Mayfair. Has been bringing young gentlemen from the* ton *to his establishment, receiving percentage of losses against own debt.*

JA confirmed as cautious gambler, no significant losses recorded. Sources indicate JA paid SH's immediate debts a month ago. Send further instruction if need more. Regards, BB.'"

She lowered the telegram, her pulse quickening. The confirmation of Sebastian's desperate financial situation solidified his motive. If Vance had threatened to expose Sebastian's scheme—bringing wealthy, young aristocrats to gambling halls and profiting from their losses—it would have meant ruin. Not merely social disgrace but perhaps even criminal charges for what amounted to fraud.

And James had paid Sebastian's debts? She thought James naïve, easily led, but this hinted at something deeper. *Loyalty? Guilt?* Or something Sebastian had over him? She wasn't sure which possibility troubled her more.

"This confirms our suspicions," she said, looking up at him. "Sebastian had every reason to want Vance silenced."

"Yes, his motive is clear now,'" he agreed, rising from his chair to pace before the fire. "But motive alone isn't enough. We still have no evidence placing him at the scene of Vance's death."

"We have the letter warning Vance about Sebastian's influence over James," she pointed out. "And now this telegram confirming Sebastian's desperate financial straits."

"But neither proves he pushed Vance down those stairs," he replied, his voice gentle but firm. "We need more, Alice. Something indisputable."

"But with the guests departing tomorrow morning, our window for gathering evidence is closing rapidly. We need to confront Sebastian directly, Baxter. Tonight after dinner."

He stopped his pacing, turning to face her with alarm. "Confront him? Alice, you can't be serious."

"I'm entirely serious," she said, rising to meet his gaze.

"Sebastian leaves tomorrow. This may be our only chance to get the truth from him."

"And you think he'll simply confess if asked?" His tone was incredulous. "Or perhaps slip up and reveal his guilt through some careless remark?"

It's possible... "People often reveal more than they intend when caught off guard."

He shook his head, his expression grave. "This isn't one of your detective novels, Alice. We can't go about accusing guests—a member of the *ton*, no less—of murder without substantial proof."

She clenched her hands. "I'm not suggesting we accuse him. We would simply ask him about his argument with Vance and see how he reacts when pressed."

"And if he refuses to speak with us? Or worse, realises what we're implying and takes offence?" He moved closer, lowering his voice. "You could create a scandal, Alice."

"A scandal?" She gave a short, humourless laugh. "Is that all you care about? My husband is dead, Baxter. Murdered on the stairs of this very house. I'm well past worrying about a scandal."

"All the more reason to proceed with caution," he urged. "If he's innocent, you risk alienating an influential family for no reason. If he's guilty, confronting him directly could be dangerous. What if he lashes out, Alice? Vance is already dead. Will you be next?"

She rolled her eyes. *He's hardly going to kill me in broad daylight, is he?* She huffed and paced away from Baxter, trying to contain her mounting exasperation. "So we do nothing. Is that what you're saying? We simply allow him to leave tomorrow and forget all about it?"

"I'm not suggesting we do nothing," he said, his tone

softening. "But confronting him directly seems foolhardy at best, dangerous at worst."

"Then what do you propose?" she asked, turning back to face him. "We have no other suspects. We've eliminated Lilly, Cordelia, and now Henry. Sebastian is the only one with both motive and opportunity. And he's leaving in the morning."

"Perhaps we could—" he began, but a sharp knock at the door interrupted him.

The door opened to reveal Stokes. "Your Grace, my lord, the dinner gong is about to be rung. The guests are assembling in the drawing room."

Blast!

"Thank you, Stokes," Baxter replied, "We'll be along shortly."

Stokes nodded, gave a slight bow, and left.

Dinner would be wasted time. They needed to continue their investigation. She turned back to Baxter. "Would it be bad form if we forgo dinner and—"

"No, Alice. We cannot miss dinner," he said firmly.

She knew he was right. She sighed. "I daresay. But then we need to speak with Sebastian after dinner. Before it's too late."

He raked a hand through his hair, then immediately smoothed it down again. "Alice, I understand your urgency, but I'm not convinced this is the right approach."

She stepped closer. "Do you have an alternative that doesn't involve letting our prime suspect walk away tomorrow morning?"

"Let me think about it over dinner. Perhaps there's a more subtle way to extract information from him."

They left the library together. The corridor stretched before them, lit by oil lamps that cast warm pools of light against the panelled walls. As they walked back to the drawing room where the other guests were gathering, her mind was made up. If Baxter couldn't be persuaded to help confront Sebastian, she would do it herself. He was reckless, entitled, and cornered. But if she had to face a man like that alone, so be it. The thought of Vance's murderer escaping the consequences was unbearable. Some things were worth risking scandal for. Justice for Vance was one of them.

32

AFTER DINNER...

The ladies rose from the dining table in a gentle rustle of silk and taffeta, responding to the Duchess of Arnwall's subtle nod that signalled the end of dinner. Alice smoothed her green skirt as she stood, exchanging polite smiles with her mother and the remaining female guests. The rich aroma of roast beef and wine lingered in the air as the ladies filed towards the door, leaving the gentlemen to their port and cigars.

The pleasantries, the chatter—it had all been intolerable tonight. Her mind had been unable to ignore the churning thoughts about Sebastian Hawthorne and the telegram from Ben Beaumont.

As she followed her mother and the others along the hallway on their way to the Green Drawing Room, a soft *click* from behind caught her attention. She glanced back over her shoulder and glimpsed her brother James and Sebastian Hawthorne slipping out through the door of the dining room, their heads bent close together in what appeared to be intense conversation.

Her steps faltered. Throughout dinner, James had pointedly ignored Sebastian, refusing to pass the salt directly to him and directing his conversation exclusively to those seated on his other side. Why, then, were the two men now leaving together?

She hesitated, torn between following the ladies as propriety demanded and satisfying her growing curiosity. The two men turned right in the corridor, heading away from her. *What are they up to?*

It was too good of an opportunity to miss. She turned and moved swiftly down the corridor to follow them. Ahead, she caught a glimpse of James' tailcoat as he and Sebastian turned into the Old Study. She slowed her pace. The Old Study was only really used by her father for formal meetings with his steward. The family much preferred the less formal library a short distance off the Painted Hall. *What shall I do?* If Sebastian was indeed Vance's murderer, confronting him alone might be dangerous. She needed Baxter, but was there time to fetch him from the dining room?

As she approached the Old Study door, she spotted Stokes emerging from a side corridor, a silver tray balanced on one hand. *Perfect!*

"Stokes," she called softly, changing course to intercept him.

The butler paused, his face betraying only the mildest surprise at finding her alone in the corridor. "Your Grace?"

"I wonder if you might convey a message to Lord Rushton," she said, keeping her voice low. "Please inform him that I request his presence in the Old Study as soon as possible. It's a matter of some urgency."

"Of course, ma'am." Stokes' eyes flickered briefly at the door before returning to her face. "I shall attend to it at once."

As the butler departed, she crossed the corridor, stopping outside the heavy oak door. As she drew closer, she could hear the muffled sounds of voices from within. Though she couldn't make out the words, the tones were unmistakably heated.

She pressed her ear to the door, straining to hear. James' voice rose suddenly, sharp with anger. "—absolutely unacceptable!"

Sebastian's reply was too low to distinguish, but the tension in his voice was clear.

She pressed her lips together, indecision gripping her. Should she wait for Baxter or intervene now? If Sebastian had murdered Vance, might James be at risk as well? The thought of losing her brother to the same hand that had taken her husband sent a chill through her veins. *It can't wait.* Drawing a deep breath, she grasped the brass doorknob and turned it decisively, pushing the door open without knocking.

Inside, the tall, lean frame of Sebastian was silhouetted against the flickering gas-lights. His fair hair was dishevelled, as if he'd been running his hands through it. Across from him, James stood with his back to the door, his shoulders squared and his hands clenched at his sides in a posture of barely contained fury.

"If you don't fix this, Seb, then I will have no choice but to tell—" James cut off abruptly, twisting to see who had interrupted them. A flicker of anger crossed his face, then it set in a guarded neutrality that failed to hide his irritation. "Alice? What are you doing here?"

Both men stared at her. *What indeed?* She racked her brain for a response. "Er, I'm sorry to interrupt," she said, closing the door behind her. She glanced around the room, improvising quickly. "I need to write a letter before the evening post leaves, and I left my stationery in here earlier."

Neither man appeared convinced by her explanation. *Well, so be it.* She was here now, and she had a job to do.

"Actually," she said, dropping the pretence, "while I have you here, Mr Hawthorne, there's something I've been meaning to ask you."

Sebastian visibly tensed, his fingers clasped together until they were white at the knuckles. "Yes, Your Grace?"

"I wondered if you might tell me about your argument with my husband on the night of the party."

"Alice!" James hissed, giving her a warning look. She ignored him and stared pointedly at Seb. The colour drained from the man's face, his pale-blue eyes widening in shock.

"I—I don't know what you mean," he stammered, his practiced charm nowhere in evidence. "His Grace and I didn't argue that evening."

"Come now, Mr Hawthorne," she replied, advancing a step in his direction. "I heard you arguing in the morning room. Vance was threatening you about something. I'd like to know what it was."

Sebastian's gaze darted to James, then back to her, a muscle twitching in his cheek. "There must be some mistake," he insisted, though his voice lacked conviction. "We exchanged pleasantries, nothing more."

So he wants to be like that, does he? She drew herself up to her full height, channeling every ounce of ducal authority she possessed. "I know about your debts to the gambling house in Mayfair, Mr Hawthorne," she said, her voice steady despite the rapid beating of her heart. "Was my husband threatening to tell your family about them?"

Sebastian's mouth opened and closed wordlessly, his composure crumbling before her eyes. He looked to James with an expression of such naked panic that she felt a momentary pang of sympathy for him despite her suspicions.

"Alice," James interjected, stepping forward with a

warning in his eyes. "Leave this, will you? I have it all in hand."

"I'm afraid I can't do that, James," she said, her voice softening but losing none of its resolve. She turned back to Sebastian, her green eyes hard. "Did you know, James, that Sebastian has been luring young men from the *ton* with more money than sense into Mr Halstead's gambling halls and taking a percentage of their losses to clear his own debts?"

James' surprise gave way to a grimmer look. "Yes. But how do *you* know that?"

So it's true then... "I have my sources." She paused. So why wasn't James doing something about it. Unless…was he, too, involved in the game? "You knew?"

James dragged his fingers through his dark hair, his mouth set in a tight line. "I knew about Seb's debts, of course," he admitted, throwing a glance at his friend. "And as I told you, I've been trying to help him. But I didn't know about how the gambling house was using him to bring in new gamblers until Vance told me that evening." He turned to Sebastian, his face hardening. "Of course I was shocked. When Vance first told me, I didn't believe it. I told him Seb wouldn't do such a thing, and we argued about it. It turns out I was the one who was wrong!"

"You've no idea what these people are like once you owe them money and can't pay," Sebastian broke in, his voice rising with desperation. "They own your soul! You have no choice but to do as they ask."

He pushed away from the fireplace, pacing a few steps before turning back to face James. "All I did was introduce them to the club," he said, a pleading note in his voice. "I didn't *make* them lose their money—they did that all by themselves!"

"That's no excuse," James shot back, his temper flaring again. "You should have refused."

"They said they would break all my limbs!" Sebastian's voice cracked on the last word, his facade of sophisticated charm completely dissolving to reveal the frightened young man beneath.

Alice studied him, noting the genuine fear in his eyes. Sebastian Hawthorne was desperate, cornered—but on that night, had he been desperate enough to kill Vance? Surely, he could've asked his parents for the money if his life was in danger? They might disapprove, but they would want to secure his safety. "Why not simply ask your father for the money?"

Sebastian gave a bitter laugh. "My father would never pay my gambling debts. He's already said he'll cut me off if I fall into debt again. I'd be penniless—and still owe the club. At least this way, while I still receive my allowance, I have a chance to get out of this one day."

The sound of the door opening behind them made all of them turn. Baxter stepped into the room, his sharp gaze taking in the scene before him. His eyes met hers, and she could read the question there as clearly as if he'd spoken it aloud: *What have you done?*

She lifted her chin slightly, refusing to be cowed. "Baxter," she said, her voice steady. "Mr Hawthorne has just admitted to arguing with Vance about his gambling debts the night he died."

Sebastian rolled his eyes and huffed. "Does everyone know about my debts?"

"What did Vance want from you?" Baxter asked as he closed the door behind him.

Sebastian looked to James, then muttered, "He wanted me to stay away from James."

"Or?"

"Or he'd tell my father."

So you had to silence him, she thought grimly.

Baxter turned to James. "Did you know anything about this scheme to lure young men into gambling halls?"

"Of course not," James said firmly. "If I had, I would've stopped it."

Alice added, "He didn't believe Vance at first. That's why they argued."

James nodded. "But later I challenged Seb about it, and he confessed."

Sebastian threw up his hands. "I *am* in the room, you know."

She ignored him. She needed him to confess. *I have to press him further—*

But Baxter interrupted. "When was that, James?"

James frowned slightly, considering. "I left Vance in the library and went to my room at around quarter past two," he said. "But what Vance had said was playing on my mind, so I went down to the first floor and knocked on Seb's door."

"At what time?" Baxter asked, and she noticed the sudden sharpness in his gaze.

"Shortly after half-past two," James replied.

She felt a jolt of realisation. The timing was critical—if James had been with Sebastian at half-past two, and Vance had died at approximately ten minutes to three...

"How long were you there?" Baxter asked, evidently following the same line of thought.

"Only about fifteen minutes," James said. "I was so angry, I left…"

She exchanged a glance with Baxter. If James had left Sebastian's room at twenty to three, that still gave him ten minutes to get to the second floor and push Vance down the stairs... "What did you do after James left?" she asked Sebastian.

"My valet came out from the adjoining room," he replied, rubbing at his bloodshot eyes. "The noise had woken him up. He made me a drink, and we talked for a short while. Then I went to bed. It must have been not long after three."

Her heart sank. Sebastian had an alibi for the time of Vance's death. He couldn't have murdered her husband. But if not him, then who?

Baxter seemed equally puzzled. "Did you see anyone as you were returning to your room, James?" he asked.

"Only one of the staff," he replied with a shrug. "But that was because I used the east wing service stairs. Seb's room was almost directly below mine, and it's much quicker than going via the main staircase."

What did he say? "Wait," she said, her stomach doing a flip. "You saw someone? Which member of staff?"

He shook his head. "I've no idea. I didn't really see them as such—I heard footsteps. They were exiting onto the second floor as I entered the stairs from below."

"Are you sure it was a member of staff?" Baxter asked sharply.

James hesitated, his brow furrowing in thought. "Well, no," he admitted finally. "As I said, I didn't see them. I assumed it was as they were using the service stairs. It could've been anyone, I suppose, but by the time I got to the second floor, they were gone." His brows drew together in confusion. "What's this all about?"

Alice ignored him. Someone had been near the service stairs just before Vance had died—someone James had heard but not seen.

A cold weight settled in her chest.

If it wasn't Sebastian... then who was it?

33

A FEW MINUTES LATER…

James' brow furrowed. "You didn't answer my question. What exactly is this all about?"

Alice opened her mouth, but nothing came out. How could she explain that they were chasing down the truth of a death no one else believed was suspicious? That they'd suspected Sebastian of murder until a moment ago? Her mind scrambled for a credible half-truth.

"It's nothing to worry about, James," Baxter jumped in with a casual shrug, strolling towards the fireplace. "We're simply trying to piece together the events of that evening. The solicitors are requesting a detailed account of His Grace's final hours for their paperwork. You understand." He gestured vaguely, as if the matter were of little consequence. "Legal formalities. Tedious but necessary."

She blinked. *That's it?* That was his grand explanation? It sounded like a terrible bluff. Too vague. Too convenient. Surely, James would see right through it?

"Paperwork?" James repeated, his expression skeptical.

I knew he wouldn't fall for it!

"Indeed," Baxter continued, seemingly warming to his

fabrication. "In cases of unexpected death, particularly when the deceased is someone of Vance's standing, the documentation required is rather extensive. We're merely gathering information."

This isn't helping! She racked her brains for something that would sound more convincing…

But James was nodding slowly, his expression clearing. "I suppose that makes sense. Vance wasn't exactly straightforward about that sort of thing."

She caught Baxter's eye as he turned to face into the room, and he gave her the smallest of winks.

He's lucky to get away with that…

Sebastian, who'd been sulking by the hearth, gave a heavy sigh. "Well, if we're finished picking over my affairs, I'd like to go and find a drink if you don't mind."

She stared at him, the hope that had sustained her through these difficult days crumbling like ash in her hands. He had an alibi. Their last suspect, eliminated in a few casual sentences about valets and nightcaps. *Now what?*

"Before you go, Hawthorne," Baxter said, his tone suddenly more serious, "if I may offer some advice?" Sebastian reluctantly nodded. "I would strongly suggest you tell your parents the truth about your situation. However uncomfortable that conversation might be, I assure you it will be preferable to remaining in debt to a man like Halstead." Sebastian paled slightly at the mention of the name. "The sooner you extract yourself from his influence, the better it will be for you—and for everyone associated with you." Baxter's eyes caught James'.

"He's right," James added, moving to stand beside his friend. "Come on, Seb. Let's get a drink and figure out the best approach to tell your father. It won't be pleasant, but I'll help you through it."

Sebastian hesitated, then lowered his head, his shoulders slumping in resignation. "I suppose you're right," he replied. "Though God knows what he'll do to me."

"Whatever it is, it can't be worse than what Halstead might do," James said firmly, guiding his friend towards the door.

Sebastian stopped as they reached it and glanced back at Alice and Baxter. "You won't say anything about this to anyone, will you?"

"Of course not," she replied, managing a small smile. Looking at him now, his usual bravado replaced by frightened eyes at the thought of facing his parents, she felt rather sorry for him. He wasn't a murderer; he was a misguided young man with weak willpower who'd got himself into a mess. She hoped he could get himself out now.

Her brother gave her a grateful look before following Sebastian out of the room and closing the door behind them with a soft *click*.

She sank into a nearby armchair, the green silk of her dress pooling around her. "At least one of them is acting like a grown-up. I hope James doesn't bail him out again."

"Do you think he might?" Baxter took the chair opposite her.

"I think he might want to," she said, "but I hope he doesn't. Sebastian needs to stand on his own two feet."

He responded with a silent nod as he raised his fingers in a steeple shape to his mouth.

The momentary distraction faded, leaving her once again confronting the reality of their situation. They'd just discarded their last real suspect. The weight of it settled over her like a shroud. "What now?" she asked, her voice hollow. "We have no suspects left. No leads. Nothing." She sighed deeply. "Everyone leaves tomorrow, and we're no closer to knowing who murdered Vance than we were when we started."

Baxter remained silent as he stared at the floor.

Perhaps it would've been better if I'd done nothing. The thought crept into her head and took hold. *If I'd simply accepted Vance's death as an accident, as everyone else has, would I have felt better than I do in this moment, knowing someone murdered him but being powerless to do anything about it?* She rose, unable to sit still. The Old Study's heavy mahogany gloom pressed in around her, matching the weight inside her chest. "All is lost, Baxter," she said, turning to face him. "We have nothing—no suspects, no evidence, nothing but questions without answers."

He looked up at her, his head still resting on his fingers. "I wouldn't say that," he replied. "We've eliminated four suspects, all who had motives. And we have something new. James saw someone on the stairs. That could be our murderer or, at least, a potential witness."

"He *heard* someone," she corrected, pacing the length of the faded carpet. "He didn't *see* them. It could have been anyone—a guest, a servant, anyone at all."

"It was shortly before Vance died."

"They would've come out on the east wing of the second floor, so they may never have gone anywhere near the main stairs, like James didn't."

"But they might have heard something," Baxter persisted. "Or seen something. We should try to discover who it was."

She stopped her pacing to stare at him incredulously. *Does he think it's that simple?* "And how do you suggest we go about that? We can hardly make an announcement over coffee, can we? 'Ladies and gentlemen, would anyone who was using the east wing service stairs at approximately quarter to three in the morning on the night my husband died kindly identify themselves?'" She rubbed her temples. "Besides, as James pointed out, it could have been a member of staff. Any one of the dozens we have here."

"We could ask George to help," he suggested. "He might be able to discreetly enquire among the staff."

She pinched her lips together. *So* now *he wants to use George!* Her eyes narrowed as she glared at him. "You didn't approve of me using him before, but *now* you want to ask him to interrogate the staff? Perhaps you should make up your mind, Baxter."

The words hung in the air between them, harsh and unfair. She regretted them immediately. It wasn't his fault that they'd reached this impasse. In fact, he'd been nothing but supportive since she'd forced him into this investigation.

He blinked up at her. "That's not what I—"

"I'm sorry," she cut him off, her voice softening. "That was unkind of me. None of this is your fault—you've been extraordinarily patient and helpful since I dragged you into this." She crossed her arms. "It's most vexing—we seem to have come to a standstill."

His expression softened. "You didn't drag me, Alice. I walked in willingly."

Her eyes twinkled with mischief. "Well, then I'll take it as proof of poor judgement on your part."

He gave a low chuckle, and a less bleak silence settled between them again.

"But what if we never find out who murdered him, Baxter?" she asked softly, voicing the fear that had been growing within her. "What if they simply walk away, and Vance never receives justice?"

"We won't allow that to happen," he replied, his quiet conviction somehow more reassuring than any passionate declaration could have been. "We'll find another approach.

Perhaps when the house has emptied and the pressure of time has lifted, we'll see something we've overlooked."

She wanted to believe him. *But will it be too late then?* Somewhere in this house, the person who murdered Vance's was walking free—and now they had no idea who it could be...

34

AN HOUR LATER...

A sharp knock at the door startled them both. Alice turned towards the noise, her heart quickening as Baxter looked up from the armchair. "Enter," she called, exchanging a curious glance with him.

The door opened to reveal George, his expression composed, the crisp lines of his uniform unruffled despite the day's demands.

"Ah, George," Baxter said, rising. "Just the man we wanted to see."

The footman blinked but inclined his head. "Your Grace. My lord."

"We've had a rather significant development in our investigation, and we could do with your help," Baxter told him, sitting down again.

George remained standing, his posture erect as befitted his position, though his eyes betrayed keen interest. "Indeed, my lord?"

"Yes," Alice said, sinking back into her chair. "We've eliminated Sebastian Hawthorne as a suspect. He has an alibi for the time of Vance's death." She briefly explained what they had learned about Sebastian's whereabouts, James' confrontation with him, and the valet who had been with Sebastian when Vance had died. George listened attentively, nodding at intervals.

"But more importantly," Baxter added, "Lord Astley heard someone on the east wing service stairs at approximately quarter to three—only minutes before the duke's death."

"But he didn't see who it was," she continued, her fingers absently tracing the edge of her chair's armrest. "He only heard footsteps ahead of him."

George's expression remained composed, though his eyes flickered briefly from her to Baxter and back. "It could have been anyone, ma'am," he said carefully. "Although given that the person had disappeared by the time his lordship reached the second floor, it seems most likely they either had a room on that floor or were a servant with duties there."

"Who had rooms in the east wing?" Baxter asked.

She ticked them off on her fingers. "Vance, of course. James. Aunt Cora. Lilly's parents, and my father's youngest brother and his wife. I think that's all."

George added, "Plus their personal staff, naturally. The east wing is mostly reserved for immediate family. The guest rooms on the first floor were occupied by the remaining visitors."

"So," Baxter said, leaning forward, "if someone used the service stairs around that time, odds are it was one of those people or their servants."

She frowned. "I cannot imagine any of the family using the services stairs. Except James, of course. But not my aunts or uncles. Remember how Aunt Cora reacted when she was asked to use them the next day, when the main staircase was out of action? She was horrified at the impropriety of it all."

"But one of them might have seen or heard something," Baxter pointed out.

"I agree with you, ma'am," George said. "Although, we cannot rule out that it could've been someone from another part of the house."

"Indeed. But it's a place to start at least," she said, feeling a spark of renewed hope after the crushing disappointment of Sebastian's alibi. "George, could you discreetly enquire among the staff? See if any of them were on the second floor of the east wing around that time? Baxter and I will tackle the family."

"Of course, ma'am," George replied with a small bow.

"Thank you, George," she said warmly. "Now—didn't you come to find *us*?"

"Yes, ma'am." George straightened. "I've spoken with both Edward and Tom regarding Lord Rivershore's presence at Francis Court that night."

She leaned forward, her heart quickening. "And?"

"It was Tom who spoke with Lord Rivershore, ma'am. He confirmed he encountered his lordship attempting to enter through the terrace doors."

"Did he say why he told Henry I was with my husband?" she asked, recalling Henry's account of being turned away by a footman who'd claimed she was unavailable.

George bowed his head. "Yes, ma'am. Tom explained he'd seen the back of the duke and a woman come in from outside and assumed it was you the duke was with."

But it hadn't been. It had been Lady Cordelia. But if she'd been wearing her cloak… *We* are *about the same height…*

"Tom was most apologetic, ma'am," George added. "He seemed quite upset that he may have caused you distress."

She smiled gently. "Please tell him it's quite all right. In fact, without knowing it, he did me a favour." The thought of an inebriated Henry coming face-to-face with Vance that day was uncomfortable at best.

"I shall convey your reassurance, ma'am," George said with another small bow as he turned and left the room, closing the door silently behind him.

Alone again, she exchanged a meaningful glance with Baxter. "Well," she said, smoothing her skirts as she stood, "it seems our investigation isn't over after all."

"Far from it," he agreed, offering her his arm. "Shall we divide and conquer? I'll take the men, you take the ladies, and we'll meet back later."

She took his arm. "Let's hope someone saw something useful."

———

The Green Drawing Room at Francis Court emptied considerably as the evening wore on. Most guests retired early to finish packing for their departures the following morning, leaving behind a quieter, more intimate atmosphere. Alice sat beside Aunt Cora on a small settee upholstered in faded emerald damask, the older woman's silver-streaked dark hair gleaming in the soft lamplight. Having already spoken with her other two aunts, where she'd learned plenty of opinion but no useful facts, she was beginning to lose hope of discovering anything worthwhile before the night's end.

"And the boys, Alice?" Aunt Cora asked, her hazel eyes sharp despite the lateness of the hour. "Have you decided when to bring them home from school?"

Alice took a sip of brandy. "Duncan has offered to collect them tomorrow," she replied. "We agree it would be best for them to come here to Francis Court for now rather than returning directly to Manning Hall."

Aunt Cora nodded, her lips pursed in consideration. "A sensible suggestion. The familiarity of their grandparents' home might provide some comfort." She paused, taking a sip of her hot whiskey. "But eventually, Alice, you *will* need to go to Manning Hall. The tenants will want to see you. The staff will need reassuring."

"I'm sure Duncan will help me with that as well," she replied, unable to keep a slight edge from her voice. The thought of returning to Manning Hall—to the house she'd shared with Vance, where every corner held memories—was simply too much to contemplate at present.

"That's all very well, Alice," Cora continued, her eyes narrowing, "but as Harold is so young, you cannot rely on your brother to manage the estate until he's of age." Her tone softened slightly as she continued, "You have a duty to your son now, my dear. You must protect his legacy and take charge of his inheritance."

Alice swallowed back a retort. She hadn't sought out Aunt Cora for a lecture on her responsibilities. She folded her hands in her lap, a nagging voice telling her Aunt Cora was right, and soon, she would have to face up to the reality of her situation. *But I'm trying to solve my husband's murder!* All of the rest of it would have to wait for the time being. "I understand," she said stiffly, reaching for her drink again to avoid meeting her aunt's penetrating gaze. "I shall consider what's best for the boys once they're here."

A brief silence fell between them while she searched for a way to steer the conversation towards the night of the party without appearing suspicious. She feigned a yawn. "I confess," she began carefully, "it feels as though the last time I had a proper night's sleep was the evening of the party." She gave a small, rueful smile. "Everything since has been rather... overwhelming."

"Oh, you poor thing," her aunt said, her tone softening as she patted Alice's arm with her free hand. "Of course you haven't slept. You've had a death, a house full of guests, and your life turned on its head. You'll feel like yourself again soon enough—especially once things settle and the house clears out. However—"

Yes?

"All I can say is that you're lucky you weren't in the east wing like me. It was like Piccadilly Circus up there that night. I barely slept at all."

Well, that did the trick. "Really? What do you mean?"

Aunt Cora waved a hand. "People coming and going at all hours," she replied with evident disapproval.

Alice's stomach flipped. This was what she wanted. "What happened?" she prompted.

"Well, I went up at about half past twelve and was in bed twenty minutes later." She tapped her finger against the arm of the settee. "My head had barely touched the pillow when I was disturbed by the door opposite mine creaking open." Her lips thinned and she huffed. "I've told Stokes it needs oiling."

Alice's pulse quickened. "Which room was that?"

"Vance's," Cora said, frowning. "And then out he went again five minutes later."

Alice quickly worked out the timing in her head. That hadn't been Vance; that matched what Lilly had told her about leaving a note in Vance's room at about one.

"I tried to drift off to sleep, but it was no use, I was wide awake. I picked up my book and read." Aunt Cora tutted. "Then at about twenty past two, the door of the room next to mine slammed open and shut. That's James' room. I'd hardly read more than a few sentences, then *bang!* out he goes again. I wanted to throw a slipper at the wall."

That matches, Alice thought. James had gone to confront Seb.

"And then, low and behold, a few minutes later, the door opposite creaked open again," Aunt Cora continued.

That must have been Vance coming up to bed. Then he'd read the letters and—

"And would you believe it?" Aunt Cora's voice rose in indignation. "He went out again barely five minutes later. What's wrong with these men? Can they not stay in one place?"

That was Vance going off to see Lilly.

"I was cold by this point," Aunt Cora said with a sigh. "So I decided to get a shawl. I'd reached my dressing room when I heard the service door—the one next to my dressing room, you know—open and close. I stayed a moment longer to fetch my shawl, then heard it go again as I stepped back into my bedchamber!"

The unknown person and then James, Alice reasoned, her heart beating faster. Had Aunt Cora heard where the first person had gone?

"It does sound busy, Aunt. Do you know who it was?"

Aunt Cora tilted her head. "I'm fairly sure the second person was James as I heard his door close next to mine when I was getting back into bed, although why he'd been using the service stairs, I hate to imagine." She pinched her lips together tightly. "As to the other person… They must have gone in the other direction as I didn't hear any other doors close at my end of the corridor."

Towards the stairs then… Her lips parted, then closed again. "Did you hear anything else?"

"Only Vance returning to his room. I was still awake. I looked at the mantle, and the clock said three."

Alice froze, her heart skipping a beat.

Vance was dead by three. Whoever had returned to his room at that time—it hadn't been him. "Did he come out again?" she asked, trying to keep her voice steady.

"I certainly hope not, Alice. It was far too late." Then she paused, as if hearing what she was saying. Her lips parted a little in confusion. "But of course he must have, or else, he wouldn't have been found downstairs…" She shook her head. "I must have drifted off."

Aunt Cora prattled on, but Alice's mind spiralled far ahead. Someone had entered Vance's room after he'd died. Had they been searching for something? Or returning the pocket watch perhaps? She tried to assemble the sequence in her head piece by piece. Something still didn't quite fit. Something was missing, but she couldn't work out what.

She pressed her fingers to her temples. This was important. They were close. She could feel it pulsing beneath the surface, just out of reach. She would not let it slip away. She *had* to find the missing link.

35

THE NEXT DAY...

Morning light spilled through the tall windows of the breakfast room, catching the silver serving dishes in a soft glow. Alice stirred her tea absently, watching the amber liquid swirl as her thoughts circled in much the same way. Despite the cheerful chatter around the table, her mind remained fixed on the revelation from Aunt Cora the previous night—someone had entered Vance's empty bedchamber at three o'clock, but Vance had died at ten to three. The question wasn't only who had returned to his room—but why?

Around her, the conversation flowed in fits and starts—small talk peppered with farewells, travel plans, and the polite exhaustion that followed a country house gathering of this magnitude. Duncan was discussing the best route to Derbyshire with their father, while their mother buttered a crumpet and chatted with Aunt Cora about the state of the London shops.

"Alice, did you hear a word I said?" Fee's voice cut through her cloudy mind, gently reproachful.

She looked up, meeting her sister-in-law's bright blue eyes. "I'm terribly sorry, Fee. My mind wandered."

"I should say it did," Fee replied with a fond smile. "You've been stirring your tea for a full five minutes. I fear it's gone quite cold."

"Here, have a fresh cup," Aunt Cora interjected, reaching for the silver teapot. "You look as though you barely slept, my dear."

She nodded gratefully as her aunt put the steaming cup down in front of her. "Thank you. You're quite right; I didn't sleep particularly well."

"Well, that's understandable given the circumstances," her father said, his voice gruff with sympathy. The duke's weathered face had grown more lined in the days since Vance's death, his normally ruddy complexion somewhat paler. "No one expects you to maintain perfect composure all the time, my dear."

She swallowed. She was lucky to have her family around her at a time like this. She picked up a piece of toast and dipped her knife in a pat of butter.

"As I was saying." Fee leaned towards her and lowered her voice to a hush. "Henry left yesterday afternoon. The poor darling seemed quite embarrassed by it all. You know— the whole turning up uninvited to the party thing and trying to find you. I told him there was no need to feel ill at ease, of course, but he left anyway."

Probably just as well…

Meanwhile, her older brother responded to their father's earlier comment. "We all are, Pops," Duncan said, his deep voice cutting through his wife's whispers. "It's been a dreadful shock."

Fee nodded at her husband, her blonde curls catching the sunlight. "Indeed it has." She turned back to Alice. "I'm returning to London today, darling. I'll stay until Oliver and Arthur break up from Eton, then I thought we might join you at Manning Hall for the summer." Her eyes softened as she looked at Alice. "We thought perhaps you might appreciate the company, and the boys always enjoy being together."

"That would be lovely," Alice replied automatically, though her head had already drifted back to the mystery at hand. Something continued to press at the edges of her mind —some detail she couldn't quite pull into focus.

She recalled her late-night conversation with Baxter in the library: how they'd reviewed everything they knew. His conversation with her two uncles had yielded nothing useful —they'd both retired early and had heard nothing unusual. The only concrete piece of information they had was Aunt Cora's testimony that someone had entered Vance's room at around three o'clock. Someone who hadn't been Vance. Someone who'd gone in after he was dead.

They'd spent an hour debating possibilities. Could it have been a servant entering for some reason? But at three in the morning? Unlikely. Could it have been the murderer, returning to place the pocket watch in Vance's room? But why take it in the first place, only to return it later? Nothing made sense, and without knowing who'd been on those service stairs, they seemed no closer to identifying the person who murdered Vance.

Alice's gaze drifted to where Tom stood at attention near the sideboard. The footman looked distinctly unwell this morning. His normally impeccable posture remained, but his face was drawn, with dark circles beneath his eyes. His hands, usually so steady when serving, trembled slightly as he moved to pour coffee for a guest. Something was clearly troubling him. Was he still upset about the confusion with Henry Rivershore? *Perhaps I should speak to him, reassure him that no harm has been done?*

"Would you like me to write to Mrs Wilson about

preparing Manning Hall?" Fee asked, apparently still discussing their plans for the summer. "She'll need time to air out the nursery and the guest rooms. I thought perhaps we could arrange some small entertainments for the children—nothing too boisterous, of course, given the circumstances but enough to keep them occupied."

"Yes, that's a wonderful idea. The boys will need distractions." Alice inclined her head, trying to focus on the conversation but failing. Last night, she and Baxter had talked about trying to account for everyone in the east wing, but the idea had quickly unravelled. Too many guests, too many servants, too many variables. It had felt like chasing smoke.

"Alice?" Fee's voice had grown concerned. "Are you quite well? You've buttered the same corner of your toast three times."

Alice blinked and forced a smile. "I'm sorry—I was miles away." She lowered the toast to her plate. "Yes, having you all in Derbyshire will be wonderful. I think the boys will thrive there this summer." She said the words, but her mind was already elsewhere again. What she needed, desperately, was time to think. Proper time—away from kind relatives and expectant glances and the weary fog of constant conversation. Every polite question felt like a pebble dropped into her already rippling thoughts. She needed stillness to see the truth clearly, to go somewhere and be alone.

She folded her napkin carefully and stood. "Would you all excuse me?" she said, setting it down in front of her forgotten cup of tea. "I should like to change before our guests begin to depart."

"Of course, my dear," her mother replied, though she exchanged a puzzled glance with Aunt Cora. "Though I'm not sure it's necessary. You look perfectly appropriate as you are."

"I'd prefer something... more suitable for saying good-bye," Alice improvised, immediately regretting the flimsy excuse. *Why didn't I simply say I have a headache?*

Baxter's clear blue eyes fixed on her with quiet concern. She summoned a reassuring smile for him. They seemed to have developed a silent language over the past few days, and she knew he understood her need to think in peace.

"Don't forget we're gathering in the Painted Hall at eleven to see everyone off," her father reminded her. "Carriages are ordered for half past."

"I'll be there," Alice promised, making her escape before anyone could question her further.

As she stepped into the corridor, she noticed George and Tom engaged in quiet conversation near a recessed window. The morning sun streaming through the leaded glass illuminated their faces in sharp relief, allowing her to observe them without being immediately noticed. She moved carefully to avoid drawing their attention. George stood with his back straight, his voice too low for her to hear but his expression serious. Tom, by contrast, looked increasingly agitated, his hands clasped tightly before him as if to stop their trembling.

Alice couldn't make out their words, but as she drew closer, she studied their lips.

"...so you didn't go to the duke's room later in the evening?" George asked.

Alice slowed, adjusting her pace to pass them naturally.

Tom shook his head emphatically. "No," he replied. "The last time I was in his room was when I saw him off for the evening. He never called for me later."

Alice's heart quickened. So it wasn't Tom who'd entered Vance's room at three. *But if not Tom, then who?* She passed the two men with a polite nod, relieved that George was following through on his promise to question the staff. His thoroughness gave her hope they might yet uncover the truth in time.

But time, however, was precisely what she didn't have. In less than two hours, the remaining guests would depart, potentially taking with them the answer to Vance's death.

She had to solve this puzzle quickly, before the truth slipped away forever.

36

FIFTEEN MINUTES LATER...

Alice sat alone in the garden room, curled in an armchair, her knees drawn up slightly, her skirt spilling in soft folds around her ankles. The morning sun threw shifting patterns onto the rug in front of her, but she barely registered the light or the warmth. Her mind was far away.

She pressed her fingers to her temples, her elbows resting on the armrests, and let herself sink into thought. She needed to sort through each piece of evidence, each conversation, each suspect. Somewhere in this tangle of information lay the truth—she was certain of it.

She began with Vance's body. The facts were clear enough: his neck broken from the fall, the bruising on his wrist suggesting he might've scuffled with someone, the sconce being knocked off, the mark on the wall, the position of his body.

Then there was the white cotton thread that had caught on his signet ring. She and George had removed it, puzzling over it. Baxter had reasoned that it could have come from anywhere. Was he right?

There was the missing pocket watch, later found in Vance's bedchamber, with its crystal cracked and its hands stopped at precisely ten minutes to three—the estimated time of his death. They knew he'd had it when he'd left Lilly's room ten minutes before he died. So someone had returned it to his room. Most likely it had been the noise Aunt Cora had heard at three that morning…

Alice massaged her temples gently. The pocket watch still troubled her. Why would someone take it from Vance's body, only to return it to his room?

She shifted in her seat, her heart beginning to pound as she moved on to what she and Maud had discovered in his room. The two letters. The first a warning from an old friend, alerting Vance to Sebastian's troubles and his influence over James. The second from Cordelia, asking for a rendezvous the next day. Someone had burned it, but who and why?

Wait! There were three letters… She'd forgotten the one from Lilly, asking to see Vance that night, the one he'd later returned. *Of course!* That was the reason they'd found the handkerchief with the initials LA that Lilly had dropped when she'd visited his room to leave him the note.

Three letters, not two…

She opened her eyes and reached for the glass of water on the small table beside her chair, taking a small sip as she continued her mental inventory of what they knew. Their suspects: Lilly, Cordelia, Henry, and Seb. She set the glass down, a frown creasing her brow. They'd systematically eliminated every suspect with a motive to kill Vance. None of them could've been on the east wing service stairs when James had heard footsteps.

None of them could have pushed Vance to his death.

So who'd been on those stairs? And who'd entered Vance's empty room at three, after he was already dead?

Alice closed her eyes again, letting the heat of the sun wash over her. There was something, some detail that nagged at the edges of her consciousness...

A loose thread.

Maud had mentioned something… *Yes…*

Could that be it?

She straightened in her chair, her heartbeat quickening. Her mind raced ahead, connecting threads she hadn't previously seen as related.

It makes sense. More sense than she wanted it to. The misdirection. The subtle avoidance. The strange phrasing— yes, that was another thing she'd missed. The peculiar way something had been said. A small lie wrapped in something that seemed harmless. But now that she saw it clearly, the lie burned like the blazing sun on a hot day.

She pressed a hand to her stomach. *No. Please no…*

But she couldn't deny the pattern her mind had drawn. It all fitted. *Too well.*

And yet… something was missing. One last thing. *A reason.* She closed her eyes, turning over her memory. There was something. She'd thought it had simply been a mistake at the time. One she hadn't questioned. But it couldn't have been, could it? Now it shimmered in her memory with terrible significance.

A chill ran down her spine as the final piece of the puzzle clicked into place. Her stomach churned with the implications of her theory. It seemed unthinkable. And yet, the clues were there. She forced herself to breathe deeply, to think rationally. She needed more evidence before she could make such a serious accusation.

Standing abruptly, she reached for the bell cord and tugged it with trembling fingers. She needed to speak with George.

37

HALF AN HOUR LATER...

The Painted Hall at Francis Court hummed with the polite murmurs of departure. Sunlight streamed through the tall windows, illuminating the marble floor and casting long shadows behind the guests as they exchanged final pleasantries. Valises were being carried down the main staircase by liveried footmen, and carriages crunched along the gravel drive outside.

Alice stood near the grand staircase, maintaining a smile that betrayed none of the urgency churning within her. Her eyes swept the hall for what felt like the hundredth time, searching for George among the footmen who moved efficiently between departing guests.

Her fingers plucked absently at the fabric of her skirt as she agreed vaguely to something her aunt, Lady Evelyn Astley, said. The older woman's words washed over her, barely registering as Alice's thoughts circled relentlessly around the theory she'd formed in the garden room.

The tall grandfather clock in the corner chimed the quarter-hour, its sonorous tones reverberating against the stone walls. *More time wasted on pleasantries while a murderer potentially walks free!* She fought to keep her impatience from showing as she kissed her aunt's cheek and said goodbye. As the woman walked away to say her farewell to Duncan and Fee, Alice let out a barely suppressed sigh. *This is taking forever!*

She scanned the hall, catching sight of Baxter engaged in conversation near the front doors. She needed to tell him about her theory. *Will he think I'm mad?*

Across the other side of the room, Lilly was speaking to Alice's parents, accepting a kiss on the cheek from her mother and a murmured word from her father. She made her way towards Alice, looking better than she had during their last conversation—some colour had returned to her cheeks, although her eyes still held a shadow of melancholy.

"Lilly," she said, summoning a genuine smile. "I hope you have a good journey back."

"Thank you again for the use of Va… sorry, I mean, your carriage," Lilly said softly, her smile small but sincere. "It's most kind of you."

"Of course. I'm glad it's of help."

Lilly hesitated, then added, "When you're settled at Manning Hall, Alice… please do visit. If you're willing."

Something in the woman's tone touched her unexpectedly. For all Lilly's earlier self-pity, there was truth in her isolation. As an only child whose husband had died before she'd borne him children, leaving her alone in a remote country house, her life must indeed be solitary. Alice, despite everything, had her sons, her brothers, Fee, Baxter—a family who would surround and support her through her grief. Lilly had no such comfort. *And anyway, she is, technically, family.* "I'd like that," she said, surprising herself with her sincerity. "I'll send word when we're settled."

Gratitude flickered across Lilly's face, quickly masked by

her usual composure. "Thank you, Alice. I wish you well until then."

As Lilly and her parents moved towards the door, then disappeared down the steps to their carriage, a cloud of lavender perfume announced Lady Cordelia's approach.

"Your Grace," Lady Cordelia purred, her silhouette striking in grey silk. "I simply couldn't leave without saying farewell." Her gaze slid past Alice, fixing on something—or someone—behind her.

She felt a presence at her shoulder and knew without looking that Baxter had positioned himself strategically by her side. She bit back a smile. *Is he using me as a human shield against Cordelia's attentions?*

"Lady Granville," she replied with perfect politeness. "I trust your stay, despite the unfortunate circumstances, was comfortable?"

"Comfortable but not quite as… convivial as I'd hoped," Cordelia replied, her eyes still fixed on Baxter. "Though I live in perpetual hope that some er… excitement may yet be forthcoming."

Baxter stiffened beside her, standing straighter as though preparing for battle. She fought to maintain her composure as Cordelia leaned closer, ostensibly to kiss her cheek in farewell.

"Lord Rushton," Cordelia murmured, her voice pitched to carry to Baxter but not beyond. "Should you find your-self in London and in need of… diversion, my door is always open to you. Day or night." She straightened, patting Alice's arm. "Dear Alice, do take care of yourself. Widowhood can be so terribly lonely without proper… company."

With that parting shot, she glided away, leaving a trail of perfume and suggestion in her wake. Alice turned to Baxter, unable to hide her amusement. "I believe you narrowly escaped being devoured, Bax."

Baxter's expression was pained. "That woman is a menace."

"Perhaps you should take her up on her offer," she suggested, her eyes dancing with suppressed laughter. "She did seem quite... enthusiastic."

"That's not remotely amusing, Alice," he growled. "The woman cornered me in the drawing room last night and asked if I'd like to see her collection of 'exotic Oriental artefacts'. I dread to think what she actually meant."

"I'm sure she meant precisely what you think she meant," she replied with a sly grin.

His expression remained unamused. "If you've quite finished enjoying my discomfort, I shall go and say my farewells to Lord and Lady Hawthorne."

Wait! She reached out and caught his arm. "Can you meet me in the garden room once this is over?" she whispered.

He looked surprised. "Do you have something new?"

She nodded. "Please."

He tilted his head. "Of course."

She watched him join Sebastian and his parents. Their farewell appeared strained but civil—Lord Hawthorne's posture stiff with barely concealed disapproval, Lady Hawthorne's smile tight but present. Sebastian himself looked pale but resolute, standing slightly apart from his parents.

"He told them," a voice murmured next to her.

She turned to face her younger brother. "And?"

"They didn't disown him on the spot, which I count as a positive sign," James said with a slight smile.

She patted his arm, relief mingling with her impatience to get these goodbyes over with. *At least something good might come of this tragedy.*

As the last of the guests departed and the great doors of Francis Court swung closed behind them, the artificial smile she'd maintained for the last hour faded from her face.

Duncan approached, patting her shoulder with brotherly affection. "I'm off to fetch the boys," he said. "We should be back by tomorrow afternoon, weather permitting."

"Thank you," she replied, reaching up and kissing him on the cheek. "I can't tell you how much I appreciate it."

Fee appeared at Duncan's side, linking her arm through his. "And I'm heading over to Francis Lodge to pack," she announced. "My train leaves at three, so I should be in London by evening." She dropped her husband's arm to give Alice a quick, fierce hug. "I'll be in London until the boys break up. But I'll come straight to you after that. Try not to worry too much about everything."

As her brothers and Fee moved away, she gave Baxter, who was standing with her parents, a glance that said, "Now," and turned in the direction of the west wing.

———

The garden room felt like a sanctuary after the forced smiles and polite farewells of the morning. Alice stood at the window for a moment, watching the leaves ripple in the breeze. *What if I'm wrong?* What if she'd misconstrued innocent coincidences, crafting a narrative of murder where there was none? But the evidence all pointed to a conclusion she could scarcely believe yet couldn't ignore.

She glanced at the small clock on the mantelpiece for the third time in as many minutes. *What is taking Baxter so long? And where is George?* Had he uncovered something that contradicted her theory? Or had he found proof that confirmed it?

She sank into one of the armchairs by the window, her hands twisting in her lap.

The door opened, and Alice started, her heart leaping into her throat. *George?* But it was Baxter, followed by Stokes carrying a silver tray with a teapot and cups. She forced herself to take a steadying breath, smoothing her expression into something resembling calm.

"Tea, Your Grace," Stokes said, setting the tray on a small table near the window. "Would you like me to pour?"

"No, that's fine, Stokes. We can manage, thank you," she replied, fighting to keep the impatience out of her voice. She couldn't discuss her suspicions with Stokes present, but every moment's delay felt like an eternity.

The butler bowed and withdrew, closing the door with a soft *click* that seemed to release some invisible tension in the room. Baxter immediately took the seat opposite her on the other side of the table and crossed his legs. "What's going on? You're as twitchy as a cat in a room full of rocking chairs."

"I've worked it out," she said, her voice tight.

He stared. "You know who murdered Vance?"

She tilted her head to one side. "Well, I have a theory. But it's rather... disturbing."

He leaned forward. "Go on."

She told him.

His eyebrows shot up in surprise. "But why on earth would—"

"I don't know the exact motive, but I have an idea," Alice interrupted, the words tumbling out now she'd started. She laid out the pieces for him one by one—the overlooked detail, the lie, the misdirection. The motive though... That was the hardest part to say aloud. "What do you think?"

He rose, his expression deeply troubled. "Alice, this is a serious accusation. Are you certain?"

Before she could respond, the door opened again, and they both turned as George entered. His tall figure seemed to fill the doorway, his expression grave as he closed the door firmly behind him. "Your Grace, my lord," he said, giving a small bow.

She stood abruptly. "Well?"

His face was solemn. He gave a single nod. "You were right, ma'am."

Her breath caught. Her knees felt weak. Part of her had hoped—prayed—she'd been wrong. But she wasn't.

She'd found Vance's murderer.

And it's all my fault...

38

TEN MINUTES LATER...

Alice paced the garden room with quick, sharp steps, her skirts whispering along the edge of the Persian rug. Her nerves prickled beneath her skin, every moment stretched tight with tension. She glanced at Baxter, who was seated in one of the leather chairs by the hearth, his forearms resting on his thighs, his hands loosely clasped. He looked calm. He always did. But his eyes followed her, steady and watchful.

"Are we right about this?" she asked quietly. "Truly? What if we're wrong?"

He looked up. "It fits, Alice. All of it. The timing. The details. But we must tread carefully. It won't do to assume too much too soon."

She nodded as she tried to steady her breathing.

"Allow me to ask the questions," he continued. "You needn't subject yourself to—"

"No," she replied, shaking her head firmly. "This is my doing, and I must deal with the consequences."

"Alice," he said, his voice dropping to a fierce whisper,

"it's not your fault. You're not responsible for someone else's actions."

Perhaps not. But I fear I'm the catalyst.

The knock came like a gunshot, jolting them both. Her mouth went dry. She swallowed as her heart leapt into her throat, her pulse suddenly thundering in her ears. This was it —the moment she would face her husband's murderer. She drew a deep breath, smoothing her skirts with hands that trembled a touch despite her resolve. "Come in," she called, surprised by the steadiness of her voice.

George entered, his expression grave. Next to him was another.

Alice's breath caught.

The other person looked almost translucent with shock, as if someone had drained all colour and substance from them. Their eyes were hollow. Guided by George, they stepped further inside like a sleepwalker. Hazel eyes, which had been fixed on the floor, slowly lifted to meet her gaze. Naked emotion flickered across a face clouded with shame and despair.

She took a deep breath. "Tom… did you push the duke down the stairs?"

The footman opened his mouth, his lips trembling. "I didn't mean to—" Tom choked out, his voice barely audible. His legs gave way beneath him, and he crumpled to the floor.

39

A MOMENT LATER...

Alice stepped back involuntarily, her hand flying to her mouth. He hadn't denied it. The last, smallest hope she'd had about being mistaken, that there was some other explanation for the evidence, evaporated like morning mist.

The room tilted slightly, the bright patterns of the Persian rug swimming before her eyes. She felt Baxter's steadying hand at her elbow as George knelt beside Tom's collapsed form.

"Is he ill, George?" she whispered, taking a step forward.

"He's fine, ma'am," George replied, helping Tom up, his limbs seemingly too heavy for him to manage alone. He deposited him in a chair by the fireplace.

Baxter handed George a glass of water, and George pressed it into Tom's trembling hands. He stared at it for a long moment before taking a small sip. The glass rattled against his teeth. No one spoke. The only sounds in the garden room were Tom's ragged breathing. Then he leaned back and bowed his head, his shoulders curved inward as if he was trying to make himself smaller.

Her heart twisted. Part of her wanted to flee, to escape the grotesque confession that was to come and the pain it would bring. But another part of her—the part that had driven her to investigate Vance's death so tenaciously—kept her rooted to the spot. She moved slowly towards him. "Tom," she said gently. "I need you to tell us what happened. All of it."

He looked up at her, his eyes red-rimmed and haunted. "I'm so sorry, Your Grace," he said, the words tumbling out as if he'd been holding them back for days. "I never meant... I don't know what came over me. I never wanted to do anything that would hurt you. You were always so kind to me. I just..." He lowered his head as he trailed off.

Baxter stepped forward, his voice firm but not unkind. "Start from the beginning, Tom. From the evening of the party. Tell us what happened step by step."

Tom wiped his face with the back of his hand and took a shuddering breath. "I helped His Grace dress for the party. He was in good spirits that night. He said he was looking forward to spending the evening with you, ma'am."

Her chest tightened. She remembered his smile as he'd led her onto the dance floor, the brief moment when it had felt like the early days of their marriage again, before the disappointment and resentment had crept in.

Tom glanced briefly at her before his eyes dropped back to the floor, and he continued, "I thought perhaps... things might be improving between you. I heard the others downstairs talking. Saying how he'd ended things with Lady Forthington—"

She felt a flicker of irritation at the thought of the servants discussing her husband's infidelities so openly, but it was quickly extinguished. She could hardly fault them for noticing what was obvious to everyone.

"I thought he'd finally come to his senses. Had realised how lucky he was—"

Her face felt impossibly hot. Tom's perception of her as some sort of wronged angel was as far from reality as it could be. Yes, Vance had been unfaithful. He had often been thoughtless and self-centred. But she'd not been the perfect, devoted wife Tom probably imagined. She'd been cold to Vance at times, had withdrawn from him emotionally years ago. Their mutual unhappiness had been simply that—mutual.

George jumped forward. "Tom, that's not your place to—"

Tom looked up with frightened eyes. "I'm sorry. I—"

Her hand shot up. "It's all right, George. Please. I'm aware of the talk downstairs. I want to hear the whole story from Tom so I can fully understand what happened and why."

George bowed his head and took a step back.

"Is that why you told Lord Rivershore I was unavailable when he asked for me?" she asked quietly. "Because you thought you were protecting me?"

Tom nodded, his shoulders slumping further. "He was in his cups, ma'am. I didn't think you would want to see him in such a state. And I didn't..." He hesitated. "I didn't trust his intentions."

"So you told him I was with my husband? You knew it wasn't me who came in with the duke from the garden. You knew it was Lady Granville, didn't you?"

A flush crept up Tom's neck, his discomfort obvious. "Yes, ma'am. I said that to make him go away."

Alice exchanged a significant glance with Baxter. This confirmed what she'd suspected when recalling George's report—Tom knew her too well to mistake another woman for her, even at night, even from behind. After all, he'd watched her grow up.

"Please continue, Tom," Baxter encouraged, his tone

neutral. "What happened after the guests began retiring for the night?"

The footman drew a shaky breath. "Mr Stokes and I were on duty, clearing up and preparing refreshments for the guests who had moved to other rooms to continue their conversations. We worked until well after two-thirty." He paused, swallowing hard.

"When did the hall boy give you Lady Granville's letter for the duke, Tom?" Alice watched his face carefully.

He couldn't meet her eyes. "Shortly after half past one. He said Lady Granville's maid had asked him to deliver it to the duke's valet."

"But you never delivered it, did you?" she said softly.

Tom shook his head, still staring at the floor. "No, ma'am. I didn't. I thought... I wanted to protect you from more hurt. I thought if the duke didn't receive it that night, perhaps he wouldn't..." He trailed off, his meaning clear.

She felt a cold certainty settle over her. Her suspicions had been correct. When she'd reconstructed the sequence of events that Aunt Cora had heard on the second floor of the east wing, she'd realised something was missing. No one had delivered Lady Cordelia's letter to Vance's room. And yet, the letter had ended up in Vance's fireplace, and Tom had told George he'd not been in the room since her husband had left to go to the party. It had seemed a trivial lie at the time, but now she understood its significance.

"Why did you burn it?" she asked, causing Baxter to look at her in surprise.

"After the duke was... after what happened," Tom replied, "I realised someone might ask about the letter, and I still had it on me. So I went to His Grace's room and burned it in his fireplace." He looked up, his expression pleading. "I thought it would look as if he'd read it and burned it himself."

"Take us back to what happened later that night, Tom," Baxter said. "After you and Stokes finished your duties."

Tom's breathing became more rapid, his hands shaking so badly that water sloshed over the rim of his glass. "Mr Stokes told me I could retire for the night. It was about twenty to three. I was making my way upstairs—I used the main staircase, though I should have used the service stairs." He looked apologetic, as if this breach of below stairs etiquette was somehow comparable to the crime he'd committed. "When I reached the first floor, I heard voices coming from the west wing. I went to see if anyone needed assistance, but when I reached the corridor entrance, I could hear it was the duke saying goodnight to someone."

That must have been Vance leaving Lilly's room.

"I thought I should hurry up to meet him at his rooms," Tom continued, his voice growing increasingly strained, "in case he needed help preparing for bed. So I ran down the east wing and up the service stairs to the second floor."

He's who James heard on the stairs.

"When I reached the second floor, the duke hadn't arrived yet. So I went back towards the main staircase to meet him." His face contorted with anguish, tears welling in his eyes again. "I only wanted to ask if he needed anything." His breath hitched. "I didn't mean for it to happen." And then he crumpled again, his head in his hands, overcome by the weight of it all.

Alice froze. The facts circled like vultures in her mind: the timing, the letter, the footsteps. It was all there.

But what exactly happened on those stairs that night?

Only two people knew. And one of them was dead.

40

SHORTLY AFTER...

T he garden room fell into a heavy silence. Alice stood motionless, her hands clutched tightly before her as she watched the footman struggle to compose himself. His shoulders shook with silent sobs, his face buried in his hands as if he could no longer bear to look at any of them.

Baxter rose sharply. "George, fetch some brandy, would you?"

George hesitated, his brow furrowed as he darted a look at Tom. "My lord, I'm not certain I should leave you alone with—"

"We'll be quite all right," Baxter assured him in a firm voice.

"Very well, my lord." George gave a short bow, his eyes lingering on Alice with concern before he turned and left the room.

She watched Tom, a quiet ache blooming in her chest. *How did it come to this?* Of all the people she'd considered, suspected, and questioned in the last several days, Tom had never truly featured. Not Tom, whose first steps on the stone flagstones of Francis Court had echoed her own. Whose father had tended the gardens with a quiet pride. Who, at fourteen, had beamed with such earnest excitement the day he'd been given his livery and taken his place as a hall boy. She and her brothers had run through the grounds with him as children—bare-kneed and mud-streaked and laughing without care. There'd been no talk of rank or station then. Just games and sunshine and the feeling of home.

And now... Now Tom sat pale and trembling before her, a man crushed under the weight of what had happened. Of what he'd done.

The door opened, interrupting her troubled thoughts. George returned with a silver tray. Baxter poured a generous measure and pressed it into Tom's hands. He drank quickly, and although he shuddered, his eyes were clearer when he looked up.

Baxter poured another glass for himself, glancing at her with a raised eyebrow. She shook her head—the thought of alcohol at this moment in time made her stomach turn.

"Tom," Baxter said, taking a sip of his drink. "We understand this is difficult, but we need you to continue. What exactly happened when you encountered the duke on the stairs?"

Tom nodded, his eyes glassy. His gaze focused on some middle distance, as if he were watching the events unfold on an invisible stage. "I met him as he reached the top of the stairs," he said, his voice oddly detached. "He seemed... somewhat in his cups. I asked if he wanted help getting ready for bed. He looked at his watch and then asked if Her Grace was in her usual room in the west wing."

He turned to her, sudden emotion cracking through his composure. "I don't know what came over me. I should have simply said yes. That was all he wanted to know. But my head was..." He paused, struggling for words. "All I could think about was how he'd been with you at dinner, then dancing with you, making you smile like… like it used to be. But then I'd seen him flirting with Lady Granville over the soup, whispering things that made her laugh behind her fan. And then he disappeared with her into the garden…"

A flush of embarrassment warmed her cheeks. Had her complicated marriage been so obvious to the servants? Had they all watched, noticing each slight, each betrayal, each moment when Vance's attention wandered to other women?

"And then I realised the voice I'd just heard," he continued, his words coming faster now, "the one saying goodnight to him—it was Lady Forthington's. He'd been in her room, and now he was asking about you, and I…" He drew a shaky breath. "I told him you'd retired for the night."

Vance wouldn't have liked that! He could be perfectly pleasant with servants—charming even—but only when they remained in their place. He lacked the easy familiarity with them that she and her family had cultivated over generations, and he wouldn't have taken kindly to Tom's deflection.

"His Grace became quite agitated," Tom said, confirming her thoughts. "He said, 'That's not what I asked you,' in that cold way he had. Then he demanded to know which room you were in." He looked down at his hands, twisting the now empty glass between his fingers. "I suggested that perhaps I should escort him to his own room," Tom continued. "I said again that you had already retired, and it might be best not to disturb you." He took a deep, shuddering breath. "That's when he grabbed me by the arm, hard, and he said—" His voice dropped to a whisper, forcing them all to lean forward to hear him. "'You're a footman. Your job is to do as you're told, nothing more. Now tell me where my wife is.'"

Alice's heart raced. She could picture it vividly. Vance's jaw set, his voice low and full of quiet fury.

Tom's eyes were now fixed on the carpet. "I don't remember exactly what happened next," he said, his voice growing strained. "It's all a blur. I know I pulled away from him—or tried to. I think I said something; I'm not sure. But I remember pushing at his chest, wanting him to let go of my arm." He looked up, his eyes wide with remembered horror. "He lost his balance. I saw him start to fall backwards, and I reached out to grab him." He faltered. "I caught his wrist. For just a second, I thought I had him. But then he was slipping. I tried to hold on, but he must have grasped at my glove. It slipped off in his fingers, and he..." He swallowed hard. "He fell. I heard... I heard the sound when he landed. I'll never forget that sound."

Alice closed her eyes. It was as if she'd seen it happen. The stumble. The hand flailing out. The ring hitting the sconce and extinguishing the light. The sudden drop. The glove still clutched in a falling hand. The *thud*. Then the silence. She lowered herself into the nearest armchair, unable to stand any longer, her limbs like water, and her heart pounding somewhere near her throat.

The room was quiet but for the faint ticking of the clock on the mantel.

Alice stared at the rug, the same pattern she'd seen since childhood, but it blurred before her eyes.

She swallowed. Her mouth was dry.

He didn't mean to do it.

She'd known him since he'd been eight. She believed him.

And yet, belief could not undo what had been done.

Vance was gone.

And someone she'd known all her life might end up paying with his.

41

A FEW MINUTES LATER...

It was Baxter who broke the silence. "Tom, why didn't you raise the alarm?" he asked. "After Vance fell?"

Tom stared into the amber liquid, his fingers trembling as they curled around the crystal. "I ran down the stairs to check on him, but... it was clear he was gone." His voice cracked. "I—I panicked. I didn't know what to do. Who would believe me? A servant. Saying I'd pushed a duke—by accident? No one would believe it wasn't deliberate. I'd be hanged, sir."

Alice's stomach twisted. "What happened next?"

He drew a shaky breath. "I'm ashamed to admit it, ma'am, but all I wanted to do was run away. To pretend I hadn't been there at all. "His Grace still had my glove clutched in his hand. I... I took it back."

"And the pocket watch?"

"I saw it as I was going back up the stairs. It must have fallen from his other hand when he…" He couldn't finish the sentence. "I was in such a panic not to be discovered with His Grace's body that I simply picked it up and put it in my pocket. I wasn't thinking clearly."

She nodded slowly, the scattered pieces fitting together at

last. "So you went to his room," she said, her voice quiet but clear. "You cleaned the watch and left it there before you burned Lady Cordelia's letter."

It wasn't a question, but Tom agreed anyway. "I was in such a state," he whispered. "I wanted to be done with it all. The next morning, I realised I'd made a mistake by burning the letter—I should have left it there as if he'd never seen it. So I went to his room to clear the ashes from the fireplace, but—"

"Maud and I arrived before you had the chance," she finished for him. She remembered the moment clearly now—Tom's strange nervousness when she'd encountered him inside Vance's room that morning, his evident resistance when she'd told him to go and take a break.

"Yes, ma'am," Tom agreed, his shoulders hunching further. "You sent me away before I could finish."

A weighted silence fell over the room. Her mind jumped to what came next—possibilities, consequences, responsibilities. The law was clear—murder meant hanging. But she believed Tom hadn't intended to kill Vance. The horror and remorse in his eyes couldn't be feigned. It had been a single push, a moment of impulse with consequences far beyond anything he could've foreseen. Would the courts show mercy for that? Or would they see only a servant who had raised his hand against his master?

But now—she would have to choose.

Justice for her husband.

Or mercy for the person who hadn't meant to kill him.

If she chose justice, then there would be a trial. Her heart squeezed tight. *Everything will come out in the open.* Vance's movements that night, his liaison with Lilly, his flirtation with Cordelia. Every sordid detail of their unhappy marriage would be dissected in court, reported in newspapers, whispered about in drawing rooms across London. The humiliation would be complete.

And not only that. Duncan's position in the House of Lords could be compromised by such a scandal. Her boys would forever be marked as the sons of a duke whose philandering had led to his death at the hands of a servant. The damage would be irreparable, extending far beyond their immediate family to affect the tenants, the staff, everyone who depended on the Astley and Manning estates for their livelihood and security.

And then Tom would be sent to the gallows. Her stomach clenched at the thought. She stole a glance at him now as he clutched his glass, his head hung low, and saw not the footman who had murdered her husband, but the boy she'd known since childhood. Memories unfurled like ribbons in the breeze, taking her back to sun-dappled summer afternoons in the gardens of Francis Court. She'd been very young, running with her brothers, when Duncan had spotted Tom, the gardener's son, watching them from behind a yew hedge, too shy to approach the children of the house. Duncan, never one to stand on ceremony even then, had promptly invited him to join their game of hide-and-seek. Their governess had been scandalised, of course, but their father had merely laughed when he'd come upon them all rolling on the lawn, their clothes grass-stained and their faces flushed with delight. "Children will be children," he'd said, dismissing the governess' concerns with a wave of his hand. "Let them play while they can."

And play they had, that summer and the next and several after that. Tom had known all the best hiding places in the gardens. He had shown them where the early strawberries grew against the south-facing wall, had taught them to recognise the songs of different birds. It hadn't been until they were older, with Alice sent off to finishing school, Duncan to Eton, and Tom appointed as hall boy at the tender age of fourteen, that the boundaries of class had reasserted themselves, transforming friendship into the more formal relationship of master and servant. But Alice had never quite forgotten those carefree days. She'd made a point of speaking to Tom whenever their paths crossed—there was a childhood bond there that remained strong. Despite the grief and confusion of the past few days, she knew with sudden clarity that she could not stand by and watch Tom hang for Vance's death.

She smoothed down her skirt as the image of Vance's crumpled body lying motionless on the half-landing made an unwelcome appearance in her mind. *How will I explain this to Harry and Freddie when they're older?* Their father dead and no one held accountable. *There has to be another way.* A solution that would see justice done without destroying everyone's lives in the process.

Her thoughts swirled as fragments of an idea formed. And then, quite suddenly, a solution began to take shape in her mind—a plan that might just work if she could find the right help.

And she knew exactly who might be able to provide it…

She had to act quickly. She turned to George, who'd been standing silently by the door throughout Tom's confession.

"George," she said, her voice steadier now she'd made a decision. "I need you to take Tom up to his room and help him pack his things. You're both coming with me to London on the next available train."

George's expression betrayed nothing beyond a slight widening of his eyes. "Very good, ma'am," he replied, moving to Tom's side. "Come along, Tom. We need to be quick about it."

Tom looked bewildered, but he rose unsteadily to his feet,

allowing George to guide him towards the door. Before they left, he turned back to Alice, his eyes filled with pain. "Your Grace," he began, his voice breaking, "I didn't mean for—"

"We'll speak later, Tom," she interrupted gently. "Go with George now. We don't have much time."

As the door closed behind them, Baxter remained where he stood, his expression a mixture of confusion and concern. "Alice, what are you doing? Surely, we need to tell Duncan about this—and the police?"

She shook her head, rising from her chair with a sudden energy. "No," she said firmly. "I have a plan."

"A plan?" Baxter echoed, his tone skeptical. "Alice, a man has confessed to killing your husband. We can't simply—"

"A trial will cause a scandal that none of us are likely to survive," Alice interrupted, her voice low but intense. "Think of the consequences, Baxter. For my sons, for Duncan, for your sister, for everyone connected to the Astley and Manning names."

Baxter frowned. "So we allow Tom to escape justice? That can't be right either."

"Of course I'm not suggesting that," she replied, moving across the room to the bell pull beside the fireplace and giving it a firm tug. "Look, I don't have time to explain everything now, but I believe I have a solution that will see justice done for Vance without destroying lives in the process." She met his gaze steadily, willing him to trust her. "I'm going to London, but I'll be back before the boys arrive tomorrow afternoon."

His frown deepened. "Then I'll escort you," he said, his tone making it clear this was not a suggestion.

"That's not necessary," she said, but he cut her off with a shake of his head.

"It is entirely necessary," he replied, a hint of steel entering his voice. "You yourself admitted that you dragged me into this investigation, Alice. You can't now exclude me before its rightful conclusion."

Hold on! Didn't he dismiss my comment and tell me he'd joined in willingly? But he was right, of course. She'd involved him from the beginning; she couldn't shut him out now.

His expression softened a touch. "Besides, whatever you're planning, you ought not to do it alone."

"Very well," she agreed with a small nod. "But we'll need to hurry if we're to catch the next train."

"Alice, are you certain about this? Whatever you're planning—"

Am I certain? No. But I must try... "I'm not certain of anything except that I can't let Tom hang for what was essentially an accident, nor can I allow my family to be ruined by a scandal. There must be a middle path, and I believe I know how to find it."

Before he could respond, a knock at the door announced Stokes' arrival.

"You rang, Your Grace?"

She straightened her shoulders. "Yes, Stokes. I need to go to London immediately," she said. "I'll be taking Maud with me to collect suitable mourning attire and to deal with some correspondence before the boys arrive here. George and Tom will accompany me as well, as long as you can spare them."

If Stokes found anything unusual in this arrangement, his expression revealed nothing. "We can manage, ma'am. I'll arrange for transport to the station as soon as possible."

What will I say to Stokes when Tom doesn't return? Alice thought as the butler departed to make the necessary arrangements. *That's tomorrow's problem.*

She drew a deep breath, steeling herself for what lay ahead. Her plan was risky, dependent on factors beyond her control. She could only hope that her instincts were correct, that the person she sought in London would be willing and able to help. For Tom's sake, for her sons' sake, for the sake of her family's future—it had to work. There was simply too much at stake for it to fail.

She was gambling with a man's life—and the future of everything she held dear.

42

THE NEXT MORNING...

The clock on the mantelpiece ticked with deliberate patience, mocking Alice's frayed nerves. She sat poised on a silk-covered chair in the morning room of Darby House, watching Baxter pace like a restless animal. His footsteps tapped rhythmically across the polished floor. With each turn, he glanced towards the tall windows that overlooked Berkeley Square, as if their visitors might materialise beneath the leafy plane trees rather than arrive at the front door like everyone else.

Up and down. Up and down.

"If you don't sit down, Baxter," she said tightly, "I may scream."

He paused mid-stride, looking almost surprised to find himself in motion. "My apologies," he said, making a visible effort to compose himself. He settled into the chair opposite her, though his fingers drummed an anxious rhythm on the arm. "Are you certain Sherlock Holmes will be able to persuade this inspector to consider your proposal? It sounds rather... extraordinary."

Alice smoothed an invisible wrinkle from her black

mourning dress. "He has considerable influence with Scotland Yard."

"So I've heard," Baxter murmured, his gaze drifting once more to the window. "Though I must say, I still find it remarkable you managed to secure his assistance so quickly. The man is notoriously selective with who he gets involved with."

A small smile tugged at Alice's lips despite her anxiety. She hadn't told Baxter about her previous dealings with Sherlock Holmes. "Perhaps he simply took pity on me." *Or because I met with him last night...*

She'd arrived at Baker Street shortly after eight, having left Tom and George at Darby House under Maud's watchful eye. Baxter, having seen her safely home, had returned to his family's residence at Langdon Place.

The famous detective had received her in his cluttered sitting room, offering her the chair across from his own. "Your Grace," he'd said, steepling his fingers beneath his chin. "This is an unexpected pleasure. I trust your train journey from Francis Court was uneventful?"

Alice had blinked in surprise. "How did you—"

"Your hair is flattened just here" —he'd made a small circling motion beside his own temple— "as it always is when you've been leaning against a window, lost in thought. The mark is distinctive and quite beyond the reach of a hairbrush. You travelled recently—and not by carriage." Then he gave a sly smile and indicated a copy of *The Society Page*. "The rest was elementary given the news of your husband's unfortunate accident at your parent's country house."

Alice had been glad Baxter had not been present. He would have noticed her childish awe at Holmes' deductions, her flustered reaction to being so thoroughly 'read' by those penetrating eyes. It had taken her a moment to regain her composure, to remember she'd come seeking his help for a very serious matter.

He'd wanted to know everything—how she and George had examined the body, what they'd discovered, how she'd ruled out each suspect in turn. But it was her reasoning about the white cotton thread that had seemed to catch his attention most.

"You remembered your maid saying the footman was darning his gloves," he'd repeated thoughtfully, "and made the connection to the thread found on your husband's signet ring? Excellent. Very few people can hold so many threads in their mind at once—pardon the pun."

She'd been thrilled. Baxter would've rolled his eyes if he'd heard Holmes say that. Then again, Baxter had looked rather stunned himself this morning when she'd casually mentioned who they were expecting.

"Sherlock Holmes?" he'd said, choking on his coffee.

"And Inspector Gregson from Scotland Yard. They'll be here by ten."

As the minute hand inched past the hour, Baxter resumed his pacing. "Are you certain they will come? And can Holmes convince this man—Gregson—to even entertain such an idea?"

"I'm sure they will be here any minute," she replied. "As for convincing him... that's up to me." She felt the weight of it all pressing down on her—the boys, Duncan's career, Tom's trembling voice, Vance's lifeless body on the tiles. If Gregson refused... *No. I have to make him see reason.*

She recalled Holmes' final words to her as she'd left his rooms last night. "I believe your proposal has merit. It would serve justice without unnecessarily destroying lives—a balance the law often fails to achieve. I will speak with Inspector Gregson of Scotland Yard personally and brief him.

He knows you already, and if anyone at Scotland Yard might be persuaded to consider such an arrangement, it would be him."

As if summoned by her will, the door opened to admit Pratt, her butler. "Mr Sherlock Holmes and Inspector Gregson of Scotland Yard, Your Grace," Pratt announced, stepping aside to admit the visitors.

She rose smoothly to her feet as the two men entered.

Holmes entered first, his tall, lean figure instantly commanding the room despite his understated attire. He moved with a contained energy, like a coiled spring, his gaze sweeping the room and seeming to absorb every detail in an instant. Behind him came Inspector Gregson, a stark contrast to Holmes' austere elegance. The inspector was broader, blunter in manner and dress, with a thick moustache and watchful eyes. He carried himself with the quiet authority of a man accustomed to command, his neat but unremarkable suit betraying occasional signs of long wear.

"Mr Holmes," she said. "Inspector. Thank you both for coming."

Holmes bowed. "Your Grace."

Gregson bowed too, then curved his lips into a faint smile. "It's a delight to see you again, Your Grace."

Baxter raise an eyebrow, his gaze catching hers. She gave him a tight smile before returning her attention to Gregson. She extended her hand. "I appreciate your willingness to hear me out, inspector."

"After your invaluable help with locating *The Nizam Blaze*, I felt it was the least I could do."

She suppressed a grin as she turned to a startled Baxter. "May I introduce Lord Rushton? His father, the Earl of Langdon, chairs the Police Committee at Quarter Sessions, I believe."

There was the briefest flicker of recognition in Gregson's eyes as he inclined his head. "Lord Rushton."

Good. He knows we have connections…

Baxter gave a quiet, measured nod. "Inspector."

"Please, gentlemen, be seated," she said, gesturing to the chairs arranged around a small table where tea waited. "Pratt, please ensure we won't be disturbed."

"Very good, ma'am," the butler replied with a bow, withdrawing and closing the door quietly behind him.

Alice took a deep breath, gathering her courage as she faced Inspector Gregson across the table. "Inspector," she began, her voice steadier than she'd dared to hope, "I find myself in a rather delicate situation. My husband's death was not an accident as was initially believed." She paused, studying his reaction. "It was the result of a momentary confrontation with a footman—a man who has served my family since childhood and who I am convinced never intended to cause my husband's death."

Gregson's expression remained carefully neutral. "Holmes has outlined the basic facts for me, Your Grace. I understand you have the man in custody here?"

"Not in custody, precisely," she replied, choosing her words with care. "But, yes, he's here at Darby House. He has made a full confession to me and Lord Rushton, and he's prepared to face the consequences of his actions." She leaned forward slightly. "But inspector, those consequences, as dictated by the law, seem disproportionate to what actually occurred."

"The law does not generally concern itself with proportionality," Gregson replied. "A man has died. If another man caused that death, even unintentionally, there must be accountability."

"I agree completely," she said quickly. "And I'm not

suggesting he should escape accountability. Rather, I'm proposing an alternative form of redress that would serve the law's purpose without ruining more lives than necessary." She took a breath, willing her heart to slow so she could hear her own voice. "Will you hear me out?"

Gregson crossed his legs and nodded.

Thank goodness...

She lifted her chin. "I want him to be allowed to plead guilty to a lesser charge than murder—to manslaughter, in fact, brought on by provocation and under duress. I would like it done quietly, out of the public eye, and that instead of prison, he's permitted to enlist in the Royal Navy. I will see that it happens. A man like him needs purpose. Discipline. A fresh start. Not a trial that will use him as a scapegoat and cast a shadow over two prominent and influential families." She emphasised the word *influential* deliberately, then waited.

The inspector raised his hand to his mouth and smoothed his bushy moustache. "I don't deny that a confession is always useful," Gregson said at last. "But the coroner will want a verdict. And the papers will want a scandal."

Her jaw tensed. "And I want neither." She took a measured breath. "Inspector, I don't condone what he did. But I understand it. He panicked. My husband fell. There was no malice, no premeditation. Only fear and a moment of madness."

Gregson gave a dry snort. "Most folk who panic don't end up with a duke dead on the floor, Your Grace."

She ignored the barb. "He's confessed. He hasn't run. He's ashamed. And I believe he will carry the burden of that night with him wherever he goes."

Gregson studied her, narrowing his eyes. "It's an unusual solution, but it has been done before." Her heart stopped. *So you can do it again...* "It is, however, not one we offer lightly.

There's paperwork. And the Navy won't want a man who doesn't want to be there."

"I believe he will agree," she replied. "I have friends at the Admiralty. I can make it so."

The inspector was silent for a long moment, then gave a single, reluctant nod. "If the Admiralty signs off and the coroner can be persuaded, then—aye. It can be done."

She thought she would burst into tears.

"But, Your Grace… you're walking a line here," he added grimly.

"I know," she said quietly. "But I believe it's the right one."

Gregson stood and placed his hat back on his head. "Then see to it. And quickly. Before someone else decides to ask questions you won't want to answer."

"I will. Thank you, Inspector Gregson," she said softly, then turned to Sherlock Holmes. "You have both been invaluable allies, and my gratitude is immeasurable."

Holmes' lips quirked in his subtle smile. "Justice tempered with humanity is a principle well worth preserving."

43

LATER THAT MORNING...

Tom arrived in the morning room with his cap in his hands, his eyes lowered. George hovered next to him, his eyes bright as he, too, waited to hear Tom's fate.

Alice was aware that the two footmen had worked together for many years before Alice had stolen George away from Francis Court in a move that Fee still referred to as 'the great George-grab' and her aunt as 'poaching Stokes' pride and joy'. George would want to see justice but would also want to see his friend judged for the truth, not merely the outcome.

She took a deep breath. "I've spoken to Inspector Gregson of Scotland Yard, Tom."

Tom flinched. "I understand I'll be taken in, Your Grace. I don't ask for mercy."

"I'm not offering mercy," she said softly. "I'm offering a way forward."

His head lifted, his eyes full of wary confusion.

"You will plead guilty to the charge of manslaughter," she continued. "Privately. There will be no trial, no headline. I've made certain of that. But instead of prison, you'll be given the chance to enlist in the Royal Navy."

He blinked. "The Navy, ma'am?"

She'd already received word from her godfather, Admiral Sir Peregrine Wexford, agreeing to accommodate her request. "A ship leaves from Portsmouth within the week. You'll be aboard if you choose to accept. It will not be easy, Tom. But it will be honest work. And it will be far from here."

Tom's throat worked as he swallowed. "And if I say no?"

Her eyes widened. Tom's refusal wasn't something she'd considered.

Baxter harrumphed behind her. "I would think very carefully about your position, Tom. Her Grace has gone to a lot of personal trouble to secure you an outcome that doesn't involve you being thrown in jail to rot."

She looked around at him, pressing her lips into a thin line. *That was scarcely necessary.* The thought of going away to sea and probably never seeing his family and friends again must be extremely daunting for someone like Tom, who'd barely left Fenshire in his life. *But he does have a point.* If Tom didn't want her help, then he was on his own… "Then I'm afraid I can't protect you, Tom," she said simply.

He stared at his cap. His fingers tightened around the brim. "It wasn't supposed to happen—" His voice broke. "I should've called for help. I know that."

"Yes. But you didn't," Baxter pointed out before she could respond. "And now you must do your best with what remains."

A long silence fell, then Tom straightened. "I'll go," he said. "I'll serve. I'll do whatever it takes."

She stood and offered him her hand. "Then I'll make sure the path is clear."

He took it with trembling fingers. "Thank you, ma'am."

She swallowed the lump caught in her throat and turned to her first footman. "George, please accompany Tom to Scotland Yard. Inspector Gregson is expecting you. You may take my carriage."

George gave a quick bob of his head and guided Tom towards the door. As they stopped in front of it, Tom hesitated and turned. "Your Grace," he said, his voice breaking a little. "I know I have no right to ask for forgiveness, but——"

"Tom," she interrupted gently, "what's done cannot be undone. But perhaps in time, we may both find peace with the past." She added softly, "Do something worthwhile with this opportunity, Tom. That's all I ask."

He nodded sadly, then turned and followed George out of the room without looking back.

Left alone with Baxter, she felt the careful composure she'd maintained begin to unravel. She sank into the nearest chair, suddenly exhausted, the events of the past days catching up with her in a rush that left her trembling. She turned to where he stood by the fireplace, his arms folded, his gaze distant. He looked tired too. "It's done," she whispered.

He moved to sit beside her. "You did the right thing, Alice," he said quietly. "Retribution but with mercy—it's more than many would have offered in your position."

She dipped her chin, her eyes burning with unshed tears. "I need to return to Francis Court as soon as possible," she said, hauling her heavy limbs out of the chair. "The boys will be arriving from school this afternoon. I should be there to meet them."

"Of course," he agreed, rising. "Would you like me to accompany you back home?"

She hesitated, then shook her head. *I need to be alone for a while.* "But there's something you can do for me, Bax.

Would you be good enough to stay here in London and oversee Tom's joining the ship? I'll leave George here to assist you."

"Certainly," he replied without hesitation. "I'll ensure everything proceeds as agreed."

He may be annoying and disapproving at times, but he's a good friend...

"Thank you," she said, moving towards the door. She turned. "Oh, and I was thinking that perhaps you and Bertie will join me and the boys at Manning Hall in a few weeks? Duncan and Fee will be there with their two. It will be... pleasant for them to have company."

His expression lightened, a smile tugging at the corners of his mouth. "Five boys all together?" he said with mock horror. "You're a braver woman than I gave you credit for, Alice."

A quiet amusement played on her lips. "I may well regret it. But I think the chaos will be a welcome distraction."

"Then we would be delighted to come," Baxter said, his tone softening. "Bertie will be thrilled at the prospect of so many companions."

She smiled again as she reached for the door handle.

"And Alice?"

She swivelled around to face him.

"I may not have always approved of your methods. And Lord only knows what you did to help the inspector and Sherlock Holmes in the past. But I think you've generally handled this entire situation with remarkable grace and wisdom," he said, his blue eyes suddenly serious. "Vance would be proud of you."

The words caught her off guard. Her throat tightened as a single tear escaped, sliding down her cheek before she could catch it. "Thank you," she whispered as she turned and walked out.

———

The train rattled through the Fenshire countryside, its wheels clacking against the rails in a steady rhythm Alice found oddly comforting. She sat alone in the first-class compartment, her black mourning dress a stark contrast to the vibrant green landscape that flashed past the window. Fields and hedgerows, farmhouses and church spires—the familiar scenery of home slipped by like pages in a book.

Had it really been less than a week since Vance's body had been discovered on the grand staircase? So much had happened, so many revelations and confrontations, leading to that final, terrible confession from Tom. And now, a resolution that felt like justice of a kind had been served. But there was no satisfaction in it, not really. Vance was still dead. Tom was facing a life alone at sea, far from everything and everyone he'd ever known, and she was on her way home to comfort two fatherless boys.

She closed her eyes, leaning her head against the plush upholstery of the seat. She thought of Vance as he'd been that last evening. Charming, infuriating, complex. A man who had loved her in his own way, even if he hadn't always known how to show it. A man who'd made mistakes—so many of them—but who hadn't deserved to die that way.

Tom hadn't meant to kill him. She believed that with every fibre of her being. It had been a tangle of hurt and anger and timing. A tragedy, not a crime.

Now she could mourn. Fully and freely.

And she could also look ahead.

There would be challenges, of course. Manning Hall was

hers to run now. Her sons would need her more than ever. The Season would resume eventually, with its endless parade of obligations and expectations. But for the first time in a long while, she felt something close to hope.

She straightened in her seat, rearranging the heavy folds of her skirts. Her family would rally around her—Duncan with his steady practicality, Fee with her warmth and energy, her parents with their unwavering support.

And Baxter. She felt a rush of gratitude for her friend's presence throughout this ordeal. His calm reason, his quiet strength, his unflagging loyalty—all had been a beacon in the darkness of the past few days. Without him, she might never have discovered the truth about Vance's death.

The train began to slow as it approached the station at East Felsham. She gathered her reticule and gloves, preparing to disembark. The thought of returning to Manning Hall for the summer with the boys no longer felt as daunting as it had done before. The familiar surroundings, the rhythm of country life, the simple pleasures of watching the children play—these things would help to heal the wounds of recent days. And having Fee and Duncan there with their sons and Baxter and his son too would provide the companionship and support she and her boys would need in the months to come.

I will ask Aunt Cora to join us. As much as her aunt tried to hide it, she loved the youthful energy of the children. And she would be a great help with household matters. Mrs Wilson, the housekeeper at Manning Hall, might not be so keen with the arrangement, but it would give Alice the chance to spend time with Thomas Renshaw, Vance's steward, and get to grips with managing the Manning Estate.

As the train pulled into the station with a hiss of steam and the squeal of brakes, she felt an unexpected sense of lightness. Grief remained and would for some time—a sadness for what was, for what might have been, for the waste of it all. But alongside it was something else: a cautious hope for what the future might hold. She might not be able to see it clearly yet, that future, but she could sense its presence on the horizon, waiting for her to be ready to embrace it.

But for now, it was enough to know it was there.

44

SEVEN WEEKS LATER...

Extract from *The Society Page* broadsheet, dated Tuesday, 21 July 1891:

Whispers from the Country: A Duchess in Retreat

It has been a most eventful Season thus far—though not without its sombre moments. Seven weeks ago, the ton was shocked to learn of the sudden passing of His Grace, the Duke of Stortford, at Francis Court, the country seat of the Duke and Duchess of Arnwall in Fenshire.

It is understood that Her Grace, the Duchess of Stortford, has retired to Manning Hall in Derbyshire with her two young sons following the untimely death of her husband. In this time of mourning, she is said to be surrounded by an intimate circle of family, including her brother, Lord Tilling, and his family; long-standing family friend, Lord Rushton, and his son; and the Duchess' aunt, the Countess of Dunmore.

Intriguingly, some note that Manning Hall lies but a few miles from the country residence of Lady Forthington—whose connection to the late Duke was spoken of in terms rather warmer than familial. Since His Grace's unexpected demise, the once-effervescent widow has retreated from public life, her household whispering of long solitary walks and tightly drawn curtains. Whether she is paralysed by grief or simply prudent enough to avoid an encounter with her cousin, the Duchess—whose presence is now quite literally on her doorstep—is unknown, but one suspects that in Derbyshire, the air is currently thick with more than simply summer roses.

While custom would suggest that the Duchess, as a woman of rank and circumstance, will remain in full mourning until the end of the year, those familiar with Her Grace's independent spirit quietly wonder whether she will defy expectation and return to Town sooner than protocol permits. After all, the Duchess has always danced gracefully along the edge of convention.

One thing is certain: when Her Grace does choose to lift her mourning veil, all of London will be watching.

———

I hope you enjoyed *A Husband is Hushed Up*. If you did, then please consider letting others know by writing a review on Amazon, Goodreads or both. Thank you.

Alice now faces a long period of mourning. **So what will she do when she receives a mysterious summons from Clarissa, Dowager Countess of Romley, to go to Lawrence House in Hampshire?** She'll go of course! *A Dowager in Done In*, is available to order now from wherever you buy your paperbacks.

Want to read more by me? Lady Beatrice is Alice's great-great-great niece on her father's side and is 17th in line to the (fictional) British throne. She is also a trouble magnet when it comes to murder! Find out how Bea and her sister's assistant (and future best friend) solved their first crime together. *A Toast To Trouble* is the introductory novel in the *A Right Royal Cozy Investigation* series and you can download the ebook for FREE when you join my readers' club at https://www.subscribepage.com/helengoldenauthor_bmatttrm or if you'd prefer you can buy the ebook or paperback in the Amazon store.

For all books by me, take a look at the back pages.

If you want to find out more about what I'm up to you can find me on Facebook at *helengoldenauthor* or on Instagram at *helengolden_author*.

Be the first to know when my next book is available. Follow Helen Golden on Amazon, BookBub, and Goodreads to get alerts whenever I have a new release, preorder, or a discount on any of my books.

CHARACTERS IN ORDER
OF APPEARANCE
A HUSBAND IS HUSHED UP

Alice, Duchess of Stortford — lives at Darby House, London. Wife of Vance. Mother of Harry and Freddie. Daughter of the Duke of Arnwall.

Maud Willis — Alice's maid.

Betty — downstairs maid at Francis Court

Stokes — butler at Francis Court

Vance, Duke of Stortford — lives at Manning Hall in Derbyshire. Husband of Alice. Father of Harry and Freddie.

Percival, 12th Duke of Arnwall — Alice's father. Resides with Ann, Duchess of Arnwall, at Francis Court in Fenshire.

Lilian 'Lilly', Lady Forthington — lives in Derbyshire. Widow of Sir Francis Forthington. Cousin of Alice. Rumoured paramour of Vance.

Henry, Earl of Rivershore — Recently inherited his stepfather's title and estate. Great admirer of Alice's.

Duncan, Lord Tilling — Alice's older brother. Husband of Fee. Future Duke of Arnwall.

Fiona 'Fee', Countess of Tilling — Married to Alice's older brother, Duncan. Alice's best friend.

Baxter, Lord Rushton — Fee's older brother and Alice's childhood friend. Future Earl of Langdon. Widowed. Father to Albert 'Bertie' Howe.

Lord James Astley — Alice's younger brother and youngest son of the Duke of Arnwall.

Lady Cordelia Granville — Predatory widow.

Lord & Lady Hawthorne — guests at the Duke of Arnwall's party. Parents to Sebastian.

George Stokes — Alice's first footman.

Cora, Countess of Dunmore — lives at Darby House. Alice's aunt on her mother's side. Widow.

Tom Gresham — footman at Francis Court assigned to be Vance's valet during the duke's stay.

Sebastian Hawthorne — Friend of Lord James Astley. Son of Lord & Lady Hawthorne.

Earl and Countess of Langdon — Fee and Baxter's parents. Great friends and neighbours of the Duke & Duchess of Arnwall.

Albert 'Bertie' Howe — Son of Baxter, Lord Rushton.

Harold 'Harry', Lord Treeble — older son of Alice and Vance. Away at school in Derbyshire.

Lord Frederick 'Freddie' Manning — younger son of Alice and Vance. Also away at school in Derbyshire.

Charlotte, Viscountess of Rushton — late wife of Baxter and mother of Bertie.

Peter — hall boy at Francis Court.

Constable Peters — local Fenshire police

Inspector Meacham — Fenshire police

James, Earl of Dunmore — Aunt Cora' late husband. Alice's uncle.

Edward 'Teddy', Lord Ashford — school friend of Vance.

Ben Beaumont — Private investigator based in London.

Cousin Lucy — a relative of Alice's. Known to have had an 'issue' that Alice helped resolve privately.

Eliza — Lilly Forthington's maid

Sir Francis Forthington — late husband of Lilly.

Mary — Cordelia Granville's maid.

Mrs Potts — Housekeeper at Francis Court

Edward — Footman at Francis Court

Mrs Wilson — Housekeeper at Manning Hall, Deryshire.

Pratt — Alice's butler at Darby House

Sherlock Holmes — Consulting detective residing at 221B Baker Street in London

Inspector Gregson — of Scotland Yard.

A BIG THANK YOU TO…

To my editor, Marina Grout—your thoughtful guidance, endless patience, and pitch-perfect mix of encouragement and constructive critique are invaluable. I'm so lucky to have you.

To Ann, Ray, Lissie, and Carolyn—for being my early readers and trusted extra pair of eyes. Your feedback helps me release the best version of my books that I can, and I'm deeply grateful.

To my amazing ARC Team—for your insightful reviews, error feedback, encouragement, and ongoing support. You make every release feel like a celebration.

To my fellow authors in the *Cozy Mystery Writers' Clubhouse*—you are a constant source of wisdom, motivation, and shared laughter. Thank you for being such a special corner of the writing world.

And finally, to you, my fabulous readers—thank you for coming along on these mysteries with me, for your loyalty, enthusiasm, and delightfully inquisitive minds.

As always, I may have taken a little dramatic license when it comes to Victorian police procedures, so any mistakes or misinterpretations, unintentional or otherwise, are my own.

THE DUCHESS OF STORTFORD MYTERIES BY HELEN GOLDEN

An introductory novella in the new The Duchess of Stortford Mystries series set in the 1890s and featuring Alice, The Duchess of Stortford.
When an heir to an earldom goes missing Alice is asked to investigate, but with the clock ticking and the gossip swirling, can Alice find the missing heir before it's too late?

It's Alice's father's 60th birthday and all of London high society has descended on Francis Court for the celebrations. But when Alice's husband is found in a heap at the bottom of the stairs, and the police declare it an accident, Alice believes it's murder. Helped by her maid and footman, can she find out what happened before the guests disburse and a killer goes free.

Widowed, bored, and stuck in black, Alice jumps at the chance to escape to a country house party—until the Dowager Countess drops dead after dinner. The doctor blames her heart. Alice suspects the hot chocolate.
With a 'big' announcement, a secret summons, and a very suspicious guest list, Alice, her loyal household sleuths, and her childhood friend, must uncover the truth—before the killer disappears for good.

Alice expected suitors during her first Season as a widow—she didn't expect one to end up dead in her garden. The police say accident, but Alice suspects murder, especially when whispers of blackmail begin to surface. With help from her loyal staff and her childhood friend, she must navigate a world of secrets where reputation is everything—and someone will kill to protect theirs.

PAPERBACKS (INCLUDING LARGE PRINT EDITIONS) ARE AVAILABLE FROM WHEREVER YOU BUY YOUR BOOKS.

A RIGHT ROYAL COZY INVESTIGATION SERIES
BY HELEN GOLDEN

A novella lenght prequal in the series A Right Royal Cozy investiation series. With Perry and Bea working against each other, can they still save the party—or will it be ruined beyond repair along with Francis Court's reputation as a gold-standard venue?

A short prequal in the series A Right Royal Cozy Investigation. Can Perry Juke and Simon Lattimore work together to solve the mystery of the missing clock before the thief disappears? FREE novelette when you sign up to my readers' club. See end of final chapter for details. Ebook only.

First book in the A Right Royal Cozy Investigation series. Amateur sleuth, Lady Beatrice, must pit her wits against Detective Chief Inspector Richard Fitzwilliam to prove her sister innocent of murder. With the help of her clever dog, her flamboyant co-interior designer and his ex-police partner, can she find the killer before him, or will she make a fool of herself?

Second book in the A Right Royal Cozy Investigation series. Amateur sleuth, Lady Beatrice, must once again go up against DCI Fitzwilliam to find a killer. With the help of Daisy, her clever companion, and her two best friends, Perry and Simon, can she catch the culprit before her childhood friend's wedding is ruined? Also in Audio format.

The third book in the A Right Royal Cozy Investigation series. When DCI Richard Fitzwilliam gets it into his head that Lady Beatrice's new beau Seb is guilty of murder, can the amateur sleuth, along with the help of Daisy, her clever westie, and her best friends Perry and Simon, find the real killer before Fitzwilliam goes ahead and arrests Seb? Also in Audio format.

A RIGHT ROYAL COZY INVESTIGATION SERIES
BY HELEN GOLDEN

A Prequel in the A Right Royal Cozy Investigation series.
When Lady Beatrice's husband James Wiltshire dies in a car crash along with the wife of a member of staff, there are questions to be answered. Why haven't the occupants of two cars seen in the accident area come forward? And what is the secret James had been keeping from her?

When the dead body of the event's planner is found at the staff ball that Lady Beatrice is hosting at Francis Court, the amateur sleuth, with help from her clever dog Daisy and best friend Perry, must catch the killer before the partygoers find out and New Year's Eve is ruined.

Snow descends on Drew Castle in Scotland cutting the castle off and forcing Lady Beatrice along with Daisy her clever dog, and her best friends Perry and Simon to cooperate with boorish DCI Fitzwilliam to catch a killer before they strike again.

A murder at Gollingham Palace sparks a hunt to find the killer. For once, Lady Beatrice is happy to let DCI Richard Fitzwilliam get on with it. But when information comes to light that indicates it could be linked to her husband's car accident fifteen years ago, she is compelled to get involved. Will she finally find out the truth behind James's tragic death?

An unforgettable bachelor weekend for Perry filled with luxury, laughter, and an unexpected death.
Can Bea, Perry, and his hen's catch the killer before the weekend is over?

A RIGHT ROYAL COZY INVESTIGATION SERIES
BY HELEN GOLDEN

Bake Off Wars is being filmed on site at Francis Court and everyone is buzzing. But when much-loved pastry chef and judge, Vera Bolt, is found dead on set, can Bea, with the help of her best friend Perry, his husband Simon, and her cute little terrier, Daisy, expose the killer before the show is over?

Even in a charming seaside town, secrets don't stay buried for long as Bea and Perry discover when they uncover the remains of a chef who disappeared 3 years ago. As they unravel a web of professional rivalries and buried grudges, they must race against time to solve the murder before the grand opening of Simon's new restaurant.

Lady Beatrice's peaceful holiday in Portugal is shattered when a Hollywood star's husband is found dead. What appears to be an accident soon reveals itself as murder. Tasked with clearing an innocent woman's name, Bea and Rich must untangle a web of lies to uncover the truth before it's too late.

Perry is excited to be playing Algernon in The Importance of Being Ernest by Oscar Wilde. But disaster strikes during rehearsals, and a leading actor is killed. And it's no accident.
Can Bea and Perry sift through the petty jealousies and diva behaviour of the larger than life characters in the theatre company to unmask the culprit before Perry's acting debut is ruined?

When the King and Queen's beloved bulldogs disappear on Christmas morning, the King turns to Bea and Rich to investigate—quietly. With suspects everywhere and clues going cold fast, their best help comes from Daisy, Bea's loyal and food-distracted dog, whose nose leads straight to the truth. A warm, funny, and festive royal caper.

PAPERBACKS (INCLUDING LARGE PRINT EDITIONS) ARE AVAILABLE FROM WHEREVER YOU BUY YOUR BOOKS.

Made in United States
North Haven, CT
07 January 2026